NATURAL
BORN
Liar

Also by Noire

Maneater
(with Mary B. Morrison)

Lifestyles of the Rich and Shameless
(with Kiki Swinson)

Published by Kensington Publishing Corp.

NATURAL BORN
Liar

NOIRE

Kensington Publishing Corp.

www.kensingtonbooks.com

DAFINA BOOKS are published by

Kensington Publishing Corp.
119 West 40th Street
New York, NY 10018

All Kensington Titles, Imprints, and Distributed Lines are available at special quantity discounts for bulk purchases for sales promotions, premiums, fundraising, and educational or institutional use. Special book excerpts or customized printings can also be created to fit specific needs. For details, write or phone the office of the Kensington special sales manager: Kensington Publishing Corp., 119 West 40th Street, New York, NY 10018, attn: Special Sales Department, Phone: 1-800-221-2647.

Dafina and the Dafina logo Reg. U.S. Pat. & TM Off.

First trade paperback printing: May 2012

ISBN-13: 978-0-7582-6608-8
ISBN-10: 0-7582-6608-1

10 9 8 7 6 5 4 3 2 1

Printed in the United States of America

This urban erotic tale is dedicated to my friends and family who watch my back, protect me from the noise, and allow me to do this thang in my own unique way every single day.

And to all the Mink LaRues out there who are enjoying a few crazy misadventures of their own, I lubya!

Acknowledgments

As usual, all props go to the Father above for blessing me with originality and creativity. Thanks to Missy, Black, Nisaa, Man, Jay, Reem, Ree, and my entire team for all you do behind the scenes to help make me a success. Big ups to my UETBC fam, and all my loyal readers and friends for hopping on the urban erotic train every time it pulls into the station.

Muahhhh!

Noire

WARNING!

This here ain't no romance
It's an urban erotic tale
A gwap is up for grabs
And Mink is gunnin' for that mail!
A missing kid was on a carton
Real cute and rich and smiling,
Mink looked into the mirror
And straight pictured herself styling!
She hopped a flight with Bunni
So they could gank on her fake fam,
They bust up in da mansion
Tryna cop a hunnerd grand!
Mink took a DNA test
Just to prove her story true,
But the boss man peeped her hustle
Even from the ICU
So this here ain't no romance
Y'all gold diggers know how we do!
Hop aboard this urban train
With con-mami Mink LaRue!

CHAPTER 1

The Rip-Off

Pussy sold for pennies on the dollar on Friday nights in Harlem, and if you were looking for a couple of hot whirly-whirlies, then Club Wood was damn sure the place to be. Located on a busy corner off 125th Street, Wood stayed packed out with coochie-sniffin' niggas who were deep on the prowl, and some of the baddest bitches in the city of New York stripped, danced, and hosted private fuck-fests in the club's back rooms.

I had twirled around the strip poles earlier in the day, but I was taking the night off so I could collect some dough from a mark that me and my best friends, Peaches and Bunni, had recently ganked.

We'd schemed up a plan to lure a switch-hittin' old head into a motel room, then we snapped a bunch of shots of him sporting a sexy red bra and taking some real thick pipe up his ass.

Dude was a high-profile principal at a private boys' school and he didn't want no trouble. He didn't want no publicity neither, and in less than five minutes he had agreed to give up twenty g's to stop a picture of his hairy balls from being posted to his teenaged daughter's Facebook page.

The lick had gone down perfectly, and I was chillin' at the bar sipping slut juice and congratulating myself for a job well done when outta nowhere I caught a funny vibe.

Something wasn't right.

I got the feeling I was being watched. I had a bag full of blackmail dough slung over my shoulder, and something in my gut told me to get the fuck up outta Dodge.

I slid down from the barstool and broke for the door, but Hova's latest banga came on, and every pole freak in the house broke out in a mass stanky stroll. The strippers jumped down from the stage and hit the floor rolling hard, booties twerkin', hips grindin', stroking their pussies and sending a wave of horny niggas rushing down the aisles straight toward me.

WHO GON' STOP ME? WHO GON' STOP ME, HUH?

I crashed into about thirty sweaty niggas as I pushed through the crowd and tried to fight my way outside. I was shaking fools offa me left and right as their horny asses pulled me in all directions and tried to feel me up. A few of my regular customers offered to get me toasted, some wanted me to slide over in the corner so we could smoke some yay, and even more begged me to go in the back room and hit 'em with my patented-move, double-hump lap dance.

Somehow I made it past them, and I was *this close* to getting my ass outta there when a strong hand clamped down on my shoulder and a deep voice boomed, "Excuse me, ma'am."

I almost shit. I didn't know if I should turn around swinging or make another break for the door, but I knew I was busted. The twenty racks I had just hustled from that principal felt like a ton of bricks weighing down my bag. This was supposed to be an easy little gank, and I couldn't believe that greasy old dick-rider had called the cops on me!

Getting arrested was gonna cause some real big problems for me. I was already on probation for writing bad checks, and a thousand lies flew through my head as I thought about the bus ride to Rikers I was about to take.

"I said, excuse me, ma'am," the deep voice boomed behind me again, "but is your name Nicki Minaj?"

I spun around so fast my pink-and-blond Chinese bangs swished across my forehead. I eyeballed the hand that was still gripping my shoulder. It sported a five-thousand-dollar platinum Versace ring on the pinkie finger, and I'd seen that fourteen-thousand-dollar Rolex Prince Cellini on sale at a jewelry store on Broadway.

"Oh! My bad." Dude busted a grin as he checked me out. I was styling pussy-pink from the top of my Glama-Glo wig all the way down to my toenails, and it was real obvious that he was feeling my flow. "You look *just like* Mizz Minaj from the back, but you're even finer than she is in the face."

I stunted on him. I was a con-mami, a pole dancer, and under the right circumstances I could be a big-ass thief. A chick like me had ninety-nine hustles but a rap star wasn't one of 'em.

I breathed a sigh of relief as I checked him out right back. Dude was handling his. He had pretty brown skin and real white teeth. His dome was freshly-lined and he stood at least six-five.

My eyes rolled over his gear as I added up his digits. Chocolate-brown Polo shirt, baggy jeans, Cool Grey Jordans. Uh-huh. He was thuggin' it and I was lovin' it. Papa was stackin' some real mean paper and he wasn't shy about flossin' it. I could almost see the fat money knots swelling up in his pockets and the hard piece of wood that was starting to rock up in his drawers too.

"I'm serious." He grinned again and hit me with his dimples. "I didn't mean no disrespect, shawty. You just look so damn fly, so damn . . . *New York*. For real. My bad."

His mistake was understandable because my shit was put

together super-tight. I was rocking Fendi from my diamond-trimmed pink shades down to my tight pink miniskirt. My jewelry was pink mother-of-pearls from Tiffany's, and my pink-polished toenails looked nice and suckable in my peep-toe heels.

"No problem." I grinned and played it sexy-classy. "Men take me for Nicki Minaj all the time."

"Hell, yeah, with that kinda body I bet the fuck they do," he growled. His voice was full of mad appreciation as he introduced himself. "My name is Dajuan," he said. "Dajuan Latrell Sullivan. What's yours?"

"They call me Tasha," I lied, sliding my shades off so he could peep my hazel eyes. "Tasha Pierce."

"Look, I don't mean to come at you, Tasha, but I'm just visiting here tonight. Me and my brother own a club in Philly and we're thinking about opening up a joint around here pretty soon too. You look like you know this city. Can I buy you a drink so we can kick it for a while?"

A businessman? A club owner? I was definitely down for that!

"Nah, I don't think so," I fronted. "I don't drink with strange dudes. For all I know you could be the Harlem River Strangler."

He laughed and pulled out a business card. "I'm a balla, not a killer," he said, passing it to me. "That's real talk. Look, I ain't tryna push up on you, I just want some good conversation, that's all. I ain't askin' you for no lap dance or nothing like that. I got a nice little spot over in the VIP joint, and we can have a few drinks together and then I'll have my driver drop you off anywhere you wanna go. You feelin' that?"

"Your driver?" I played him off, but I had never been the type to turn my back on a knockin' opportunity.

He looked through the glass doors and pointed toward the corner where a shiny black limo was parked right at the curb.

An old white man was sitting behind the wheel, and when Dajuan waved at him the old man smiled and waved back.

I glanced down at his business card. The lights in the club were pretty dim, but I could tell it was made of thick, cream-colored card stock with heavy gold trim. The initials D.L.S. were scripted and embossed in large red letters, and a bunch of other words were printed on it real small.

That right there did it. I felt a rush coming on. God, I loved this fuckin' hustle! Hoodwinking niggas felt as good as the first hit on a crack pipe, and I had to stop myself from squealing with excitement. This Philly fool was gwapped out. Swimming in cream! Did I wanna sit in his VIP booth and have a drink with him? Did a wino piss on the stairs?

I shook my head again. I was wide open but I still had a role to play.

"Nah, I can't. I got other plans for tonight."

I was praying he'd push up on me just one more time, 'cause I could tell his deep-ass pockets were dying to get tricked out.

"So that's how y'all treat company around here? A Philly nigga can't get no Big Apple love?"

My bag was already full of dough, but a hustlin' chick like me was always good for one more con. I did the math in my head as I let Dajuan hold me by my waist and lead me back through the crowd. I was in debt with some real dangerous cats for some real crazy cash, and this was gonna be a great opportunity to get my weight up. Between his watch and his ring alone I could probably rack up at least ten grand at the pawn-shop around the corner.

I switched my plump apple ass toward the VIP booth while Dajuan walked behind me watching it move. He seemed like an all right cat, but he was on the young side too. He was fine, but he didn't look like no genius. I was planning on getting his horny ass naked and doing a quick little dip and zip.

Peaches and Bunni were expecting me to show up at the crib soon, and I figured I could lure Dajuan into the hotel next door and get the whole bizz over and done with in less than an hour.

I slid into the VIP booth just a' crackin' up inside. Some-body's mama shoulda warned him about pickin' up strangers 'cause this was about to be a mismatch. But what the hell *ever*! Niggas these days were just beggin' to get got, and even with a pocketbook full of cash I could always find time to roll an un-suspecting mark with nothing but pussy on his brain!

CHAPTER 2

We sat in the VIP booth sipping on tall glasses of Red Devil that Dajuan had ordered for us. The Friday-nite special at Woods was always a fifty percent off club-wide affair. That meant half off for lap dances, hand-jobs, and mixed drinks too. The VIP area was crowded and noisy, and I was steady schemin' on Dajuan's jewelry as we drank and flirted back and forth and talked sexy shit.

I was a girly-girl from head to toe. I sat there looking like a strawberry milkshake with a nipple on the top. My frame was banging. My titties was puffed up and bulging outta the top of my jacket, and my body gave off that fuck-a-licious scent that men picked up on right away.

Dajuan was no exception. I had him wide open and right where I wanted him. He could hardly keep his eyes on my face because they were so busy rolling all over my body and peeling off my clothes.

I threw my femininity down hard on his ass. I crossed my legs and struck a dainty pose on the stool and ran my tongue over my straw as I sipped my syrupy-sweet mixed drink. I didn't give a damn how fine this nigga was, my focus was strictly on getting next to his shine, and while there was a whole lotta hot, horny lust in his eyes, there were nothing but mad dollar signs in mine.

Dajuan was telling me all about the club he owned in Philly and how Club Wood was all good, but if he opened a joint in the city he would do his set up a whole lot different. He went all into where he would place his stage, his bar, and post up his security. He told me how many chicks would be grindin' on his poles at one time, how much he would charge for drinks, and all that kinda bullshit. I could tell he was young and optimistic so I let him blab, but all that mess he was talking sounded like a pipe dream to me.

Blah-blah-blah. His sexy eyes moved like pinballs as he ran his mouth non-stop. *Bing! Bing! Bing!* They ricocheted off my banana-colored curves as he damn-near drooled over my nipples as they poked through my top. Ten minutes later Dajuan ordered us another round of drinks and his wack-ass convo had moved on from his future titty-bar to some of the hot record executives he was down with.

My ears perked up when I heard that, and I opened my mouth to ask him who he fucked with, but instead a huge yawn came out. I blinked my eyes real fast. Dajuan's lips were steady moving, but now I could barely follow him. That Red Devil shit had me buzzin' and feeling kinda tipsy. I felt like I was losing focus and slidin' off my game.

"So what do you do?" Dajuan asked me. "I mean, you're fine as hell, Tasha Fierce. Sexy as fuck. I'm not tryna be slick with it or nothing, but if I had to guess what you did for a living I'd say you were probably a high-powered model. I mean, look at you. You could be some kind of fashion designer."

I laughed real loud. This nigga just didn't know! Ms. Mink LaRue *told lies* for a living, and I was damn good at it too.

"Yeah okay, what*ever*!" I said. "I mean, I thought about becoming a model at one time, but I got way too much ass to squeeze into them tiny little clothes so I changed my mind."

"Yeah, you holding it down back there, baby." He was

straight-up impressed. "I mean you sittin' on at least ten pounds of ass in each cheek right there. But"—his voice dipped real low and all of a sudden my mouth started watering and this nigga looked sexy as hell—"I can also picture you being a hot star in the adult sex industry. You know, one of those amazing big-booty chicks you see on the cover of joints like *King* magazine and *XXL*. I'm just saying . . . and no, I ain't no agent or nothing like that, but you just have that type of body, that's all. I mean it as a compliment."

Wasn't no need in checking him. I knew I had a prime package and I wasn't offended in the least. Dajuan was right on point with all that. I had taken my share of ass-shots over the years, and if the money was right and *XXL* or one of them type of mags came calling I would toot it up for the cameras over and over again.

"But for real though, you prolly should try to get an agent," Dajuan suggested. "You're just so amazingly sexy. A chick like you would be a breakout in the film business. I know Nicki got the rap game on lock, but can you act?"

Could I act? I laughed so damn hard I almost threw myself off the freakin' barstool. My head was spinning and I knew for sure I was slippin' now, but I couldn't help myself. All of a sudden I felt real hot and free. Like I wanted to take my jacket off and let my titties get some air. I was turned the fuck on too, like I had guzzled a whole gallon of slut juice.

I stared real hard at Dajuan, and for the first time ever I was ready to put pleasure before the game. My pussy was tingling. I wanted to duck down under the table and get my uterus dug out, and I wanted long-legged Dajuan Latrell Sullivan to pull out his shovel and do the digging.

He chuckled. "Yo, I'm serious baby. A chick with your kinda star quality should be in the movies."

Fuck a con game. My lips flapped loose and all the nasty thoughts on my mind rolled straight outta my mouth.

"Yo, you real cool, Dajuan, and I'ma ga'head and suck ya

dick and give you some pussy too, 'kay? But you got some real white-boy shit going on witcha self boo. I ain't wanna be the one to tell you, but you walk like you got a blunt stuck up your ass!"

"A blunt?" he said. "Up my ass?"

"Uh-huh." I nodded and took another gulp of my drink, and suddenly the whole room seemed like it went on high buzz. It was real confusing. Everybody in the VIP area seemed like they was talking extra loud, but Dajuan's words sounded like silky whispers in my ear. I pushed that damn drink away.

"Super Bass" blasted through the speakers, and right away my juices got to flowing. Fuck a Nicki! I was *Mink* Minaj and I started singing real loud and grindin' my ass on the chair like I was giving the seat cushion one of my hump-a-lump lap dances.

"Oh, that's my shit right there! That fuckin' super bass feels *good*!"

"Finish your drink." Dajuan pushed that evil red liquid back at me. "And I promise you, Tasha, you's about to feel *real* good, baby. At least for tonight."

"Yo," I slurred. I took the little straw outta my glass and sniffed the tip. "What the fuck is in this shit?"

"The devil," Dajuan said with a slick grin.

He put his arm around me and helped me stand up on my wobbly feet. I stumbled outta the VIP lounge and walked through Club Wood hugged up on that dude like he was my boo. We dipped into the hotel next door and he took me straight to the elevator. When we got on I bust out laughing as I tried to count all them pink reflections the panel of dirty mirrors was throwing back at me. I was counting those babies out loud too, but I kept getting stuck and forgetting which number came after two and went before four.

"So you think I walk like a white boy, huh?" Dajuan asked as we rode up the elevator shaft.

My tongue was so damn heavy all I could do was nod.

Dajuan grabbed my hand and pressed it up against his bulging dick. "I bet you ain't never ran across no white boy who was packing meat like this."

That nigga was all over me. He tongued me down like a starving man, and I moaned as my steamy pussy melted. He sucked on my bottom lip and stroked my ass until my thong was nice and wet.

"Your body is fuckin' killer crazy," Dajuan said as we got off the elevator.

I stumbled into a room so big it had to be the penthouse suite.

"Know what? Your ass looks like a choo-choo train with an extra-wide caboose."

"You so fuckin' corny!" I squealed as I tossed my bag down on the chipped wooden nightstand. My damn hands had a mind of their own as I helped him strip off his Polo shirt and unbuckle his belt. There was a big basketball emblem on his buckle, and that shit hit the floor hard as he dropped his jeans and his boxers too.

"Ah shit . . ." I sucked in my breath as he stood there almost naked. His long black dick stuck straight out in front of him and curved a little bit to the left. A tiny drop of pre-cum hung from the tip and I wanted to get down on my knees and slurp it up before it dripped. Instead I giggled.

"I see *somebody* wants some *pussy!*"

"That ain't all I want."

Out of nowhere he was holding a Crown latex in his hand. I staggered over to him and snatched the condom and ripped the wrapper off with my teeth.

"Lemme do it," I slurred. His dick looked so delicious it made my mouth water. That sucker had me in a trance. It was the color of chocolate M&Ms, and it looked just as sweet. I squeezed my thighs together and panted as I rolled the latex down over his thick shaft.

I was about to jack that beautiful dick half to death, but then something made me ask, "Do you wanna see a show?"

I kicked off my heels and stripped down to my hot-pink thong and satin half-bra. Then I unsnapped my garter belt and inched my pink fishnet stockings down my thick yellow thighs that never failed to drive niggas wild. I flung my right stocking up high in the air, and I cracked the hell up when it fluttered down and landed on Dajuan's head. I twirled the other stocking around my neck and wore it like a scarf.

Dajuan ate me with his eyes as I drooled over his muscular shoulders, rocked up stomach, and heavily-veined dick. I wanted that damn dick! No, I blinked. I wanted both of his dicks. No, hold up. This nigga was packin' three fat pieces of meat!

The room started swimming and I closed my eyes and tried to fight off a big wave of dizziness. When I opened my eyes again Dajuan was licking his lips and staring at my crotch. "I smell your pussy," he panted.

"But you got three dicks . . . ," I whined as every damn thing in the room shifted and flipped upside down.

He grabbed my shoulders and held me up.

"Relax."

Gripping my elbows, he eased me down on the bed. I thought I was onstage at Club Wood, so I spread my legs open wide and brought my knees up to my shoulders and got ready to go into one of my twerk 'em routines, but before I could get it poppin' Dajuan buried his face in my pussy and went to work with his tongue.

I screamed when his lips touched me. I arched my back and grabbed his head and started grinding my pussy all over his lips, nose, and chin. His tongue was so damn good I wiped my nookie juice on his forehead and I didn't give a damn if he liked it or not!

I came twice before Dajuan let my ass up. Then he turned over on his back and held my hips as I lowered myself down on his thickness, sucking all ten inches of him up inside of me. That stiff dick rammed straight through me. I felt like I had a sausage coming up outta my throat.

My titties jiggled as he worked his meat like he owned a slaughterhouse. I rode him like a jockey, giddy-upping him to death. The next thing I knew I was on my hands and knees in the middle of the large bed. Dajuan was crouched down lickin' my cat out from the back.

He palmed my ass and spread my lumps open wide, and I gyrated my hips in crazy circles as he stuck his tongue in my twat and slurped up my slippery juices.

"Ahhh, yeah!" I tooted up that na-na and urged him to get up in there even deeper. Dajuan stretched his tongue out like it was a plumber's snake, massaging my clit with the tip and then thrusting it deep inside my pussy before withdrawing and slithering it up to my asshole. He plunged two fingers into my juicy hole and licked that back door all the way from my puckered crack, up to my lower back.

I was whimpering with pleasure when he gripped his dick and rammed it back into my pussy hard enough to make me scream. I busted me another one as he deep-drilled me until my backbone hurt.

"Dajuan!" I screeched as he pumped wood into me doggy-style. Cries of ecstasy flew from my lips. I arched my back as sweat seeped from under my pink wig and dripped into my eyes.

"Kill this pussy . . . ," I muttered, suddenly feeling light-headed and totally dick-whipped. "*Yeah*, white boy!" I shouted over my shoulder. "Bang this pussy up!"

"Call me Daddy," he instructed as he gripped the back of

my slender neck and drove home all up in my wet-wet. He pounded my guts so hard the flesh on my ass rippled like delicious sea waves. "That's right, baby," he panted. "I wanna hear you call me Daddy."

"*Daaadeee* . . . ," I whispered as he hit me with a powerful down stroke. And then my knees straight buckled. I fell face-down on the bed as Mister D.L.S. proceeded to grip my plump ass and fuck my lights completely out.

CHAPTER 3

Club Wood was still on fiyah when a very tall college basketball player walked out of the hotel next door. Upstairs, in the very best room they had, he'd left a sweet, luscious piece of ass slobbering on a pillow. They'd torn the room up and fucked like a pair of wild tigers, and his dick was sore and throbbing as he walked toward a white, late-model Chrysler 300.

He grinned as the driver's window slid down.

"Hey wassup! Sorry about the wait." He laughed. "I got kinda caught up in a lil something, ya feel me?"

The driver shrugged. He was a distinguished-looking black man in his late forties, and the smell of cigars and expensive cologne drifted out from the car's interior.

"Well, did you have a good time?"

"C'mon now! You saw that chick's ass!" the handsome balla from Philly answered. "That was the best piece of pussy I had in years."

He reached into his jacket pocket and pulled out a thick package of money. It was in a plastic bag and still had traces of tape wrapped around it. "Twenty g's! I counted it as soon as she passed out." He tossed the package to the driver, then started taking off the jewels he wore. He handed them to the

man in the car, who strapped the fifteen-thousand-dollar
watch onto his wrist and slid the Versace diamond ring back
on his finger.

He held out his hand. "My cologne?"

"Ahh!" The young balla grinned as he pulled a six-hundred-
dollar bottle of Ambre Topkapi from his other pocket. "You
got me, yo! You got me!"

The older gentleman dug into the plastic bag full of cash
and slid a hunk of hundred-dollar bills from the top of the
stack. He counted off ten pieces of paper and handed them to
his favorite nephew.

"Good looking out," he said as they dapped. "I can always
count on you to put in work, D."

"Thanks, Unc. And thanks for sponsoring my team's prac-
tice jerseys too. Temple is getting real cheap with the gear."

The older man nodded his understanding. Temple was his
alma mater too. "Summer school going okay?"

"Yeah. It's a'ight. You coming out to our next scrimmage?"

His uncle nodded before pulling off. "Damn right. You can
count on it. I haven't missed one yet."

CHAPTER 4

I knew I had been fucked the moment I opened my eyes. My cell phone was ringing like crazy. I reached out wildly tryna find the noise and kill it, and I damn-near fell outta the bed because that bad boy was on the floor.

I pressed the TALK button, then rolled over back on the bed.

"H-h-hello?"

"Bitch, wake up!" a loud-ass voice screamed in my ear.

It was Bowlegged Bunni Baines, my best friend and partner-in-grime.

Tangled in the old cotton sheets, I was butt-naked with my head resting on a flat, unfamiliar pillow. My aching legs were stretched wide-open, and my neatly trimmed triangle was still moist and sore from last night's stunts.

I opened one crusty, bloodshot eye and peered at the clock on the ancient nightstand. It was after ten o'clock in the morning and I had been out cold the whole night. My hand shot to the top of my head and I patted around for my strawberry-blond Glama-Glo wig. It was gone. And so were my diamond earrings and my matching braided-diamond bracelet too.

"Girl, did you hear what I said? Wake your ass up!"

"W-w-what?" I croaked. My voice came out ripped and

rusty, like I'd been humping some nigga's good wood all night and screaming out his name.

"Gurlfriend . . . ," Bunni said in her classic hood drawl, "I'ma need you to open your eyes and pull yourself together, okay? You ain't gonna believe this shit, but guess where me and Peaches just seent your picture at?"

I swallowed a mouthful of sleep dust then blurted out, "On a wanted poster?"

Bunni cracked up. "Nah, baby. I seent your mug on the back of a *milk carton!*"

I groaned and rolled over in the lumpy king-sized bed.

"Stop playing, Bunni. It's too early in the morning for all that bullshit."

"Oh, 'scuse me, my bad." She had the nerve to cop a little attitude. Bunni was ghetto-dipped in shiesty sauce, but she had one of the slickest con games in Harlem. We'd been best friends since the fifth grade, and even though we butted heads sometimes, she was exactly the kind of chick I liked having on my team.

"Where the hell are you anyway? You was supposed to get that twenty large and come straight back last night!"

Twenty grand.

Suddenly I was wide-awake. I had a vivid flashback of getting nasty-knocked by some young dude I'd been trying to vic, and my stomach flipped over. Dropping the phone, I swept my foot around under the sheets and came up cold.

Cursing, I sat straight up. My eyes darted all around the big, run-down suite and reality slammed into me like a big, black cannon.

My mark had dipped.

His name flashed in my head. *Dajuan Latrell Sullivan.*

"Oh, shit!" I leaped from the bed and dashed across the room. My pink-and-blond wig was draped over a lampshade, and my oversized Fendi bag was laying on a large coffee table.

I turned it over and shook it. Two mints, a tampon, my makeup bag, and my ID fell out.

Other than that, it was empty.

"Awwww, *shit!*" I ran over to the crusty, linoleum-tiled bathroom and flung open the door. Empty.

I jetted back across the room and peeked inside the large walk-in closet. Other than a rickety ironing board, some crooked clothes hangers, and two empty plastic bags, that shit was empty too.

Back at the table, I picked up my bag again and saw the expensive-looking business card laying underneath it. The letters on it read *D.L.S.* in bright-red, extra-large script. I squinted hard to read the tiny print below the initials, then I blinked a few times until I could make out the horrifying words and a telephone number.

D.L.S. aka Daddy Long Stroke. 1-900-FUK-A-LOT.

I stared at the tangled bed where just hours earlier that nigga had had me moaning like a punk and getting my back blown out. The last thing I remembered was being dug out deliciously from behind, and then everything faded straight into fuzzy after that.

My ass had been stole! I'd been got real good!

And now, the only thing that was left to remind me of the long-legged Philly balla who had dropped something in my drink and lured me up to his penthouse suite, the so-called mark that I had been planning to gank for his watch, his ring, and every dime he had in his knotty-ass pockets, was a dent in the pillow where his head had lain!

Hater-bitches ran real thick in Harlem, and every time I went around Bunni's way some stupid chicks wanted to fight me. Well, I was ready for them chickens today. The street where Bunni lived was hot and funky. Somebody's dog had busted into some garbage bags that were lined up on the curb, and they overflowed with beer bottles and dirty pampers. Little kids wore crushed soda cans on their feet and slid across the pavement like they had on skates.

The porch monkeys were sitting on the front stoop puffin' yay when I got off the number three train. I took off my shoes and walked up on them bitches like I was ready to throw down. Heffas musta sensed my heat 'cause none of them so much as looked my way. They just sat on them little plastic chairs smokin' blunts and twirling that cheap-ass hair weave they bought from the ninety-nine-cent store.

"Yeah," I straight busted on them outta nowhere. "Check this out. The next time one of y'all hallway-hoes got something to say about me, say that shit to my face!"

They looked at me like I was crazy, but I wasn't fooled. One of these saggy-titty bitches had gone and blabbed to Punchie Collins that I was undercutting his drug sales by intercepting his customers before they could get upstairs to his dope house. Everything they'd said was true, but I dared one of these chicks to spit something clever out they mouths today because I was already steaming. That bandit-nigga Dajuan had jacked me for my dough, my earrings, my tennis bracelet, and my hot-pink thong too. I'd had to take the train home and sneak up under the turnstile with no drawers on just to get back uptown! Oh, *yeahhhh*. I would fuck a bitch up today!

With my mug set in a hard grill, I ran up the steps holding my breath and dodging mad piss puddles. Bunni lived on the third floor, and when I got to the top of the stairs I hesitated for a second, wondering if I should tell my best friends a bold-faced lie. The last thing in the world I wanted to do was step up in that crib and admit how bad I'd fucked up with our cash.

The three of us had needed that twenty grand, and me losing it was gonna put everybody in a bind. Peaches and Bunni were three months behind on their rent, and not only was I due in court on Monday to face a summons for writing bad checks, but Gutta, my thug nigga and gangsta boo, was getting sprung from the bing in less than a month, and I had lost his apartment and tricked up almost every dime of the twenty-five grand in cash that he had left me holding for him until he got out.

We had targeted that pillow-biting principal for a gank because Peaches had seen him out flossin' and figured he had big loot. The take was supposed to be a three-way split, and since Bunni and Peaches had done all the real work, all I had to do was go make the pick up and bring home the cream. But now that I had lost it all, what the hell was I supposed to tell them?

Think, bitch, think! I screamed inside as I tried to figure out my next move. I pushed through the stairwell door, and I was so busy concentrating on coming up with a lie that I forgot to look out for Punchie Collins.

I gasped as the weight of cold steel was pressed against my neck and I was shoved right back through the door. I stepped dead in the piss puddle that I had just dodged, and I flinched as Punchie hurled me up against the concrete wall.

Pain exploded in my shoulder, but that was nothing compared to the hot fire that detonated in my back when he flung my ass down hard on the stairs.

I shoulda known better than to fuck with Punchie Collins. That psycho nigga was medication-certified, and if I hadn't been so scared of Gutta coming home and cutting my throat I woulda never violated Punchie's little trap game the way I did.

"Where my fuckin' money at, Mink, huh? Nah, don't get up. Stay ya ass down on the grimy steps where you belong. This ya office, right? This where you been conducting all my business without paying me my taxes?"

Punchie was a big, shiny-black drug slanga who had a screw or two loose. He lived in apartment 3F, which was one

of the busiest drug holes on the block. The crib belonged to
Punchie's grandmother, and him and his street crew sold crack,
yay, and wet from the joint twenty-four-seven, around the
clock.

He stood over me smoking a Newport and grilling me like
he wanted to X me out. He wore a doo-rag tied over his long
cornrows, and a scary-looking SIG automatic was stuck down
in his waistband.

"Look"—I stared into his crazy eyes as my knees shook
and I worked up a lie—"I wasn't tryna fuck with your product, Punchie! For real. I swear I didn't even know this was you.
The only one I was tryna fuck with was ya boy, Moolah. Me
and that dude go way back to third grade, man! His whole
family is grimy! I didn't know he was puttin' in work for you,
cause if I did I never woulda messed with him."

That fool swung on me so hard my head whipped over my
shoulder and grit from the dirty tenement stairs filled my
mouth. My ass was shook. I hadn't been slapped real good in a
minute and I didn't know how to take it.

"Bitch don't you *ever* fuck with my money!" Punchie
screamed.

I was so shocked I felt frozen. I slid down two steps and my
ass went *bump, bump*. I pressed my fingers to my lip and realized
it was bleeding.

"But I thought I was fuckin' with Moolah!" I cried out my
bullshit.

Oh, this nigga had some screws loose, all right. Shit, them
screws was rolling around inside his head like colorful little
marbles.

"What? You think somebody stupid, Mink? I know you
was tryna jack me, bitch! Catchin' my cash on the stairs like
you got some weight behind you or something! You and that
grimy bitch across the hall was eatin' off me like fuckin' staircase rats! I oughta break ya fuckin'…"

Suddenly shit changed. Punchie took a deep pull on his cigarette as his beady eyes raped me from my ankles all the way up to the hem in my skirt. He eyeballed me like he had X-ray vision and could see my naked pussy beneath my clothes.

"Yo... you wanna square up with me, Mink?"

I played dumb. Punchie had access to plenty of freaks. Crackheads out the ass woulda lined up to suck his dick down to the bone if he wanted them to, but he didn't. That psycho fool wanted what I had between my legs.

"Um, I can try to tear you off some change when I get a few dollars, Punchie. But that's all I can do."

"Nah, nah." He waved me off. "I don't want your money...all that pink you got on make a nigga wanna get up in them guts. Let's step inside my crib for a few minutes so we can both get straight."

I smirked. Punchie was feeling himself. Playing dirty. Ever since Gutta got knocked all kinds of shiesty niggas had been tryna play me. Punchie was coming up real nice on the streets, and he was making enough cash to keep me laced in glitter and shine. All I had to do was pull up my skirt and let him lick my sore pussy out, and he woulda forgiven me for violating his bizz, and handed me enough paper to replace what I had just lost, no questions asked.

But I wasn't going out like that. I was greasy, not sleazy. I was grimy, hell I wasn't slimy. I was an opportunist, but I damn sure wasn't no fuckin' idiot. If Gutta found out Punchie was trampling on his gushy and boning me out, that beast was likely to come home and go on a killing spree.

"C'mon, Miss Body." He reached in his pocket and pulled out a fat roll of bills. He grinned as he started peeling them off. "I'm feening for a hit of that dick-bricking ass you got, ma. I'm ready to get up in them guts and dig into that gushy right now, girl. How much is a slice of that sweet pussy gonna set me back?"

"Nigga don't even play me like that!" I based. Just because he had knocked me on my ass didn't mean it was up for sale. "You might be moving weight and all, but that don't mean shit to me. It's all about Team Gutta in this camp, and my gorilla ain't gonna be locked up in the zoo forever! You better chill with all that noise before he comes home and twists your doo-rag back!"

"Fuck that bitch-ass nigga Gutta! That fool ain't nobody slick!"

"I bet you won't be talkin' none of that shit when his ass rolls back on the block!"

"Bitch!" Punchie snatched his tool outta his pants and brought it up like he was gonna backhand me with it, but then somebody kicked the exit door open and cold smashed that fool's head in with a Glock.

"I wish yo fuckin' ass would," Peaches spit and *click-clacked* a round in the head of his gat. He had on a red teddy top and a pair of flame-colored booty shorts. His size-fifteen feet wobbled in the three-inch heels he had ordered from the online drag queen store, and he stared down at Punchie's dropped ass with one arched eyebrow raised up high on his forehead.

"Yo, Big P," Punchie moaned and rolled over with his hands up in surrender. "Yo, my nig, she was—"

"Shut the fuck up!" Peaches barked. The veins in his thick neck bulged and his broad chest strained against his tiny silk top.

"Get up, Madame Mink! Did this muthafucka touch you?"

"I didn't touch—"

Peaches punted that nigga straight in the balls with his pointy-toed shoe.

"If you ain't touch her then why the fuck is she bleeding, muthafucka? I done told you"—Peaches reached down and drilled Punchie in the nose with a solid left—"'bout putting ya hands on women!"

Blood sprayed outta Punchie's nose and he tried to sit up. Peaches kneed him under the chin, and Punchie's head snapped back and cracked against the concrete steps. "You wanna fight a bitch?" Peaches growled, popping his neck. "Then fight me!"

With his tool steady trained on Punchie's grill, Peaches bent over in his high heels and grabbed that nigga's gat and his foot too. With one powerful arm he dragged Punchie straight through that puddle of piss and into the hallway.

"I'm telling you, nigga," Peaches warned. "You better not say a goddamn thing to Madame Mink no more, you hear me? 'Cause if you do, I'ma stick my big dick so far up your narrow ass you gonna think I busted a cap in your colon!"

Peaches stuck Punchie's pistol down in the front of his short-shorts and grabbed my hand as we headed toward his apartment. Both of us knew better than to turn our backs on crazy Punchie Collins. That loony tune probably had another burner stuck down in his sock.

Keeping our eyes plastered on him, me and Peaches moon-walked backward until we reached the apartment door, then we turned around and switched our asses as we hurried the hell up inside.

Before I hooked up with Gutta I had been living with Peaches and Bunni off and on for years. Gutter came from a big family of Haitians, and he was a true gangsta in every sense of the word. Rolling with him had been like a dream come true. He ran a tight crew of hoodlums who moved weight on Lenox Ave, collected payoffs for the local kingpins, punished niggas when they got outta pocket, and generally rode rough through the streets of Harlem.

Gutta was one of those fearless hoods who would blast a cat in the blink of an eye, and even the hardest dudes running game out there gave him a lot of room to move. He had six scary-ass brothers, and all of them were in and out of jail at

various times, and on various charges. Right now his two oldest brothers were upstate doing bids for murdering an entire
set on the Lower East Side, and just like everybody else in
Harlem, I hoped like hell they would never get out.

Before I met Gutta I had been tricking off a low-level guy
who worked in the post office, but I hopped on Gutta's team
when one of his manz started scoping on me. Dude made a big
mistake when he took me around his way to show me off to
his street crew. Me and Gutta busted one look at each other,
and whatever I had going with that other hustler was instantly
a dead deal.

Standing close to six-four, not only was Gutta a biggun
like I liked 'em, he had a ruthless swagger about him that reminded me a lot of my daddy, Big Moe LaRue. Gutta stayed
strapped up with a heavy tool, but his rep was so cold, and he
was so fuckin' brutal and intimidating that he could shake a
nigga off his spot with just a look.

Right after me and him met, I watched him bum-rush a
prime corner from three rival hustlers who were known to be
hardbody killers in our hood. My dude walked right up on
that profitable piece of concrete and claimed that shit, and all
three of those cocky niggas got to scattin' with a quickness as
they relinquished their territory and ran for their lives.

I was in awe of his ass after that. I went home with Gutta
and dropped my drawers that same night, and after he slung
that dick on me the same way he slung that dope on the
streets, I got hooked on his game and moved into his crib just
like that.

At first Gutta kept me outta his bizz and outta his heart.
He told me if he so much as turned his head he didn't trust no
chicken to keep her mouth shut or her fingers outta his
dough. But after I got picked up twice and the cops tried to
squeeze on me to get next to him, I showed his ass how tight I
rolled. I pretended I was one of them 'Licious Lovers. Those

three Harlem rappers who were known for their closed lips. I got up in that precinct and bit the shit outta my tongue, and I was still chewing on it when they booked my ass and sent me for a ride to Rikers Island.

The cops were only gunning for Gutta, and they didn't really have nothing they could put on me, so I only stayed locked down in Rosie for a few weeks. But that was long enough to show my boo that not only did I have his back, I had mad heart too, and from that day forward he knew I was his loyal ride or die.

Gutta was waiting at the gate when they let me out of Rosie, and he took me back to his crib and treated me like a queen. He ran me a hot bubble bath, brought me dinner in bed, and showed me just how much he had missed me for those two weeks I was gone.

And then, after we finished fuckin' and we was laying up in each other's funky, sweaty arms, Gutta reached under the pillow and came out with a box. He slipped a white-gold diamond ring on my finger and told me how special I was to him and how much he was feeling me.

Then he reached under his pillow again, but this time he came out with a blade. He held that shit up in the air and told me he woulda straight up cut my throat if I had so much as *squeaked* about him to those goddamn cops, and on the real tip, I believed him.

But still, knowing Gutta was a certified fool didn't stop me from dipping my hand in his dough when he got knocked. At first it was only a couple of dollars at a time. A hundred here, a hundred there. Shit, it cost money to accept all those collect phone calls and to be taking that funky Prison Gap bus upstate! And since Gutta liked me to look good I always went shopping before a visit, and in addition to my designer wear, my wigs and shoes and jewelry and stuff was not cheap!

I used to send him packages and put money on his commissary and stuff like that too, but he told me to stop all that real quick.

"My boyz got me while I'm in here, Mink. Don't be sending me no money orders or nothin' 'cause they holding me down real righteous and I'm straight. All I want you to do is take out enough to pay my rent, and then your ass better stand guard over the rest of my cash, ya heard?"

Well what the hell am I supposed to live on? I had thought to myself, and Gutta's evil ass had straight-up read my mind.

"You still slick, right? And you's a damn good liar, too. Do whatever you was doing before I met you, yo. Just don't fuck over my dough 'cause that's the closest thing to my heart, you feel me?"

That shoulda been enough of a warning to keep my fingers outta his stash, but it was in my nature to dip, and being Gutta's chick had put me in a bind. The come-ups were biting at my ankles, but none of the major playas wanted to fuck with me. I mean, they all wanted to *fuck* me, but none of them wanted to *fuck with* me. Gutta was violent. He was a certified killer. They knew his ass wasn't gonna be locked up for long, and the potential trouble I could cause them just wasn't worth it.

That meant the only dudes I could hit were squares who were too low-level to be noticed, or dudes from other boroughs who came with their own ride or die bitches and their own set of problems.

True shit, I loved me some Gutta. I feened for his ass. Yeah, I was scared of him too, but that kind of danger just excited me even more. From his bed game to his head game, everything about that dude turned me on. We both had a thing for living on the edge, and I couldn't wait for my boo to get back out on the streets so we could show the world what we was working with.

But first I had to replenish his stash. I had to get it up to where it was when he got knocked. There was no way around that shit neither. I mean, I knew my man really had feelings for me, but above all else Gutta was first and foremost a product of the streets. And now that I had lost his apartment and blew through his dough, whether I was his favorite boo or not, if he hit those bricks and his stash was short, the law of the streets dictated that he take his money straight outta my ass.

CHAPTER 5

When I walked into Bunni's kitchen she was standing by the table looking laced from head to toe. Bunni Baines looked just like a chocolate brownie with a cherry on top. A spiral of fire-red dreadlocks sprouted all over her head like a burning halo, and the silver earrings she had boosted from Nordstrom dangled sexily above her shoulders.

Me and Bunni was almost opposite in our looks, and even though our styles were nothing alike, when we worked the poles together dudes had a real hard time deciding which one of us they should throw their money on.

Bunni was about five-nine, and she looked a lot like Lauryn Hill in the face, although her hips and ass were way curvier. She had big eyes and extra-long fake eyelashes, and her pretty brown skin was smooth and clear.

We were both shopaholic label-whores and we loved looking good, but I liked the weird and the extreme, while Bunni went for the slutty and the sexy. Today she had on a pair of tight-fitting white Armani riding pants, a clingy red Donna Karan belly top that showed off her deep navel and flat abs, and a wide silver jockey belt that I had picked up for her at Neiman Marcus. She was perched in a pair of six-inch hot-red gladiator sandals, and there was enough room between her bowlegs to drive a freakin' motorcycle through them without touching either one of her knees.

Bunni always kept her shit looking extra-stylish, but that wasn't what kept men feening after her though. Nah, dudes chased Bunni because of her vicious hoe gap. Her super-fat camel toe. The thick hunk of her pussy lips that she accentuated with every outfit she wore. You would never catch Bunni wearing a skirt or a dress because that type of shit didn't show off her glamorous Venus mound. Bunni's chunky monkey was her very best asset, and she put that gushy on front-row display every chance she got.

I wasn't even in the kitchen good when she got up in my face and looked at me real close. "Oh hell yeah, it's you all right. You's a missing child, Mink! Word! Your mug is on the back of every milk carton in Food Land. Trick, please! We been friends all these years and you ain't never told me your ass was adopted!"

"Please," I said and rolled my eyes. "Go 'head with that." I kicked off my shoes and pulled off my wig. "I ain't got nothing but LaRue blood running through my veins. Besides, when's the last time you seen a kid on a damn milk carton anyway?"

"*Today*, dammit! They doing that shit again to help find kids who've been missing for a long time, and for real Mink. It's you in that picture girl! I looked it up on the Web site, and there's a rich family searching for you. I think you need to let 'em find your ass."

"Your ass is *crazy*," I said and walked past Bunni and went into her bedroom. The outside of the five-story tenement looked a mess, but inside the two-bedroom apartment that Bunni and Peaches shared was some of the finest shit that had ever fallen off the back of a truck.

Bunni's room was painted fuck-me fuchsia and decorated with butterflies made from thick silver glitter. Her fluffy bed was covered in designer pillows that had ended up in Harlem by way of a hijacked delivery van from a downtown furniture store, and there was all kinds of other stolen shit scattered everywhere.

Me and Bunni went back for a good long minute. She had beat up three bully-ass girls for me when we were in the seventh grade, and she was the only real friend I ever had. I had slept on a fold-up cot in her bedroom from the time I was thirteen until I moved in with Gutta, and no matter what misadventures life took us through, me and Bunni were sistahs for life.

I stepped out of my dirty Fendi outfit and threw it in a pile of clothes that needed to go to the cleaners, then I dug down in a laundry basket full of clean clothes and pulled out one of Bunni's raggedy bathrobes. I put it on, then peeled off my fishnet stockings and went back into the kitchen looking ratchet as hell.

I sat down at the cluttered table where Peaches was plucking his eyebrows.

"Good looking out, Peaches. That fool Punchie almost had my ass out there!"

He pursed his red-painted lips. "Errm-herrm . . . ," he said, sounding like Madeah. "You lucky I was lookin' out the window and saw you come in the building, Madame Mink. It seemed like it was taking you forever to get up here so I came to see where you was."

"Punchie caught me sleepin'." I shook my head. "Crazy ass!"

"You better watch yourself, Mink. You fucked with that fool's money and he ain't going away, you know. I tried to tell you and Bunni that lil 'catch-a-crackhead' scam was way too risky, but y'all just didn't wanna listen. And speaking of scams, where the hell was you all night long?"

I hated to tell them, but I knew I had to. "Y'all ain't gonna believe this shit." I leaned my elbows on the table and pushed a half-eaten bowl of Apple Jacks outta my way. "But I lost the damn money."

Bunni bucked her eyes. "The money? *Girl*? What the hell you mean you lost the money?"

"Like I said, I lost the money!"

"You mean your ass stayed out all night and you didn't go pick up that money?"

"Nah, I went and got it." Hot shame had my cheeks burning red. "But then I lost it."

"You lost the fuckin' *money*?" Bunni shrieked. With her hands on her hips she swayed back, posing with a bitch-no-you-didn't look on her face. "How the hell did you do that shit, Mink? How much did you lose?"

I dropped my eyes. "The whole twenty large."

"*Mink!*" Bunni shrieked again. "Gutta is gonna *kill* your ass!"

"*Our* asses!" I snapped. "Gutta's gonna kill *our* asses, Bunni! We tricked that dough off *together*, baby, remember? Don't go getting amnesia on me now. Just look at your damn shoes!"

Bunni glanced down at her feet.

"Them butter bitches cost damn-near half a grand! And your earrings!"

Her hands flew up to her earlobes.

"Those are Zintys, baby! That's another two yards right there! I ain't even gonna mention all the rest of the clothes, liquor, weed, and partying his dough been financing for the last five months!"

"But *Mink* . . . all you had to do was pick up the cash and dip," Bunni wailed. "You was supposed to get the package and then jump in a cab and come straight back! Why you didn't just stick to the damn plan?"

I swallowed hard. I was so humiliated.

"I tried."

"You tried? And what the hell happened?"

I barely whispered, "I got ganked."

"You got *ganked*?"

"Yeah. I was leaving the hotel when a mark stepped to me. I thought he was green, but he was out working too. He told me he was a balla from Philly and got me open. We slid into the VIP lounge for drinks, and the next thing I knew I was waking up in an empty fuckin' hotel room! He musta seen me at the club and decided to roll me. He got me good too. My earrings, my bracelet . . . my thong . . ." I got mad just remembering how that cool breeze had felt on my coochie when I snuck on the train and squatted down under the turnstile with no drawers on.

My friends stared at me in shock. Bunni shook her head in disbelief. Peaches just sat there looking prissy and swinging that muscular leg he had crossed over his knee.

I put my forehead in my hands. "I don't know how that shit happened, y'all. Dude's name was Daddy Long Stroke and he caught me out there," I added quickly. "I swear he looked like an easy mark. He was adorned in jewels out the ass, and the cologne coming off him cost six-fifty a bottle! It musta been the liquor. He hit me with some jiggle juice. He musta paid somebody at the bar to slip it in my drink."

"Oh, he slipped sumpthin' in your sumpthin' all right." Bunni side-eyed me with a disgusted smirk. "With all them hickeys on your neck I'ma hafta say he slipped his *dick* in your *twat*!"

"Madame Mink . . . ," Peaches admonished me calmly as he put down his tweezers and began fussing with his bob-cut weave. He was feminine and flamboyant. Fabulous and queer. There weren't a whole lotta people in this world that I paid much attention to, but when Peaches had something to say I was usually all ears. After all, Peaches was a master of the con game and he had taught me everything I knew. He had shown me and Bunni how to do our makeup and style our hair, how to show off our bodies and how to hook a man. And when we were thirteen years old, it had been Peaches who taught us both how to use a tampon.

"So you think you got ganked, huh?" He chuckled dryly and picked up his tweezers again. "Oh, that wasn't a gank, my darling. What you got caught in was a flimflam."

I frowned. "A flimflam? You mean them fools trapped me in a cross-con? Are you serious?" I stared at him. "You think that old head principal set me up?"

"Errm-herrm." Peaches bit his top lip as he plucked a real long hair outta his nose. "Damn right he did. We sent you to rip him off, and he sent Daddy Long Stroke to rip you off right back." He shrugged and peered up his right nostril through the mirror. "It happens sometimes, but it's usually hard to flam somebody like you who's so gifted in the grift."

I didn't wanna believe it, but when I thought back carefully, everything Peaches was saying made perfect sense. That principal had read our asses like a coloring book. He was a slick muthafucka!

"Sorry, y'all. I fucked up. I know we all needed that money, but don't worry. I'll think of something else."

Bunni sat down beside me. Her eyes looked all big in her crafty little face. "Well you ain't gotta think too hard." She reached for the carton of milk that was still sitting out on the table and spun it around so the back was facing us.

"Check her out. This you right here, Mink!" Bunni giggled. "Girl, this chick is so *you!*"

I stared at the two black-and-white photos that were printed on the carton of milk and my breath caught in my throat. The picture on the top was of a cute little girl with two long ponytails and a real big smile. She was pretty and looked like a regular little happy kid, but the picture on the bottom damn-near knocked me out. It had been aged progressed by about 18 years, and there was no doubt about it. Bunni had that shit right. Even in black-and-white it was easy to see that the chick looked just like me. We had almost the exact same face and big bright smile.

I shrugged. "Yeah, okay. We favor. So what? There's a whole lotta 'Bad News LaRues' out there. Hell, there's about a hundred of them right here in New York, and ninety-nine of their trifling asses look just me."

"Uh-huh." Bunni shoved the milk carton up closer to me. "But they wasn't all born on the same damn day, was they? On your birthday?"

I read the words that were printed under the photo. Sho nuff, not only did the girl in the picture look just like me, but we had the same birthday too.

"That's real tight." I frowned. "Who is this chick?"

"Her name is Sable Dominion," Bunni said. "She went missing in Midtown when she was only three years old. I Googled that ass, and lil mama got a rich-ass daddy!"

Peaches chuckled again. He was caking a tube of mascara on his short eyelashes.

"What's so funny?" I asked.

He shrugged. "Her name is Sable. Mink and Sable. You get it?"

I kinda got it, but I still couldn't take my eyes off the picture. "Go get your laptop," I told Bunni. "I wanna check her out real quick."

Bunni ran in her bedroom and got her laptop, and a few minutes later me, her, and Peaches were all eyeball-deep on a Web site for missing and exploited children. Bunni typed in the name 'Sable Dominion' and the little girl's picture popped right up.

"Damn. They lost her up in a Duane Reade's," I said as I skimmed the Web site.

Peaches tsked deep in his throat. "Please. How the hell do you lose a three-year-old?"

"Easy," Bunni said. "Her ghetto-ass mama probably wasn't payin' her no attention."

I shook my head. "Her mother ain't even ghetto, Bunni. Her family is from Texas. It says so right here. They came to New York for a vacation and that's when their daughter got snatched."

"What? They ain't got no ghettos in Texas?"

I slid the laptop away from Bunni and my fingers flew across the keyboard. I opened a new window and clicked on Google and punched in Sable's name again.

"Yeah," I said as my eyes flew across the screen and landed on a newspaper article that had a video next to it. "They got ghettos in Texas, Bunni." I clicked on the page and read all the way down to the bottom and then added, "But you can bet your left titty that Sable's paid-ass mama and daddy damn sure don't live in one!"

CHAPTER 6

The Dominion name rang big bells down in Texas. They were a super-rich black family who owned their own oil company, and when I went to their Web site their mugs looked better than the Obamas, and they flossed harder too.

The info on their site confirmed what we had read everywhere else. Sable Dominion was about to turn twenty-one, just like me. But while I was broke as shit, her ass was gonna come into a hundred-thousand-dollar inheritance if she ever turned up alive. I was getting more and more hyped by the second, and Bunni was too.

There were two videos linked to their Web site, and Bunni clicked the one on top first. A news lady came on and she talked about some kinda explosion on an oil rig where seven people were killed and four had been injured. She said Viceroy Dominion, the president and CEO of Dominion Oil, was one of the people involved and that he had a serious head injury and was in critical care at a Houston Hospital.

The news lady talked for a good minute about how Dominion Oil got started and about the dangers of rig explosions, and then she introduced a real pretty black woman who she said was Viceroy's wife, Selah Ducane Dominion.

Mami had on a bad-ass black Prada dress and she looked like she was about to bust out crying in just a second. I figured she was holding a press conference or something right there at the hospital, because she was posted up in front of a micro-phone and surrounded by doctors and nurses.

I checked her out. She was light-skinned like me, and she had a heart-shaped face and a whole lot of long, butter hair that definitely wasn't a weave. She had some style about her and she was on the skinny side, but she was definitely polished up right. The earrings she wore glittered under the camera lights, and I had seen a pair almost like them in Tiffany's that were way smaller and were going for seventeen grand. She sounded East Coast and she came off kinda bougie with her flow, and she had one of those model stances like she was used to struttin' her shit on a runway.

Selah Dominion stared dead into the camera as she asked everybody to pray for the families of all the people who had been killed in the explosion, and then she asked for prayers for her husband, who was still in the hospital, and the other three people who had been injured too.

The video went off and Bunni clicked on the second link before I could get the words outta my mouth. You coulda heard a rat fart in our kitchen when that bad boy started play-ing. Selah Dominion popped up on the screen again. She had on the same clothes and the background was still the same. She still looked real sad too, but this time instead of talking about her husband, she was pleading with the public for information that could help them find their long-lost daughter, Sable Do-minion, who had been snatched from a crowded New York City drugstore when she was just a little girl.

"For the past eighteen years my family has lived with a hole in our hearts. Our baby daughter, Sable, was taken from us by an unknown stranger right after her third birthday. We have searched endlessly for our daughter, and today, as we approach her twenty-first birthday, and with my husband, Viceroy, so gravely injured, we believe finding Sable will give Viceroy the strength he needs to fight for his life. Please. *Please.* If you have any information, any small shred of knowledge at all, that might help us find our daughter, please contact us immediately."

"Get to the money part!" Bunni feened. "Hurry up and say something about the money part!"

Tears flowed from Selah's eyes as she looked into the camera and continued making her plea. "Also . . ."

I was kinda surprised that she didn't sound all proper like you woulda expected from a rich chick, but her voice was real smoove and you could tell she was used to talking in public.

"Just as we have in the past, our family continues to offer a cash reward for any information that leads to Sable's safe return. We realize it's been a long time and memories fade, but if you know anything, or remember *anything* at all . . . even a tiny shred of information that may seem insignificant to you might be the piece that helps us solve this puzzle. We beg of you. Call the number on the bottom of your screen. Our daughter belongs with us. We want her to come home! Home to see her father . . . while there's still time. Won't you help us, please?"

The news lady from the first video came back on as a phone number flashed on the bottom of the screen. "Well, there you have it," she said. "Tonight the Dominion family is in a situation that no family ever wants to be in. Not only are they praying for the recovery of their esteemed husband and father, they are also praying for the safe return of their daughter, Sable, and any information you have can be reported by calling the number on the bottom of your screen. This is Crystal Hunter for Channel Seven news."

I let my fingers fly over the keyboard and went to a celebrity gossip site. They were sorta like the online version of the *Star* or the *Enquirer*, and they loved to talk shit about the rich and sexy. The site had all kinds of juicy stuff posted up about the Dominions, and I found an article that talked about their daughter's hundred-grand inheritance and a twenty-five-thousand-dollar reward the family was offering for information leading to Sable's return. Bunni was all over that shit. She almost jumped outta her skin as she went bonkers about the reward money.

"Twenty-five large?" she shouted. Bunni scooted her chair real close to mine and started drumrollin' her feet on the floor like an excited little kid.

"A'ight now, Mink! You know what you gotta do don'tchu girl?"

I looked at her and giggled. "Are you fuckin' serious?"

"C'mon, heffa! You look *just like* that chick. Your own *mama* couldn't tell y'all apart. You should do it, Mink! Go to Texas! Just do it!"

I shook my head. "Uh-uh. Them rich people ain't gonna be stupid enough to fall for that kinda scam, Bunni."

"Why the hell not? Remember last year when somebody stole your identity and caught all them cases over in Philly? Now you got a chance to steal somebody else's identity and get you some money and some payback too—at the same time!"

A hundred grand. I added up the twenty-five grand I owed Gutta and all the fines and interest that had been tacked onto my bad-check-writing restitution payments. If I had just a little more time I could scramble me up a hustle and get all that weight off my back. But time was *not* on my side. Gutta would be home in a few weeks, and if my ass didn't show up in court on Monday morning the judge was gonna issue a warrant for my arrest.

"Nah." I shook my head. "I don't know shit about Texas, Bunni, and I ain't hardly getting my ass on no airplane by myself."

Before she could open her mouth to bitch, I snapped the laptop closed and pushed that shit way to the other side of the table. "Yeah, you be coming up with some crazy-ass schemes Bunni-baby, but this ridiculous shit right here just straight-up takes the cake!"

CHAPTER 7

Bunni used to have a lil sherm fuck buddy named Red, and Red had a lil sherm homeboy named Borne. Borne was a regular nigga who drove a beat-up Ford and worked for the post office, and whenever Gutta got locked up I kicked it off and on with Borne.

Borne was a square. He wasn't in the game and he wasn't really street-worthy neither. But one thing he definitely was, was reliable. He was always good for a couple of quick dollars in a clutch, and when my life got too shitty Borne had no problem kicking his little chickens out the side door so I could bunk with him in the basement apartment he rented out from his super-religious mother and father.

I had been back and forth between Bunni's house and Borne's basement ever since I lost Gutta's apartment and had to put all his furniture in a storage facility. Borne's parents were old as shit. His moms couldn't stand the sight of me. I heard her tell Borne I was a greedy little freak, but his father seemed to like me a lot. His old senile ass thought I was some porn star chick from back in the day, and if Borne wasn't around that old man would whip out his lil crispy two-inch dick and try to rub it on me in a minute.

Borne had picked me up in his beat-up clunker on Saturday night, and the next morning he snuck upstairs to cook me some breakfast while his mother and father were at early church services. But when he came back downstairs with a plate of French toast and turkey sausage I was so uptight I couldn't eat. I was too busy worrying about my court appointment the next day. I owed the city of New York a whole lotta cheddar, and all the judge had to do was say the word and my ass would be riding a dirty-ass bus over the bridge to Rikers Island.

"Yo, I keep telling you," Borne said as he stuffed his face with his food and mine too. He was skinny as hell for somebody who ate so much, and all his weight musta went straight to his dick 'cause he wasn't nothing like his little burnt hot dog daddy. That lil nigga was *hung*.

"It's gonna be all right, girl. I got you boo. Ya boy just got his first credit card, nah'mean? You gonna be straight, shawty. Stop worrying, baby girl. You gonna be straight."

I was sitting cross-legged on his bumpy little bed. Borne dipped his finger in some syrup and dotted it on my bottom lip. I stuck my tongue out to lick it, and he slipped his finger in my mouth so I could suck it.

His other hand crawled up my thigh and grabbed my titty. He squeezed it gently, then swept his thumb back and forth across my nipple until heat got to rising in me and I started to relax.

He leaned me back, and I unfolded my legs and stretched out flat. "Raise up," he told me, then stuck a pillow under my head tryna make sure I was comfortable. I closed my eyes and sighed as I felt his fingers wandering over me. He lifted up my top and stared at my titties. My twins sat up straight in the air, and my nipples were aimed at the ceiling.

Borne slipped his fingers under the elastic band of my boy shorts. He inched them down over my hips, and then slid them past my knees and tossed them on the floor.

"Open up them legs," he said, and dove nose-first into my pussy. He braced his elbows on the sides of my hips, and he slid his palms under my ass and gripped my booty cheeks as he licked all over my clit.

I shivered and moaned as he ate me for a while, then let my ass go and licked his middle finger. He inserted it between my pussy lips and I couldn't help grabbing his wrist and guiding him to the right spot. My shit was soppy like a sponge inside. His fingers moved in and out of me as my pussy made wet, squishy noises that drove both of us wild.

Borne finger-fucked me and kissed up and down my smooth thighs. He nibbled on me so good I started moaning and clamping my insides down on his finger like I had a dick inside of me.

He flattened his hand so he could put his mouth on my pussy again. My whole body quivered as he licked my little firecracker and dug his fingers all up in my guts.

That shit felt so good I arched my back and pushed back with my heels. My head bumped up against the wall, and Borne came off of me and grabbed me by the ankles and pulled me down the bed until my legs were hanging off the sides.

A big-ass bedspring was sticking me in the back but I didn't give a damn. I raised my legs in the air and opened them wide as Borne went back to lunch. His tongue game was magnificent, but I wanted me some dick too.

"You better fuck me right," I warned him when he came up for air and started wrapping his joint up. "You better fuck me right!"

His dick was amazing. It shoulda been on a nigga twice his size. "I need it hard," I reminded him. "You gots to bring it right, okay?"

Borne had no problem pounding me out. That nigga was groaning and making crazy noises in the back of his throat as he pulled my legs open wide and rubbed the head of his monster all over my clit. He went in for the kill and got real gutter with it too. I let my coochie muscles completely relax as he drilled me. My shit was like a slushy and my insides got totally scuffed as my clit started screaming with pleasure.

Ten minutes later we had fucked our way around to the long side of the bed. I propped one leg up on the wall and the whole bed damn-near tipped over. I had forgot that shit was nigga-rigged up on piles of old books, but Borne got us balanced and that lil beast thrust his meat so deep in my stuff that I screamed and my pussy muscles clenched down hard on him as I came like a mutha.

Borne took that as a cue to go for his. He swept his hand between us and got some of my juice, then stuck his finger in his mouth and grunted real loud. And then he spread my legs wider and licked all over my chest as he cracked his lower back until he nutted real hard too.

It took both of us a minute to come down off that one. Borne grabbed the flat little pillow and stuck it up under my head again. I laid there in his sweaty, linted up sheets as he ran his hands over damn-near every inch of my body. By the time he finished rubbing and squeezing my flesh like he expected juice to squirt outta my skin, I was breathing steady again and back to worrying about every last one of my money problems.

CHAPTER 8

I crashed real hard after that sex action Borne put on me, and we spent the rest of the day in the basement watching old movies. The next thing I knew Monday morning rolled in and it was time to head to court. Bunni met me at Borne's crib, and all three of us took the train downtown to the business district.

Borne mighta busted my coochie out in his cramped lil basement, but being seen with him on the streets in broad daylight was straight up embarrassing. His skinny legs looked real funny in his little post office shorts, and one of his black socks was always too short and forever sliding down in his shoe.

"Yo, Mink," he yapped as we walked from the train station to the courthouse. Last night was over, and I didn't like the way he was clocking me today. He had tried to hold my hand when we got on the train, and when he put his arm around my waist I bumped his skinny ass off with my hip.

"I don't want you worrying about nuthin' baby, okay? Remember, I got you in my pocket, girl. Plus, I got a feeling something dope is gonna go down today. Nah'm sayin'? Last night I dreamt the fuckin' judge tossed all your shit out! He

just went ahead and cancelled *everything*, ma! And you walked
up outta there, girl! That's word, your fine ass just *walked*!"

Bunni shot me a crazy look, and I just shook my head.
Borne was too damn hyped and he was playing me too damn
close. The only reason I had let him come with me was because of that new credit card that he couldn't stop bragging
about. It had a one-thousand-dollar limit, and he told me he
was willing to roll the whole grand on my court fees because I
was just that fine.

I was no stranger to the Manhattan Criminal Court. Matter fact, 100 Centre Street shoulda been my forwarding address
as many times as I had pushed through those revolving doors.
The inscription on the outside of the building read, *Only the
Just Man Enjoys Peace of Mind,* but there was absolutely no
peace in my mind as we walked inside and took the elevator
upstairs.

It was only nine o'clock and the courtroom was already
packed out. All kinds of criminal-minded folks was in the
house. Me, Bunni, and Borne sat in the second row right behind my slick-lipped public defender, and about ten crusty-
lookin' dudes in orange jumpsuits were chained together on a
holding bench on the far side of the wall.

In my latest brush with the law I had gotten busted in a
check-cashing scheme that almost landed my ass in jail. My
lawyer had pretty-pleased the judge into putting me on probation, and instead of serving time I was ordered to pay a restitution fee of five hundred dollars a month and to stay outta any
kind of trouble.

In almost a year I had only made one payment, and that
was the one I needed to make before they would let my ass
outta jail. My lawyer had warned me that the judge could re-
mand me to the court, and that meant instead of catching the
subway back to Harlem in my Prada pin-striped pantsuit and
matching black-and-white wing-tip pumps, I would be styling
a cotton jumpsuit and going back to lockup in Rosie.

We waited for damn-near two hours as case after case was called. There was the low-level drug slanga who told the judge he was scared to go to jail because he was a pretty boy and light in the ass, a mother-daughter booster team who had run through a bunch of stores in Midtown and wracked up mad charges, a young chick who had gone up to her son's school and stomped out his teacher, and a skinny white boy who had gotten busted for dog fighting and who was about to get a beat-down from the bailiffs 'cause he couldn't keep his hands outta his pockets like he was told.

Finally, it was my turn to stand in the hot spot.

"Your Honor," my court-appointed attorney addressed the fat white judge, "my client had every intention of fulfilling the terms of our previous agreement. Right after your sentencing she found a job and was about to begin making her payments as ordered. However, she became a victim of identity theft, and her mother had a tragic car accident where she nearly drowned. My client's mother sustained significant brain damage in the accident and she was placed in a nursing home. She was recently transferred to a facility outside of the city, and my client was forced to choose between paying her court costs or providing for her mother. And only a heartless person would neglect their own mother under those conditions."

I stood up there listening to my lawyer with my eyes closed real tight. I squeezed out tear after tear after tear, and I didn't bother to wipe none of them shits as they ran down my face and fucked up my makeup. That old lawyer-man was laying it on the judge like a real pro. He was saying everything I had told him to say, and he wasn't really lying neither. My mother *did* have an accident, and yeah, she *was* in a nursing home.

But all that had happened the summer I turned thirteen. She had gotten up one morning and decided to drive her car into the Hudson River, and if two joggers hadn't jumped in and pulled her out she woulda drowned right there where she sat. Even still, by the time the ambulance got there she had been under all that water for too long and she ended up with some brain damage. I went to see her in the nursing home as much as I could, and most of the time all she did was cry.

"Miss LaRue," the judge fussed at me, "this is your third time coming in front of me, and despite your mother's horrible situation I'm not feeling sympathetic toward you at all. Looking at your record I can see you are a habitual criminal. A petty criminal, but still a criminal. I'll tell you what I'm going to do. I'm going to give you thirty days to come current with your restitution payments, do you understand? That means, not only must you make your next payment on time, but your account must also be brought current with the courts too."

He shuffled through a folder full of papers in front of him.

"Right now you're almost a year delinquent in your payments. That means you now owe nine thousand dollars, plus fees, to this court. I'm putting you on my calendar in forty-five days. At that time I want to see a receipt from the court clerk verifying that you have made your monthly payments and paid your lump sum back payment as well, or a warrant *will* be issued for your arrest. Do you understand?"

"Yes sir," I said softly and squeezed out another tear. *Ya fat-ass bastard!* I wanted to scream. This fool knew damn well I didn't have no nine thousand dollars to be donating to the city of fuckin' New York! I wanted to tell his old bald-headed ass something real slick, but I wanted to walk up outta that building a free woman too. So I bowed my head humbly and said, "Thank you, Your Honor. God bless you, sir. Thank you."

I was mad as hell as I stomped out of the building and walked toward the train station with Bunni walking right beside me. Borne had headed across town so he could go to work, and me and Bunni were headed back to Harlem.

"You gonna put that thousand down for me?" I had asked Borne when we walked outta the courtroom. That little nigga had slid his hand in his pocket where his credit card was and shook his head. "Don't make no sense to do that, baby. You owe them people over nine grand. My little one grand ain't even gonna be no help."

Bunni was just as pressed out behind all this mess as I was.

"That judge was a muthafucka!" she said as we walked down the crowded city streets turning heads left and right. Me and Bunni always attracted mad attention when we were out together, and in a city full of hot chicks like New York, that wasn't easy to do.

"This city is full of madness!" Bunni complained real loud. "What the fuck? If you was paid like that you wouldn'ta been out there cashing other people's checks in the first place! And then they got the nerve to tack on all them damn administration fees and shit! That's prolly gonna be a whole 'nother grand. The court system got hustlers out here gankin' each other just to stay outta jail. What kinda gangsta government lick is that?"

"I know," I said, agreeing with her. "But I'da been straight if my ass hadn't lost that twenty grand to Daddy Long Stroke. I guess I'ma have to rob a damn bank now."

We ran down the stairs to the train station, and after scanning the area for cops, both of us ducked and went under the turnstile.

"Yo, I'm telling you this is a sign," Bunni said as we waited on the platform for the train to come.

"A sign like what?"

"You know, a signal-sign."

"Here we go again." I rolled my eyes. Bunni swore she was a psychic. "You and your damn paranormal signals. I know, I know . . . your left titty is itchin', right?"

She bust out laughing. "Damn right it is."

"Okay, twist your nipple and find out what the hell I'm supposed to do then, goddammit! I got that fool Punchie lurkin' on the staircase tryna pop me at your crib, Borne's mama wants him to toss my ass outta his raggedy basement, the judge is about to slap me with a W and throw me in the bing, and Gutta is gonna hit the bricks in a minute and come gunnin' for his goddamn money. What is your left nipple sayin' Bunni?" I laughed. "Should I go rob a bank, or do I get strapped and go stick up a liquor store?"

"Nah," Bunni giggled as she gripped her titty and shook it at me. "My nipple ain't even feeling New York, honey. It's pointing straight toward the south. I'm telling you, Mink. You need to flam that inheritance shit! My nipple is sayin' you need to take your ass on down to Texas and hook up with your rich-ass mama so you can get paid!"

I stopped laughing and looked at her. Shit, after what the judge had just said I couldn't help but be interested. Desperate times called for grimy capers. "You really think we could pull some shit like that off?"

"You can do it, girl." Bunni nodded with confidence. "Hell, fuckin' yeah! You can do it!"

"I said *we,* goddammit! You slippin' hard, girl. Somebody's gotta get that twenty-five-grand reward money. Don't you want it to be you? Do you think *we* can do it?"

Bunni locked in on the words *reward money,* and her eyes got big. "You *damn* right we can do it!" she hollered as the roaring train pulled into the station.

"We can do it, Mink. Yes! We! Can!"

CHAPTER 9

"Hold up. I don't get it," I told Bunni. We were eyeball-deep in mad Internet articles and finding out more and more about the Dominion family of Dallas, Texas. They were way richer than I had thought, and the father was so cold he even had his own Wiki page.

"Sable ain't even their real daughter, though," I said as I read Viceroy Dominion's bio. "It says right here that they have three adopted kids and two real kids. Barron, Dane, Sable, Grayson and Fallon. Sable is the oldest girl, and they adopted her right after she was born. Why the hell are they breakin' their necks to find her and give her a slice of their pie when she ain't even their real child?"

"Maybe they loved her," Bunni said. "It don't have to be your real kid for you to love it, you know."

"Adopted kids *are* real kids." Peaches sniffed like he had raised a bunch of babies of his own. "Look at Angelina Jolie and all her chirren. She ain't giving the crusty ends of the bread to the kids she adopted and saving the soft slices in the middle for the ones she pushed out. All them lil bad-ass kids probably came into millions as soon as they learned how to piss in the potty."

I half-listened to them as I kept reading Viceroy Dominion's Wiki page. I stared at his picture. He was dark-skinned
and fine as a muh'fucka. Dude was living larger than any brother
I had ever seen before. I clicked on a link and saw there was a
whole section on him in Who's Who of Texas Businessmen
that talked about how he had stacked his loot in a shady stock
deal and shrewdly built his oil company into a multimillion-
dollar business. I was impressed. Papa seemed like he had some
street hustle in his flow.

"Look at these damn pictures!" I told Bunni after I clicked
on another link. "This one here is from their last Fourth of
July barbeque. It says here they have houses all over Texas, but
every year they throw a big 'que at their family mansion outside of Dallas."

"The Fourth is coming up," Bunni said as she reached past
me and swiped her finger on the laptop's keypad. She scrolled
through the photos that were posted on some local Texas
celebrity sites. "Their shit is sick," Bunni muttered and stared
at a shot of their multi-wing mansion that had been taken
from up in the air. "Just fuckin' sick!"

I peered at that shit and my nose got open too. The picture
showed mad cars and pools and tennis courts, and there was
even some kinda jet parked off to one side of the house and
covered by an awning. I had never seen nothing like this at no
black person's crib before, and I couldn't even imagine what
kinda cash flow it took for them to stunt like that every day.

I clicked on another tab and Sable's age-progressed picture
came back up on the screen. I dragged the corners and made it
real big, then I stared at it from all angles and went over every
little feature that me and her had alike.

Almost all of them.

I pulled up the Web site where Selah Dominion had
pleaded with the public to help find her daughter. I watched
the entire video clip again, and when she was finished talking I
stared at the telephone number that flashed on the screen.

"Are you finally thinking what my ass *been* thinking?" Bunni said from over my shoulder.

"I don't know," I clowned. "What you been thinking?"

"My ass been thinking you need to let me make that call and tell them people I found the daughter they lost!" She snatched up the piece of paper that I had scribbled the telephone number on two days ago. "Gimme the phone, Mink. So I can call that goddamn number!"

Bunni shoulda got an award for the performance she threw down on the phone. Instead of reaching Selah Dominion like we thought she would, she got connected to a private investigator.

"Hi, my name is Bunita Baines and I have some information I think you might be interested in."

I couldn't hear what old boy was saying on his end, but if he was grillin' Bunni she was damn sure grillin' him right back.

"So how much is that reward again? Uh-huh. Twenty-five thousand? And I get it laid on me just for hooking you up with the girl I think is Sable, right? Oh, hold up. I only get paid if the girl can *prove* she's Sable, huh? Right, I gotcha. A'ight, well I got that information for you, then. Oh, hell yeah it's her. I *know* it's her. Matter fact, she's sitting here right now. You wanna talk to her?"

She passed me the phone.

"Hello?"

The private investigator introduced himself as Sam somebody and then he gave my ass the third degree. He wanted to know when I was born, where I was born, who my mama and daddy was, if I had ever been locked up or arrested, did I have any kids, did I know I was adopted, and if I had any drug addictions or weird habits.

He hit me with mad questions and I hit him back even harder with my clever, skillful answers. He tried to rattle me, but I hung with his ass for the whole ride, going toe-to-toe and using my gift of the gab to the fullest. It took me a whole lotta lying and convincing, but it was all good because after all, those were the things I did best.

Sam took my phone number and told me he would pass my information on to a representative of the Dominion family. He said if they were interested in pursuing the matter any further they would give me a call.

Less than thirty minutes later my cell phone rang. I didn't recognize the number on my caller ID, but Peaches and Bunni were jumping up and down screaming, "Answer that shit! Answer that shit!"

So I did.

"Hello?"

"Good afternoon. My name is Selah Ducane Dominion. I understand you contacted Mr. Samuel George and asked to speak to me?"

I coughed real loud to hide the sound of me putting her on speakerphone. I knew these rich people wasn't gonna want no hood-rat for a long-lost daughter, so I called forth my best hootie tootie black bougie voice and put my smooth tongue to work.

"Excuse me! Hi, yes. My name is Mink LaRue and I'm from New York. I saw your press conference on a Web site and I think"—I paused like I had to gather my emotions and said tearfully—"I think I might be Sable. Your daughter."

Selah's voice was cool as crushed ice. "Is that right? What makes you think so?"

"Well," I said keeping my voice soft and innocent, "for one thing, I was born on July fifteenth, 1991, just like your daughter was, and when I saw that little girl's picture on the back of a milk carton I knew it was me right off the bat."

"Oh, did you now?" Mami sounded kinda New York-salty, like she had some snap about herself. "So who are your parents? Who raised you?"

"My mother's name was Jude Jackson," I said, which was the truth. "She raised me by herself. She was a single parent." That part was mostly true.

"Well, did you think Ms. Jackson was really your birth mother? Or did she tell you that you were adopted?"

I swallowed hard again and sighed. "My mother had a really hard time admitting that I'd been adopted," I lied, "but when I was about to graduate from high school she couldn't come up with my birth certificate. I thought that was kinda suspicious, and it made me wonder if there was more to my story. I finally got her to admit that I wasn't her biological child and I started searching for my birth family. After seeing my picture on the milk carton, I searched the Internet and found you."

"Yes," she said dryly. "I'm sure you did."

I could tell I was losing her. Hell, if I had been expecting Mama Dominion to start jumping up and down and wiring me some of that cool Dominion cash, I was shit outta luck.

"It was good of you to call. . . What did you say your name was again?"

"Mink. Mink LaRue."

"Mink, huh? Cute," she said, and gave me one of those yeah-right-bitch chuckles. "Well Mink, I'm sure you know we get lots of calls like this from young ladies who claim to be our daughter Sable. I must say that one or two were quite convincing. But our daughter's DNA is on file, and to this day nobody we tested has ever proven to be a match."

DNA? I pumped my brakes.

They actually checked for that shit? How the hell was I gonna pass a goddamn DNA test?

"Oh, I'd be more than willing to take a DNA test," I said eagerly. "I can—"

She cut me off. "Oh, that's probably not necessary. There are other less complicated methods we use for screening these types of calls. You see our daughter has the sickle cell trait—"

"I have the sickle cell trait!" I damn-near shouted. I had forgotten all about it, but I definitely had it.

"Yes, but our daughter also had six toes."

"*I* had six toes!" I shouted for real. "On both my feet! They chopped off the little nubs when I was a baby, but I can still see the scars from where they used to be!"

"That's great, but like I said, before we can talk any further you'll be required to take a DNA test."

"That's not a problem," I assured her. "I live real close to Harlem Hospital. I'm sure they can do a test."

"Sorry." She dropped a bomb on me. "We'd need to have that test run by our own lab. It's called Exclusively DNA, and it's right here in Dallas."

How the hell was I supposed to get around *that*?

Craziness rolled outta my mouth before I could stop myself. "I understand, Mrs. Dominion. I think I can come to your lab and have the test done. That won't be a problem either."

"At what age did you say you were you were adopted?" she sounded a little bit more interested now.

"I guess I was about three," I said quickly. "But all my life I knew I was different."

"Hmm, different? How so?"

I got to spinning the wacky tale that me, Bunnie, and Peaches had come up with, and less than two minutes after I started talking I knew Selah Dominion was sitting in the palm of my hand. I had Mama's ass! I had her good!

My little conversation with Selah Dominion had gone down exactly the way I wanted it to. The only thing I was stuck on was how to get around that damn DNA test, but then Bunni looked up the lab on the Internet and came up with a hustle of her own.

"All we gotta do is get on the inside," she said. "Labs fuck shit up all the time, Mink. People get false results on all kinds of tests. Why can't you get one?"

"Why can't I get one what?"

"A fake test result, dummy! Yo." Bunni slid the laptop closer to her and brought up Google. "Girl, don't you watch *CSI*? What lab did the mother tell you to go to again?"

I looked down at all the notes I had scribbled. "Exclusively DNA. It's in Dallas."

"Cool." Bunni tapped on the keyboard and brought up the lab's Web site.

"Check this out. They offer immigration DNA, paternity DNA, and siblingship DNA." I looked over her shoulder as she clicked on a tab that brought up another page. "They got four people working for them and thank God one of them is a dude."

"Why?" I asked as we both stared at the smiling pictures of the lab's staff members. There were three white chicks and one black man. The man's name was Kelvin Merchant and he was light-skinned and big as hell.

"Because, stupid," Bunni said with a real slick grin, "the dude is the one I'm gonna go after."

CHAPTER 10

Barron Dominion was in chill mode as he rode down the mean streets of Dallas. He was on his way to a meeting with the shareholders of his father's company, and he nodded his head to the sounds of Jay-Z that blasted from the luxury automobile's twenty-one strategically placed speakers.

The rear roof was wide open, and the sun was on full beam as he slid his finger across his iPad and checked the latest stock reports from Dominion Oil. His father, Viceroy Dominion, was a cutthroat oil baron who had come up in the slums of Houston and made his money the good old-fashioned way: he stole that shit.

Rumor had it that Viceroy had come into his mega-millions by swindling one of his business partners in a crooked oil stock deal. The two had invested in a start-up company as equal partners, but at the end of the day it had been Earl Washington who ended up bleeding in the gutter, and Viceroy Dominion who stood on the throne pissing down on him.

At just twenty-five, Barron was one of the state's best and brightest corporate attorneys, and he had graduated from top-tier schools. He had watched his father bum-rush and connive his way into power positions with some of the richest men in the oil industry, and although Viceroy had learned to walk and talk like an upstanding man of means, there was always that slick hint of hood in him, that switch-blade-carrying, dice-throwing nigga from the trenches that lived just beneath the surface of his skin.

Barron was cruising in the backseat of his 1.5 million-dollar whip and studying the bylaws of the company's stock-holder's agreement when his cell phone vibrated and the front display lit up brightly. He glanced at the caller ID, then pressed a button on a side panel and spoke into the intercom in the white-on-white 2012 Maybach Landaulet.

"Yo, roll it up, Charlie. I gotta take a call."

The smoked-glass panel that separated the chauffeur's compartment from the rear seat area in the luxury sedan slid up smoothly, giving Barron complete privacy.

"Hi Ma. How you feeling today?"

Barron was a momma's boy and he didn't give a damn who knew it. Although he had his father's sharp mind for business and could come off shrewd and cocky with his corporate op-ponents, Barron had nothing but love for his beautiful mother, Selah Ducane Dominion.

"Hello, baby," Selah Dominion greeted her oldest son. "I'm doing okay. But I want you to know I got an exciting telephone call from Sam George earlier today."

Barron sat up straighter in his seat. His moms was tipsy. He could hear the old familiar slur in her voice even though she was trying hard to control it. He adjusted his tie and pinched the razor-sharp crease in his pants.

"What did he want? What, he found another Sable wanna-be? I guess that Internet news conference is getting a lot of hits, and people wanna see what they can get out of us. I'm telling you, Ma, you better brace yourself. With Daddy in the hospital all kinds of nuts are gonna start scurrying around us like project roaches."

"Hmmm . . . ," Selah said. "Maybe. But this one seemed

kind of promising. She called our hotline and they patched her through to Sam. He said he spoke to her for a little while, and she really impressed him. He gave me her number and I called her."

Barron frowned. The scenery outside had changed from an urban hood to the Dallas business district, and the buzz of a small but vibrant city was in the air.

"Come on now, Ma. You shouldn't even be talking to those people. They chase stories like ours just for the hell of it. Most of them are just schemers and con artists. They'll tell you anything to play on your heart and get in your pockets. With Daddy being so sick you just don't need that kind of distraction right now. Forget about this girl, and I'll give Sam a call and remind him not to bother you when stuff like this comes up."

"But I already spoke to her, Barron. I couldn't tell a lot about her over the telephone, but there *are* a lot of similarities between her and Sable. She lives in New York, but she's flying to Texas on Monday to take a DNA test, and we're gonna get together and have lunch or something."

Barron cursed under his breath. Sam's dumb ass was about to get fucked up. Viceroy had been tearing him off under the table for years to keep the Sable imposters away from Selah, and as soon as his father got laid up this fool let one slip through the cracks.

"So did this girl take a DNA test yet? Sam shouldn't even be calling you unless there's some DNA results on the table."

"No, she hasn't taken the test yet. She's going to do that when she flies in on Monday."

Barron sighed. "Mama, I know it's hard on you, but it's been almost eighteen years now. Eighteen long years, and every last girl who's called has either been a mental case or a broke opportunist, and I can't see this girl being any different. How much cash did she ask you for?"

"None, Barron. She didn't ask me for a dime."

"Not even to buy her a plane ticket to get down here?"

"She didn't ask me for anything. Nothing at all."

Barron pressed his cell phone to his chest and pressed on the Maybach's intercom button again.

"Turn it around, Charlie, and get Brian on the phone and tell him to cancel the board meeting. Tell him something came up and we'll have to reschedule. Cancel my lunch date with my cousin Pilar too. Run me back to the estate real quick," Barron ordered as his driver made an illegal U-Turn, then muttered under his breath, "So I can see what the hell is going on with my mother."

Twenty minutes after taking his mother's call, Barron walked through the front door of the Dominion Estate. His cousin, Pilar Ducane, was standing in the large foyer talking on her cell phone, and she ended the call and stuffed the phone inside her purse the moment she saw him.

"Barron! What the *hell*—?"

"What are you doing here?" he asked. "I thought you had a meeting in the city today?"

"I thought you had one too!" she said. "That's why I wanted us to go to lunch. What the hell happened?" she asked, rushing at him with a frown on her gorgeous face. Pilar was a sexy-ass socialite and the spoiled only daughter of Barron's uncle Digger. Her and Barron had grown up together and they'd always been tight, but lately Pilar had been playing him close and tossing around some steamy hints that let Barron know she wanted them to be a whole lot closer.

"You promised to take me to lunch today, B, and then Charlie calls and says you're ditching out. What's up with that?"

"Something came up," Barron told her. He caught the pissed-off look that flashed across her face as he rushed past. "I'll take you out tomorrow. I promise."

"That's what you said last week!" Pilar whined, and then

she smirked at his back. "What? Let me guess. Carla's got your ass running around in circles again, right? How come every time me and you are supposed to hook up that little hater tries to pull something slick?"

"It's not Carla," Barron said over his shoulder as he strode toward the parlor. "I gotta talk to Mama real quick. I just found out there's another chick out there claiming to be Sable. I'll tell you more about it later. After I handle this business."

Pilar crossed her arms across her breasts and her stylish jewelry sparkled. "Oh, I've got some business for you to handle," she muttered under her breath. "You can believe that."

"A'ight, so we've got another nutcase on our hands," Barron said as he stepped into the stunning, two-story parlor. Selah sat on an expensive sofa drinking a vodka tonic. She jumped up when her son entered the room, and there was excitement mixed with alcohol and hope in her eyes.

"I just got off the phone with Sam," Barron told her. "He said to tell you he's sorry for calling you with all that nonsense. The next girl who calls him thinking she's Sable is gonna get sent straight to the lab."

Barron had lit a fire under Sam's ass and had the dumb dick apologizing until he was out of breath. For years, Viceroy had been sliding that fool big chunks of cool cash to keep this kind of shit away from Selah. But now that Sam had fucked around and let this crazy broad from New York slide through, all of that extra paper was about to be dead.

"So it's all good, Ma. He won't be calling you with no more nonsense."

"But I told you I'm not really sure it's nonsense this time," Selah said as she raked her fingers through her silky, blow-dried hair. The liquor had broken her out in a sweat, even though the temperature in the mansion was always kept extra-cool.

"This girl seems like she might be the real thing, Barron. She had all the right answers. She has the same birthday as Sable, she was adopted at the right age, she has the sickle cell trait—she even has the same genetic mutation that causes babies to be born with six toes just like Sable was. I don't know . . . something tells me she could be the one."

Barron stuck his hands down in the pockets of his tailored Brioni suit. "That's the same thing you said about the last two girls, Mama. One of them freaks was trying to get a sex-change operation, and the other one wanted you to give away all your money because the world was coming to an end. C'mon." He put his arm around her as they walked over to the window. "Right now Pops is enough for you to worry about. I don't want you to go getting your hopes up high again on Sable."

"Sable is still my baby," Selah said as she sipped on her drink. At forty-eight she was still beautiful and classy, and she could have easily passed for thirty. She had a cool, distant air about her, but those who really knew her understood that she was fragile inside and could get broken down by too much stress.

"For real, Ma. I mean it," Barron warned her.

"I hear what you're saying, Barron. But for some reason this girl just seemed different to me. She was so *convincing*. I can't explain it. I just have a gut feeling this time. Call it a mother's intuition or whatever you wanna call it, but I have it."

Selah stood at the window and stared out over the sprawling forty-two-acre estate that her husband had built for her more than twenty-five years ago. She had grown up in a cold Brooklyn tenement, and now she lived in a dream house. A twenty-room mansion that she had helped design and had spent years decorating to her tastes. They had horses, cattle, swimming pools, tennis courts, ponds, and countless fine cars. Her children hadn't been raised like she was raised—beneath a roaring elevated New York train station with city grime falling down on their heads, but instead, they'd grown up right here in the lap of luxury. And even though she had more money than she could ever spend, and the entire world was at her fingertips, Selah still wasn't happy.

"A'ight," Barron said as he stood beside her. He hated it when she got all silent on him. "So what's her name this time? Where is she from?"

"Her name is Mink, and she's from right there in New York. Harlem."

Barron laughed. "Mink? Mama! Come on now. What? You hold a press conference and tell the world you're looking for a missing child named Sable, and all of a sudden up pops some broad named Mink? Who's gonna be on the phone next? A hood chick named Chinchilla? C'mon, Ma. Forget about this girl. I hate to say this, but it's been a long time, and we don't even know if Sable is still out there anymore."

Selah hugged her son. For Barron to be adopted, it was funny how much like Viceroy he was. But Selah knew how to handle both of them. She wasn't about to forget about finding Sable. She'd taken her eyes off her baby for just a few minutes and she'd lost her to a stranger. What kind of mother could forget that?

"You don't have to tell me how long it's been, Barron. I relive that day almost every night in my dreams. And all I can say is I'm sorry. I'm sorry for Sable, and I'm sorry for you too."

"I know. But it's okay, Ma. Everything is cool." Barron put his arms around her again. If nobody else understood the pain she felt over losing Sable, he sure did. After all, the blame was partly his too. He was the oldest. He had been the one in charge. Sable had been snatched out of her stroller right in front of his eyes, and he hadn't been able to do a damn thing about it.

"You were seven years old," Selah said, reading his guilty thoughts. "Seven. It was my fault for leaving you alone with two babies. That lady was going to take Sable no matter what, and there wasn't a damn thing you could have done about it. Nothing."

Barron nodded and kissed the top of his mother's head. She'd been telling him that same bullshit for over eighteen years.

Maybe one day he'd believe her.

CHAPTER 11

Kelvin Merchant was real easy to find on Facebook. Dude musta had his finger on the CONFIRM button because Bunni sent him a friend request and he approved it quick fast. We stalked his Facebook page and laughed like crazy as we read all his freaky info. He looked a good three hundred and fifty pounds in his pictures, and in the hobby section he had the nerve to put in "pain slut" and list a Web site called meninpain.com

Bunni loved that shit!

"Oooh, I'ma join that group and look for him," she said and pulled the site up on the screen. We hollered when a picture came up of a white dude hanging upside down with his balls wrapped in chains. He was dangling by his feet with both his arms tied behind his back. A skinny blond chick wearing nipple pasties and a black garter belt was grinning wickedly over her shoulder as she yanked his hair and ass-muffed his nose.

Sure enough, Mr. Pain Slut was already registered on the Web site.

"Damn, Kelvin is a pain slut for real!" I said as Bunni

clicked on the registration box and started filling it out. "You really gonna join that shit?"

She smirked. "Hell fuckin' yeah! I don't mind beating a nigga's ass when a nigga needs his ass beat!"

"Freak!" I screamed. "You's a nasty little *freak!*"

"Look at this!" Bunni giggled as she read ol' boy's profile. "Mr. Pain Slut likes humiliation, inescapable bondage, boot worship, ass-lickin', face-slappin', butt-spanking, and *dick torture!*"

"Stop lying!" I squinted at the screen and then bust out laughing. "You gonna have some fun whippin' on that ass!"

"Damn right," Bunni said, and her eyes got big with excitement. "I'ma hafta order me some tools and stretch out real good before I go in hard on him, 'cause that's a big ol' dude and he's got a whole lotta ass to whip!"

Kelvin and Bunni had the instant messages flying back and forth and they were getting real thick up in the mix. He invited her into an S & M chat room and they started turning each other on with all kinds of kinky torture talk and dark fantasies. Bunni told Kelvin she liked to dominate men and treat them like dog shit, and he confessed that he was passive and submissive, and he loved being spanked and slapped, especially on his face, dick, and ass.

He also told her that he walked around wearing a metal dick clamp up under his clothes, and he said one of his hottest fantasies involved having a woman torture him, then force him to eat her pussy out.

I was known to be the freak of the week, but all that pain shit didn't turn me on not one damn bit. But Bunni was all for it. She got dude to tell her his safe word, and when he asked her if they could meet in person she cursed him out and told him she made the damn rules and said he never knew when she was gonna pop up outta the bushes and fuck his sissy ass up.

Peaches had all kinds of good ideas about what kinda whips and shit Bunni should take with her in her torture kit when we flew down to Texas.

"Girl, you should get you some of them Tenga toys! They got cock studs, and deep throat cups, and all that!"

"Handle ya bizz," I told Bunni as I thought about my own plans. I had to make a stop or two before I dipped up outta New York. The first thing on my list was to get a ride to the nursing home where my mother had been living for the past seven years. "For real, I don't care what you gotta do so your pain slut can get him a nut. Just make sure he takes damn good care of our asses when we get down there."

Mama was in one of them state-run nursing homes where all kinds of violations went down unchecked. I hated visiting her. Not because I didn't love her and wanna see her, but because every time I went there I ended up wanting to kick somebody's ass for not doing their job and taking care of her.

"Mama," I called her name and sat on the side of her bed. She smelled like she had been soaking in old pee, and only God knew when the last time her diaper had been changed. "It's Mink, Mama. I came to see you."

Even with her face stiff and her hands twisted inward like claws, my mother was still beautiful. Every time I visited her I brought a comb and brush and some pretty headbands and clips for her hair. I did her makeup and polished her fingernails, and I ran my mouth talking to her a mile a minute.

Going up there was bad enough, but leaving her was hard too, because she'd start reaching out for me and talking nonsense, and then all kinds of tears would roll down her face like it was breaking her heart to see me go.

As a teenager I knew my mother had done something real twisted and wrong when she drove her car into that river, but by the time I was grown I had come to understand more about that kinda thing. And even though in my heart I had forgiven her for what she did, I had never been able to say those words out loud to her.

"I gotta go outta town for a little while," I told Mama as I brushed her soft, pretty hair and dabbed lipstick on her mouth. "Guess where I'm going? Down to Texas! You never been to Texas, huh? Well, I'm gonna be doing some acting work down there," I lied. "I'ma be gone for a couple of weeks but I'll be back to see you right after my birthday okay?"

A strange look came into my mama's eyes. Like she was real scared of something. She started drooling a little bit and moving her lips around like she was tryna tell me something real important. Her twisted hands reached out to touch me and I grabbed them and kissed them.

"You gonna be all right," I shushed her as loud moans came from her throat. I pressed her stiff hands to my chest and rocked her back and forth. "The doctors have my number, Mama. They'll call me if you need me and I'll come right back, okay?"

I always hated to leave my mama, but I couldn't wait to get outta that damn nursing home. Peaches was waiting outside for me in his boyfriend's car, and when I got in beside him his eyes was full of understanding. Peaches was good to me, and he was the only person in the whole world who really understood my soul. The woman laying in there in that bed mighta gave birth to me, but Peaches had been my mother when it really counted.

"You good, Madame Mink?" he asked softly.

I felt like shit inside, but a gwap was on the line so I wiped my tears and put on my game face and nodded.

Peaches touched my hair and smiled, and then we headed on back to Harlem.

CHAPTER 12

It was time to go! Me and Bunni were ready to blow New York and put a hella hurtin' on the city of Dallas. The Fourth of July was falling on a Thursday, so we decided to fly to Texas that Friday morning, just in time for the Dominions' annual barbeque. I knew the DNA lab was gonna be closed for the whole weekend, but I figured we could just play dumb and talk our way into the Dominion mansion and put our feet up for the weekend.

Borne had charged both of us a one-way ticket on his little credit card, and after I put some hot booty whammy on him he tore me off a couple of hundred dollars in cash for my pockets too.

Of course Mink Minaj was itchin' to floss real gully down in Texas, and Peaches and his crew went on a boosting spree for me and Bunni, and he even came through with some extra ends that helped us out a lot.

"I got two hundred dollars," Peaches told me. He looked real dainty as he took a little white hankie outta his bra, and when he opened it there were two yards inside folded up in small squares. "This is my last little bit of play, you hear? So y'all betta get down south and *work!*"

The flight was only a few hours long, but me and Bunni were runway-dressed from our shades to our shoes and loaded down with Yves St. Laurent luggage full of boosted gear.

"Don't forget," I warned Bunni for about the tenth time before we left. My girl wasn't adaptable like me. I had practiced playing so many roles over the years that I could call one up just like that. But Bunni was always the same chick, no matter what. She looked the part of an uptown diva, but when she opened her mouth all kinds of ghettoisms were prone to jump out.

"Them Dominions are rich and Selah sounded bougie as hell. So keep in mind what I told you," I cautioned her. "Whatever you do, don't let 'em peep your real game, you dig? You just keep smiling and looking good, that's all you really gotta do. If they ask you a bunch of questions just nod a little bit and play 'em off. We ain't gonna steal shit while we're down there, and we definitely ain't tryna get locked up in Texas where they deep-fry niggas and drizzle gravy over them for lunch, okay? We're just gonna dip in, work 'em over until we get 'em nice and soft, then wait for my birthday to roll around so we can cash that fat check. You got it?"

Bunni nodded.

"Good!" I squealed. "Leggo!"

It was blazing hot in Dallas when we landed at the airport. We'd gone on a mini shopping spree in an airport store, and I had twenty-two dollars left to my name and Bunni had forty. We got our brand-new designer bags off the merry-go-round thingie, then jumped in a yellow cab and gave the driver the address to Selah Dominion's mansion.

"What if them rich fools don't wanna let us stay with them?" Bunni asked. Neither one of us had ever been so far away from New York before and she sounded kinda shaky.

"Oh, they gonna let us stay!" I said. "If they wanna get their daughter back they *better* let us stay."

On the real, between me and Bunni we barely had enough money to pay the damn cab driver, and we could forget about tryna get a hotel room over a holiday weekend. But one way or another our asses was getting up in that house!

As we drove away from the airport I checked out the sights. From what I could see Dallas was nothing like New York. Instead of skyscrapers and congested highways and people scattering around like roaches everywhere, the landscape was flat, the traffic was pretty light, and it was too damn hot for anybody to be walking around any damn where.

I sat back and tried to look at every little thing we passed.

"What kinda crazy shit is this?" Bunni laughed as we rode down the highway and passed some big houses that were on huge patches of farmland. She started rapping. "Horses in da front yard, llamas in the back! Cowboys on da porch drinkin' gin like that!"

I was actually digging all the differences between here and home. I had always been a dreamer, and when I was little I had fantasized about visiting all kinds of places from London to Liberia. I used to steal luxury real estate magazines from vendors and cut out pictures of the super-mansions I wanted to live in one day and all the luxury cars I wanted to drive, then tape them on the wall next to my bed.

I had done that kinda stuff for years, and I knew rich when I saw it, but I hadn't seen a damn thing to get me ready for the sprawling estate the cabbie drove onto or the mega-mansion that sat at the end of the long, circular driveway.

"What the *fuck!*" Bunni was wide open on that shit. Two Bentleys and a flashy Rolls Royce sat in the wide driveway under a huge brick awning, and a black Mercedes Benz, a slammin' Lamborghini race car, and a bone-white 2012 Maybach were parked right in front of the house.

I elbowed her real hard. "Get it together, Bunni! I done told you! Don't get up in there cursing all loud or smacking your damn food, and whatever you do, please don't get to twisting them nasty pieces of toilet tissue up your nose the way you do when you get sleepy. Pull yourself together and let's act like we're about something, okay? There's money to get up in this bitch so let's go get it!"

But Bunni wasn't the only one wide open. I had never in my life seen black people living like this before. We had picked the right day to bust up on them too, because the estate was sho nuff jumping as they prepped for their big Fourth of July cookout. Waiters and workmen were everywhere. An old black man was bent over shining the rims on the Maybach, and another old dude was polishing up the brass fixtures on the front door.

We tossed the cab driver forty bucks even though the meter said we owed him forty-two, and me and Bunni were barely outta the taxi when a tall, killer-looking security guard in a hot black suit came at us real hard.

"Wrong address," he told the cab driver as he tried to shoo our asses back inside. "This is private property. Go back out and take a left on the main road. You should be able to find your way from there."

"Um, no," I said with a bold smile. I had on a pale yellow mermaid skirt, a sheer white belly tee, and a curly mint-green wig with pale yellow streaks. Bunni was wearing a pair of gold coochie-cutter shorts and a matching halter. I switched my ass and baby-stepped toward him like my ankles was tied together in my mint-green shoes, as Bunni posted up and struck a perfect pussy-print pose. "Nah, I think we're in the right place, boo. This is the Dominion Estate, isn't it?"

Dude hesitated like, *wtf.* He stared at me and then at Bunni, and then back to me. He was young and wit' it and I busted his groove. He was a high-priced security guard and he mighta been all strapped up in his monkey suit, but he wasn't immune to all that New York sex appeal that me and Bunni were throwing down on him.

"My name is Mink LaRue. Mrs. Dominion is expecting me."

Ol' boy left our bags sitting in the driveway and we followed him to the front door of the mansion. We stepped into a huge foyer that was cool and smelled like flowers, and I wanted to slap the shit outta Bunni when outta nowhere she started stomping her feet and squealing like a damn idiot.

"This shit is nice as *hell*!" Bunni was loud as a mutha as she hugged all on my neck and started jumping up and down. "We 'bout to get it yo! We 'bout to get it!"

"Wait right here," the security dude told us. He gave Bunni a hungry look, and as soon as he walked away a skinny white dude rushed over and tried to show our asses right back to the door.

"Good afternoon, ladies," he said, gripping our elbows and turning us around at the same time. "I apologize, but Mrs. Dominion isn't available right now. As you can see we're preparing for a family event. She asks that you come back on Monday, after you've taken care of all the necessary business you were instructed to attend to."

I put on my brakes and smiled dead in his face. He was talking about me hitting the lab to take that DNA test, but he wasn't getting my ass back out that door!

"Oh, there's a family event taking place?" I said, leaning into him and swinging him and Bunni both around in a wide U-turn. "Well *I'm* family!"

He smiled stiffly. "That's wonderful, Miss . . . er . . ."

"LaRue. Mink LaRue. I'm so sorry." I pressed my hand to my chest in a real dainty move. "I must have misunderstood my instructions." I smiled again and blinked innocently, turning on the charm. "We arrived in Dallas this morning and went directly to the address Mrs. Dominion gave me. For some reason the lab was closed, so we decided to come here instead."

"It's a holiday weekend," the assistant explained. "Most

businesses were closed yesterday and today. But they'll reopen on Monday, and you should head back to the lab again at that time."

"Oh for real, I will," I agreed as I stood my ground. "But see, I'm only gonna be down here for one day. I don't have a problem going back to the lab on Monday, but like you said, it's a holiday weekend, and there's no way we can get a room around here today. Every joint within a hundred miles is already sold out."

"I'm sorry, ma'am. I really don't know what to tell you. Perhaps you could call around and try to find some last-minute accommodations, or you might want to return home and come back next week, but you really can't—"

"Thank you, Albert," a feminine but firm voice interrupted him. A tall, slim lady walked into the parlor wearing a rose-colored skirt and a sleeveless silk shift. I recognized the outfit as Chanel and the woman wearing it as Selah Dominion. My stomach quivered in awe. It was like Michelle Obama had stepped up in the joint, or maybe even Patti LaBelle. I figured Bunni's ass was finally struck speechless too because I didn't hear so much as a squeak outta her.

"Hello." The woman extended her hand. "I'm Selah Dominion."

All I could do was stare at her. She was even flyer in person than she'd looked in the videos. She had perfect features and her whipped hair hung down below her shoulders. She rocked delicate shine from her neck and ears that had obviously cost big bank, but at the same time her style was tasteful and real classy.

"I'm Mink LaRue, and this is my best friend Bunita Baines."

Selah barely glanced at Bunni. She was too busy staring at me, and it was hard for me to handle the emotions on her face.

"Your eyes," she said, peering at me closely. "They're hazel. My daughter Sable's eyes were gray when she was a baby, but by the time she was four months old they'd turned hazel. Just like yours."

I gave Selah both of my dimples and all thirty-two of my perfect pearly whites. There was something about my smile that had always made people trust me, and Selah was no exception. Hell yeah, she was rich as shit, and that made her kinda wary, but I could tell how bad this chick really wanted me to be her long-lost daughter, which damn sure woulda been right up my alley too!

"Come on inside," Selah invited us with a smile. She took us through the parlor and down a real long hall. My beady little eyes were everywhere as I tried to take it all in. The walls were done up in some real fancy gold wallpaper, and a bunch of large-framed family photos were hung everywhere.

I felt a sharp sting on the back of my upper arm and I almost hollered "ouch" as I whirled around.

Bunni had pinched the shit outta me. She was back there grinning her ass off as she pointed and checked out all the fancy sculptures and shit that was part of the décor.

We gone get paid! she mouthed as she wiggled her hips down the wide hall. *We gone get paid!*

I swung at her and missed as we both hurried to keep up with Selah.

She led us into a super-large living room that looked out on a huge yard. A sliding glass door stretched from one wall to the other, and there were a bunch of colorful leather couches arranged in front of the biggest flat-screen televisions that I had ever seen.

"We're having a little Texas barbeque today for some friends and family," she said as she gestured toward all the workmen outside who were cutting grass, setting up tables, and positioning ice chests.

"Oh, I'm sorry. I hope I'm not intruding or anything," I said quickly, using my best white girl voice and pretending like I had some manners. "I thought the lab was gonna be open today. I didn't even think about the Fourth falling on Thursday and businesses closing down on Friday to celebrate. I guess I should have tried to get a hotel room anyway. New York is just a little bit too far to do a round-trip in one day."

Selah smiled and said the words that I had practically pushed into her mouth. "It's no problem. Since you're here now you might as well stay. It's a big house and we have plenty of room. Actually, you came at the perfect time. Since most of the family will be here this afternoon it'll be a good opportunity for you to meet my children."

I grinned happily. Ya damn skippy I wanted to meet the rest of the crew. After all, they'd gotten their sweet little hundred-grand inheritance, and I was damn sure gonna get mine too!

CHAPTER 13

"Now *that* looks damn good on you," Nellie Marciano gushed as her friend Pilar Ducane modeled a bright yellow Dolce & Gabbana dress that hugged her scrumptious curves and highlighted the best features of her firm, luscious body. "I wish I had your breasts," Nellie complained and gripped her flat chest with both hands. "Raheem loves big tits. I'm gonna have to find a good plastic surgeon."

"Oh, these babies are real." Pilar cupped her firm knockers and admired herself in the mirror. "They're all mine." She turned around to check out the precious booty and was satisfied with the way it rounded out the back of the tight dress.

Pilar was out doing some early morning shopping with two of her white girlfriends, Nellie and Vicky. Their fathers were all moguls in the oil transportation industry, and Pilar's father, Digger, had actually introduced Nellie's father to the business and sold him his first fleet of trucks.

The three girls had just hit NorthPark Center, which was one of the ritziest malls in Texas. They were only in their first store and already their arms were loaded down with merchandise. Pilar had picked out a bangin' Fourth of July dress to wear to the barbeque her aunt was having later that day, and she'd found the perfect red and white bikini to complement her caramel skin tone and show off her curves.

Her adopted cousin Barron, aka Bump, was gonna be at the barbeque with his blond fiancée, Carla, and Pilar wanted to give him a hot visual to remind him of what kind of ass he could have been banging if he was engaged to her instead of that bony chick who had hooked him when he was a star football player in college.

Pilar was in a so-called serious relationship with a fat financial analyst named Ray, but Bump was her dream man, and even though her father and his mother were sister and brother, Pilar knew nabbing a husband like Barron could set her up and bankroll her for life.

And bankrolled was definitely what Pilar wanted to be today. She'd been shopping with her friends for forty-five minutes and she had picked up all the highest-priced shit, which was only right since out of the three of them her father made the most money.

Her arms overflowed with thousand-dollar skirts, crazy expensive dresses, belts and earrings that cost more than the average man's weekly salary, and the shoes she planned to buy were all to die for.

"Just put it on my account." Pilar waved her hand as their personal shopping representative rang up her merchandise totaling six thousand, two hundred and forty-one dollars.

"Absolutely," the young lady said as she punched a few numbers into her register. Pilar and her girls were chatting away as the shopping rep peered closely at her screen.

"Er, excuse me, Miss Ducane, but there must be a problem with our system. Your account has a hold on it. The computer won't allow me to input any additional charges. I apologize. It must be some kind of glitch."

Pilar smiled at the girl sweetly. "If there's a problem with your system, darling, then why don't you go find someone who can fix it?"

Pilar grinned wickedly at Vicky and Nellie as the rep hurried off. But minutes later the girl was back with her manager, who quickly checked the system then tried to pull Pilar discreetly off to the side.

"Pardon me, Miss Ducane. Can I speak with you privately for a moment?"

Pillar wasn't having it. "What's the big problem? I've been shopping here for years and I spend a lot of damn money in this store!"

"I understand that, Miss Ducane, and I apologize for any inconvenience this may cause you. But Sheila is right. We're unable to add any additional charges to your account until your current balance has been settled. However, if you'd like to pay for your merchandise by credit card, I'd be happy to personally complete your transaction."

Hater! Pilar gave the woman a real deep look. This old bitch was embarrassing her in front of her friends on purpose.

"Here!" She slipped a platinum American Express card from her wallet and flung it at the manager. "I hope you know this is gonna be the last damn time any of us shop in your store!"

She fumed as the woman processed her transaction. She could feel Nellie's and Vicky's eyes crawling all over her back, and she wanted to turn around and fuck both of their snobby asses up.

"Miss Ducane"—the store manager wore a grim look on her face as she handed Pilar her card—"again, I do apologize—"

"Don't fuckin' apologize to me. Apologize to whoever owns this raggedy joint because business is about to get bad for everybody around here! You can keep your apologies, honey. Just get my shit wrapped and bagged so we can get the hell out of here!"

The manager grilled her. She'd spent years catering to rich

bitches like Pilar, and it always felt good when she was in a position to stick the toe of her shoe up one of their spoiled asses.

"I'm afraid I'm going to have to apologize again, Miss Ducane. I won't be able to 'wrap and bag' any of this merchandise today, because unfortunately your credit card has also been declined."

"What?" Pilar nutted up, ready to cause a scene to hide her embarrassment. "You've gotta be fuckin' kidding me!"

Hot shame flashed through her body. She swung her arm wildly and swept everything off the counter. Thousands of dollars' worth of merchandise hit the floor, including the items that had been on display and half the clothes that Nellie had set up on the counter too. Pilar lifted her feet and stomped all over that shit before she pushed past the manager and stormed out of the store.

Speed-walking back to her car, she wanted to kick some ass! How could her father let this happen to her? With the current oil crisis going on she'd known her father's business was having a little trouble, but he'd told her not to worry because he had it all under control!

Pilar tossed her valet stub at the parking attendant, then snapped her fingers for him to hurry the hell up and bring her freshly-detailed Lexus around. Nellie and Vicky must have stayed back at the store to pay for their new clothes, which was good because Pilar was too ashamed to face them. The only reason she had asked them to go shopping in the first place was because it gave her a boost when she out-spent their asses!

She climbed behind the wheel of her ride and floored it out of the parking lot. Something was going to have to change in her life, and real damn fast too. If her last name had been Dominion instead of Ducane this kind of shit would have never happened. This was gonna be the last damn time she shopped with Vicky or Nellie too. She'd been way too humiliated and her pride wouldn't let her face those snobby bitches again. At least Vicky had turned away and pretended to be interested in a purse when the drama went down, but that blue-eyed NFL groupie Nellie had been down Pilar's throat the whole time. She reminded Pilar of Barron's flat-assed fiancée, Carla. Neither one of those greedy white chicks deserved the rich black men they had!

CHAPTER 14

One of the houseboys took us upstairs to our rooms. I was kinda anxious 'cause it hadn't been a good hour yet and Bunni was already actin' ig'nant. We each got our own rooms, which were really two big suites that had a connecting door. They were laid the hell out with the kind of prime, quality shit that I had only seen in pictures of the most upscale five-star hotels.

Bunni's ass was awestruck. Our rooms were separated by some pretty French doors, and she ran straight through my suite and dove face-first on the four-poster king-sized bed in her room.

"Look at this shit!" She got on her knees, then stood up on the bed and started jumping up and down like a little kid.

"Calm ya ass down!" I told her. "Don't be acting like you never saw a bed before, Bunni. Damn."

I was fussin' at Bunni, but on the real I was open too. I'd seen a lot of nice houses in magazines, but I had never been in-side a real live mansion before, and everything in here was just like I had imagined it would be in my dreams.

All the furniture went together. The bed actually matched

the dressers and the night tables, and everything had been polished until it glowed. The carpet was fuckin' luscious. The
spreads matched the sheets, the blankets, and the drapes. The
set-up was completely perfect, and it was exactly what I had
always wanted.

I was tiptoeing around my room scared to touch anything,
while next door Bunni was wildin' out like she was back in the
hood.

"Mink! Girl, did you see the bathroom? Check out that
shower! These mofos are *rich*! Even the toilet seat is beast!"

Our suitcases were delivered to our rooms by a couple of
servants, and they brought up a tray with fruit, cookies, dough-
nuts, and cake too. Me and Bunni decided to take a shower
and change into some different clothes. We went to our own
bathrooms, and when we were done we met back in my room
to pick out our outfits for the barbeque.

Of course Bunni was bent on showing off that camel toe.
She chose a pair of white satin jeggings that rode low on her
curvy hips and stopped right below her knees. The pants
showed every bit of her bomb-ass shape, including her monkey, and she set them off with a silver and black belt, a lime-
green tank, and some matching jewelry. She sprayed her locks
down with water and scrunched them around with her
hands, then pushed her hair back with a cute lime-green
headband. She put on some mascara and lipstick, and she
was set.

I tried to approach my gear with a little bit more thought.
I knew my choice in clothes could be weird and over the top,
and since I was tryna make a good impression I suppressed my
natural desires and decided to play it safe and sexy. I wanted to
give the Dominions a hint of what I was packing, but not the
whole thing. I chose a stark-white halter dress that Peaches had
boosted from Neiman Marcus. It was cut low enough in the

front to show a little cleavage, but not so low that my rack was jumpin' out atcha.

The dress tied behind my neck and exploded in a V down my back. It fit kinda loose, but the tapered waist made it clear that I had a big ass without making my booty look ghetto. I decided to wear a platinum-white wig that was bobbed in the front and long in the back. It was so white it matched my dress perfectly, and when I added some dangling Jerome Berrion chrome earrings and a pair of matching chrome snake bracelets that wrapped around my arms almost up to my elbows, everything came together just right.

Or almost just right.

Something was missing, but I couldn't put my finger on it. I dug into my jewelry bag and took out a sparkly diamond necklace that looked like a doughnut. It dangled on a thick silver chain, and it looked real dope when I fastened it around my neck.

Hell yeah. I grinned as I looked in the mirror. My shit was set.

I was itchin' to get up in the crowd that had started to gather in the Dominions' huge backyard, and I went to get Bunni outta her room so we could bust up on the scene and start us a little trouble. Bunni's joint was trashed. She had left shit everywhere, just like she did when she was back in New York in her own damn crib.

"Girl, ain't you gonna pick some of that stuff up off the floor?" I shook my head. "You gonna have these rich people thinking we cluckin' like chickens."

Bunni checked her hair in the streak-free mirror and shrugged. "Shut up, Mink. As long as we get that loot I don't give a damn what these people think."

I didn't like the way that sounded. Bunni was known to

sabotage shit when she got too salty, and I didn't put it past her to fuck up our grand entrance just because she was mad at me. I needed Bunni to be down in order to pull this off, and Bunni knew it, so I bit my tongue and followed my girl downstairs.

New York City had been hot and sticky, but the Texas heat was dry as dust. Me and Bunni walked down the grand staircase and went out back. A lot of people had already shown up and they were already sitting at tables with big umbrellas and being served colorful drinks by a staff of waiters and waitresses in fancy uniforms.

We walked down the stone path to the pool area where mad little kids was running around laughing and spraying each other with water guns. The music was blasting and teenagers were getting their swag on. A sweet hickory scent was in the air, and three split-barrel barbeque grills were smoking Texas-style.

"Mink." Selah stood up to welcome us. She was sitting at a table that was covered by an umbrella so damn big it looked like a flying saucer. "Nice dress. Come on over here so I can introduce you and Bunni to some of my family."

She led us over to a long table where a bunch of people sat around grubbing.

"Everybody, this is Mink LaRue and her friend Bunni. They're visiting us from New York. Mink and Bunni, everybody here is family. They're either part of the Ducane clan from Brooklyn, where I grew up, or they're Dominions from Houston where my husband Viceroy was raised. Either way, they love to eat and they came to party!"

Uh-huh. I knew it! I laughed inside as I checked out her crew and listened to some of their convo. All that Oreo-ass bougie shit she had put out in them online video clips was a real front. These folks were hood-rich. They had money out the ass, but the street was in their blood. Most of them looked deep-ghetto, and they were getting busy playing spades and bones, and a few thug-lookin' fools were shooting Cee-Low up against a big chest full of ice and making that "*ahht!*" sound every time the dice rolled over and hit the ground.

I smiled real cool and shook everybody's hand as we were introduced. A few of the older women hugged me and complimented me on my diamond doughnut. I recognized some of the closer members of the family, and I was able to match a lot of faces to the names I had already read about on the Internet and memorized.

"This is my oldest son, Barron," Selah said as we walked up to a dude who looked like a younger version of that buff chocolate nigga Terrell Owens. Dude was even finer in person than he had looked in his pictures. His body was beastly, the kinda cut-up physique you expected to see on a star football player. He got up to shake my hand and we caught a whiff of each other's flow. I wasn't surprised when he put his arm around Selah and pulled her close to him like I was some kinda ghetto vampire out to suck his mama's blood.

"Unh!" Bunni grunted behind me. "Nigga fine!" she whispered with her lips damn-near on my neck. "Get 'em! Get 'em! Shit, y'all ain't related! Y'all was both *adopted!*"

"It's nice to meet you." I gave him a soft smile. I had read all about Barron Dominion and I wasn't tryna throw no suspicious vibes his way. *GQ* had done a spread on him, and I knew he was the tight-ass lawyer type. I had seen pictures of him on the Internet with his skinny, snow-bunny girlfriend, and I damn sure wasn't surprised. He was the oldest of the Dominion children, and like Bunni said, he had been adopted just like Sable.

"And your name is again?" Barron barked as he shook my hand real loose like I had cooties on my fingers. I wasn't even pressed. This nigga probably already knew just as much about me as I did about him.

"My name is Mink," I repeated. "Mink LaRue." I turned and smiled at Bunni. "And this is my best friend, Bunni Baines."

Barron looked at us like he wanted to throw both of our gutta asses on the hot grill and drown us in barbeque sauce. "Yeah. Uh-huh." He sized me up with his sexy dark eyes. "Good to meet you too."

Selah grabbed my hand and walked us around the pool and picnic areas so we could meet the rest of the crew. Little kids was running around everywhere. Black ones, white ones, and Asian ones too. It looked like Selah and Viceroy had a whole lotta family and friends, and between the Dominions and the Ducanes, the whole rich-ass posse was getting it in.

Their hood relatives from Houston had turned out by the vanload. There was a crew of thuggish-lookin' teenagers chillin' over on the other side of the tables listening to the kinda music that made pole professionals like me and Bunni wanna strip outta our clothes and make it rain all up in the joint.

Selah introduced us to Barron's fiancée, Carla, who was real pretty and real friendly. She said hi and gave me a simple little white girl smile, and something about that smile made me like her right away. I figured most of the clear folks running around were probably her family members, and I spotted an older white woman who I could tell was her mother.

Then Selah took us over to meet her two real kids. Her son, Grayson, who everybody called Jock, and her daughter, Fallon. They were the two youngest Dominions, and even though one was seventeen and the other was eighteen, both of them were about to be seniors in high school.

I checked out the son, with his Viceroy-lookin' self. I'd smoked enough weed to know a dro-head when I saw one, and Jock looked high as hell. He was tall and cute and pressed out in his gear just like the young'uns who slung rock on the corners in Harlem. He was adorned in hood shine and sagging, and his fitted was turned around backward over a red doo-rag. Jock didn't really pay me no attention, but he zeroed in on Bunni's camel toe right off the bat, and them smoked-out eyes of his stayed on her twat the whole time we was being introduced.

Fallon was a hot seventeen-year-old Texas beauty queen, and she was chillin' with about four of her teeny-bopper girl-friends. They were styling some skimpy bikinis for the thugs across the way, and giggling as they profiled their hot little bodies.

Mami was a rich little bitch, so I didn't know if she was gonna have her ass on her shoulders or what, and as soon as we were introduced she let me know how she was rollin' right off the bat.

"Mink, this is Fallon. Fallon, this is Mink."

"*Mink?*" She put her hands on her curvy hips. Her titties were high and tight in her hot pink bikini, and a cute gold charm dangled from her belly button. I could tell Miss Thang was spoiled and used to being the only chick in the house, but we was about to see about all that. She turned her little nose up at me, and then smirked as her eyes swept over me from head to toe. "Oh, yeah. Pilar told me about you." She tossed her long hair and turned away from us, giving me her ass like I was straight dismissed. I looked at her young behind like, damn! I mean, I wasn't expecting her to jump up and down with no long-lost big sister love, but her prissy ass didn't have to diss me like that neither!

"Mink, this is my niece, Pilar," Selah said as we walked on for a second, then paused beside a chick who was stretched out on a lounge chair with an open book covering her face. She had on a skimpy tangerine-colored bikini and her light-brown skin was slick and shiny with baby oil. I peeped her package and had to admit the chick was holding in all areas.

"Hey Pilar," Selah said. "Sit up, baby. I want you to meet

Mink LaRue and her friend, Bunita. They're visiting us from New York."

At the sound of Selah's voice the girl slid the book off her face. She was a few years older than me and real pretty. She blinked a few times and then sat up.

My antenna was up and I busted her groove right away. This bitch was just like Fallon. Stank.

"So what did y'all *really* come down here for?" She skipped all over the bullshit and grilled me and Bunni like she was a psychic who had just peeped our game.

I grinned at her like, bring it baby, bring it! I was *so* used to birds stepping to me. We checked each other like two hot battle bitches. My eyes were honey-hazel and Pilar's were stormy gray. Uh-huh. Shiesty was sure nuff up on shiesty. I had done the project stare-down with the best of them and I wasn't about to look away first. If this trick wanted some ass, she was gonna have to bring some too. She was giving me the bizz and I was handing her that shit right back.

Selah stepped in and tried to smooth our little nonverbal thang over.

"Mink, Pilar is my only niece and she's really more like a daughter. My brother Digger is her father, and you'll get a chance to meet him when him and Pilar's boyfriend, Ray, come back from playing golf."

I nodded and gave Pilar a real slick smile as we walked away. This little country chicken must didn't know! We bit tender bitches like her for breakfast up in Harlem.

When Selah finished introducing us to everybody we went back to the picnic area. Waiters were going around picking up behind the kids and throwing away half-eaten plates of food and bringing beer and drinks to all the grown folks.

"Y'all must be hungry," Selah said and I nodded. I had heard a lot of good things about Texas barbeques, and the smells coming off the grills had my stomach rumbling. "We have a wonderful cook on staff, but Katie's getting up in years and she keeps setting kitchen fires, so we hired chefs to cook the meat and catered the rest of the food."

Me and Bunni were fixing our plates when a dude came outta nowhere and spoke up behind us.

"So you're Mink, huh?"

I turned around. A brown-skinned guy wearing nothing but a pair of sky-blue swim trunks stood there us checking us out.

"Who's *you*?" Bunni blurted out, and for once I couldn't blame her.

He grinned and flashed us a perfect set of bright whites. I'd seen a lot of fine-ass men so far today, but this one here had a few drops of New York grime on him and he was packing mad sex appeal.

He had short, wavy dreadlock twists that looked nice and fresh. His skin was cocoa-butter smooth and his hairline looked like it had been edged up with a straight razor. I could tell he lifted weights 'cause his chest was rocked up just right, and his lumpy six-pack had a curly river of fur that ran from his navel into his swim trunks.

"I'm Dane." He grinned. "Better known as the black devil of the family."

"Brother Dane!" I laughed. Just like Barron and Sable, he had been adopted as an infant by the Dominions too. "Oh *you're* the black devil?" I cracked the hell up. "That's what I just called that chick Pilar!"

Dane laughed, and him and Bunni both got a plate full of barbeque ribs while I just took a spoonful of potato salad, a barbequed wing, and a little bit of Texas baked beans. There were big pans of fried chicken, macaroni and cheese, collard greens, and peach cobbler. I wanted to slap Bunni as she licked her fingers then picked all through the pan of franks tryna find a burnt one. There were two large champagne coolers full of ice, juice, and bottled water, and I got me an apple juice and we all sat down at a table.

A bunch of little kids were jumping rope right across from us, and Bunni pushed her plate away when she spotted them.

"Ooooh! I wanna jump!" she said, and jetted before I could check her.

Bunni showed the little girls how to take two ropes and stretch them out to play double-Dutch. Most of the little black girls already knew how to jump, but them little Asian girls were all over Bunni, and the white girls were too. They was loving her up. All the grown folks were watching and smiling as they sat around having a good time. Shit was all good while Bunni was showing them how to turn and how to jump in for double-Dutch, but when they put the ropes down my girl took it to the hood and started showing them lil kids how to play some project hand games like "I Tagged you, Miss New Booty" and "Under the Sheets Is Where We Gotta Meet!"

I fuckin' *cringed* as Bunni got them kids to recite a real loud chant that talked about peeing and farting and doing things under a blanket that no little kid shoulda been thinking about doing.

I was really done when she hit 'em with a throw-back guessing game that we used to do in the projects when we were real young.

"Half past?" she went around asking all the little girls. "Half past?" she demanded, grilling them babies with her Harlem hood-wrecker face on. They were supposed to guess the time of day she was thinking of, but of course none of them did, so she finally blurted it out to them. "Half past a monkey's ass, a quarter to his *balls!*"

"Bunni!" I hissed tryna get her attention. "Bunni!"

Ignoring my whispers, she walked right past me and dug

into one of the brass ice coolers and pulled out a bottle of Fuji. My ghetto girlfriend posed, holding that expensive-ass water up real high in the air, then twisted up her lips and said loud enough for the whole damn world to hear, "Hey now! Forget all this here *fancy* shit! Y'all got any quarter-waters or maybe some real sweet red Kool-Aid?"

CHAPTER 15

We had just finished eating when Barron came over carrying a big-ass shopping bag and squeezed in between me and Dane. He waved at the DJ and gave him the cut signal, and when the music stopped he waited for a few seconds and then hollered at the crowd.

"Listen up!" Barron said real loud, and almost instantly he got everybody's attention. He was all in my mug. Staring me down. Looking in my eyes like he was a mean cop and I was supposed to break down and confess to all my crimes.

"I wanna thank everybody for joining us today, and for all the prayers you've been sending up for my father. Today is not just a Fourth of July celebration. It's also a celebration of God's grace and mercy for allowing our father to survive a whole month with the kind of injuries he got in that rig explosion, so please keep praying for his complete recovery."

Every hand on the property clapped in applause. A lot of "Praise Gods" and "Bless him Lords" went up in the air too.

"By now," Barron said, keeping it moving, "you've all probably met Mink LaRue, and you know she's here in Texas because she thinks she might be my little sister, Sable. Let's welcome Mink with a round of applause."

Everybody smiled and started clapping again, and me and Bunni sat there looking real sweet and innocent as we cheesed our asses off right back at them. Barron opened his shopping bag and whipped out a big ol' gold-framed picture of three little kids sitting stair-step between each other's legs. He held the picture up and turned it from side to side so everybody could see it.

"This is a portrait my parents had done of me, Dane, and Sable," he announced. "Right before Sable was taken away from us."

I put my fork down and crossed my legs as everybody got real quiet. I knew it was hot-seat time and I was ready. All eyes had been on me since the moment I stepped outta the house, and it was all good. I had shit buzzin'. I could hear their lips flappin'. They were grillin' me hard, tryna figure out if my game was legit or if I had a hustler's heart.

"Mink," Barron said like I was a prisoner and he was interrogating me. "Do you remember this picture?"

"Oh!" I said after a soft pause. I had always wanted to be an actress and this was my chance to shine. I made sure my bottom lip trembled a little bit as I stared at the kids in the picture and went into lie-mode. "I've never really seen any photos of myself this young before. I can't believe how happy I look."

I touched my napkin to my eyes and blinked a few times. "My mother—the woman who raised me—just wasn't into taking pictures and that kinda thing. She was always ... sick. I don't think I took a real picture until I was in the third grade...."

I waited a few seconds for that to sink in, then I looked up like I had been taking a solo trip down memory lane. "I ... I'm sorry. I didn't mean to go there. It's just that parents usually take pictures of their children as a sign of their love. I never had much of that when I was a child."

My last line fucked Selah up. I heard her gasp, and then she clutched her throat. One of her girlfriends reached over and started patting her hand.

"Tell everybody where you grew up, Mink," Barron said all loud. "Did you go to college? What kind of work do you do?" He gave me a fake-ass grin then gestured at me like, *Speak up, bitch, speak up!*

I pushed my chair back and stood up real straight. I had everybody's attention so I knew I had to make it good.

I flashed the crowd a sweet, bright smile and let about ten gallons of honey just ooze all outta my pores. "First of all, hi everybody, I'm Mink LaRue. Thanks for welcoming me to the great state of Texas!"

A bunch of "Welcome, Mink's" flew up in the air. All the dudes were checking me out with big grins on their faces, but the sistahs were looking at me like I was an intruder tryna snatch up their men and their money, so I needed to hook them with a little bit of honey too.

"Wow. I just can't believe I'm here," I said, talking in my phony white girl voice again. I looked around slowly, like I was taking it all in. "It's so good to see such a beautiful group of family and friends. Everyone is just so lovely, especially the ladies. Growing up, I never had a sister or a close aunt, and I'd like to thank all the women here for being so warm and welcoming me with love. You ladies really know the meaning of Southern hospitality. Thank you."

I had 'em. Now all the women were smiling too, especially the older ones. I caught Selah's eye and she nodded her head and beamed like she was a proud mama for real.

I thought about all the gutter shit Barron had probably dug up to use against me and I decided to mess him up by throwing it out there first.

"As you've probably heard already, I grew up in New York City. In one of the poorest of the city's housing projects. I didn't have a lot when it came to material things, but I always had a great imagination and an eye for the unusual. My mother couldn't afford to send me to college, so after high school I enrolled at a small art school in Manhattan."

I smiled, then gestured at my wig and my clothes.

"As you can tell, everything about me is pretty unique, and I think it just comes from me being so *lonely* when I was a kid. My mother worked two jobs trying to keep us off the streets and out of homeless shelters, and sometimes she trusted the wrong people to look after me. And as an innocent little girl I really suffered because of that."

I spun them suckers a hard-knock tale about how I had been dragged through drug dens, approached by pimps, chased by rapists, and robbed at gunpoint, and I swore all out that even though I had made some mistakes from time to time, I had still managed to hold tight to my dreams by believing there was a better future waiting for me somewhere under a flippin' rainbow.

I had them suckas softer than butter, and when I finished yakking everybody started clapping again. My girl Bunni clapped the loudest. She knew how bad I was lying so she was impressed the most.

"So what are you doing with your life now, Mink?" Barron took another dig at me before the applause was even over. "Do you have any special talents? I know you said you're creative, so does that mean you model, or sing, or maybe you like to . . . dance?"

I flashed him my brightest grin and nodded. Oh yes, muthafucka! I knew where he was tryna take me, and hell yeah I went there!

"I work part-time in an art gallery, but actually, I do a little bit of everything you mentioned Barron. I sing a little, and I like to model and I definitely dance too. On a stage, and sometimes in front of the camera. Matter fact, I landed a contract last year with that hot urban clothing line called Birthday Cake. You know, the one Marshall George and all the bigwigs in hip-hop fashion are promoting on TV? I danced and modeled in a lot of their videos, and I did photo shoots all over New York, and they want me to come back in a couple of months to do a few more sessions. I'll admit I love the camera and I come across pretty sexy on film." I clasped my hands in front of me, grinned, and lowered my gaze. "But it's all a front for corporate advertising. I'm much shyer than that in my private life."

I kept my cool as Barron mean-mugged me again. I winked to let him know I wasn't scared of his ass. He knew exactly what the hell he was doing when he brought that damn picture outside. I had just played his game and used it to my advantage.

Pilar went in for hers next. She was sitting next to Ray, a chubby dude with a huge, gorilla dome. He was Pilar's boo, and he looked like the last dude on earth I woulda expected her high-flossin' ass to be fuckin' with.

"Does your family know you're here in Texas, Mink? I mean, do they know what you came down here to try to do? I know I would be like, "yeah, right" if somebody in my family woke up claiming to be somebody else after all these years."

I gave a real gentle shrug. "My aunts and cousins know I'm here. But my mother? Unfortunately, my mother died," I lied softly, and a bunch of hushed *awwws* rang out. "Yes," I sniffed. "She suffered from liver disease," I said, which was definitely true. "From being an alcoholic." Which was even truer.

My last line seemed like it punched Selah in the gut. I heard her gasp and then she clutched her throat again. Tears welled up in her eyes and that doofus-ass Barron was by her side before the first one could fall.

"It's okay, Mama." He shot me a "bitch, *please*" look as Pilar rushed to hold Selah up on the other side. "C'mon, now. You don't need to get upset."

I could tell my little child-of-the-ghetto story had all the ladies feeling me.

All of them except Cousin Pilar.

Her lips were still twisted as she eyeballed me with the shit-look. Mami was cool on me, and I was cool on that ass too. Pilar might not have been from the projects, but she was damn sure living on the shady side of the street, and I had peeped her game when I first came out the house.

Yeah, while Barron's cute little thing thang Carla was sitting off to the side conversating with big-headed Ray, Miss Pilar had been over there chomping on Barron's jock like a meat-lover with a sausage jones.

I beamed inside as I enjoyed the sympathetic looks that were plastered on everybody's face. I knew Barron regretted putting my ass on blast now, because my little sob story ended up being a buster on everybody's mood. He tried to kick the party energy back up by waving at the DJ and hollering that it was time for all the swimmers to get in the pool. I stood there and grinned as he picked up some of the little kids and they laughed and squealed as he tossed their butts in the shallow water.

Almost everybody was heading toward the pool when Pilar came over to get at me again. I had to give it to her. This rich bitch was bold. She glanced at the framed picture I was holding in my hands, and then that trick had the nerve to get up real close in my face.

"Sable doesn't look a goddamn thing like you."

I looked at Bunni and both of us busted out giggling.

"No?" I held the picture up next to my smiling face. "You don't think so?" I straight clowned that trick as I cracked the hell up right in her mug. "That's okay, my cousin. Trust and believe, by the time I roll up outta Texas me and Sable are gonna look just like *twins!*"

CHAPTER 16

The party around the pool was starting to kick up real live. They had some T.I. and Gucci Mane blasting from the outdoor speakers, and the waiters were bringing around cold beer, Cîroc, Hen Dog, and Krug. A bunch of the cousins from Houston were hanging out by the pool, while Jock and Dane spit some of their gangsta lyrics and their hood relatives played Cee-Low right at my feet.

"I didn't even know rich people got down like this," I told Dane as I slurped down some cranberry Cîroc and watched the dice roll and the money change hands. I liked Dane's vibe, and he didn't seem to be all tight in the ass like Barron was. "I figured y'all would be drinking lemon water and listening to Beethoven or some high siddity mess like that."

Dane laughed. "Everybody out here ain't rich, so don't get us twisted, Mink. Besides, my mother and father are both from the hood. We livin' pretty large with the servants and the cars, but look around, baby. This is the fam. My father grew up poor as shit in Houston, and when we were little me and Barron spent every summer right there in his old house with his aunt. We fought, stole, and played basketball and football with bad-ass kids who went to bed hungry every night. Pops made us bang up with real people who had real lives, because he wasn't gonna have his sons growing up soft."

I nodded. "So is this *all* of the family?"

"Uh-uh." Dane shook his head. "Hell no. There are a whole lot more of us than this, mostly cousins. My moms has a sister who we haven't seen in years, and Pops has a younger brother that he's real close to. Uncle Suge." Dane laughed and took a swig from his Corona. "Now that nigga there is a straight-up playa. He throws that gangsta love down real hard. You'll see what I mean when you meet him."

Me and Bunni chilled and drank with Dane and his cousins for a little while longer, then we jetted upstairs to change into the cute little bathing suits we had brought with us so we could really show our shit.

Walking back into our rooms was crazy exciting. The servants had unpacked our bags and turned down the bedspreads and put two mints on our pillows. The fruit and doughnut tray they had brought up earlier was gone, but there was an ice bucket with bottled water and a tray of crackers, chips, and pretzels sitting out.

I was hyped beyond belief, and it was hard for me to take in how fly everything was. My suite had a window that overlooked the back of the house, and I could see the swimming pool, the big, colorful garden, and the stone walkway that led down to a huge Jacuzzi that was surrounded by a tall row of privacy bushes.

I stood in the window and watched Pilar work her gushy all up on Barron over by the Jacuzzi. Their asses musta thought nobody was gonna peep their game behind all them damn bushes, but I could see them just fine from the second floor.

I couldn't believe everybody was sleepin' on their shit. Cousins my ass. Them two was fucking. I also couldn't believe how Barron's clueless girlfriend was sitting all off to the side talking to Ray while Pilar had her tongue wrapped around her man's ear. Carla musta heard me thinking, because I saw her look around, then get up and walk down the path toward the Jacuzzi.

She rounded all those bushes and took them by surprise. As soon as Barron saw her he jumped his ass straight into that bubbly water, and I was just about to call Bunni to come look at what shoulda been a good fight getting started when I heard a crash and the sound of glass breaking coming from her suite.

"Bunni! What the hell was that?"

"A freakin' soap dish!" she hollered. "Do you know they bought all this fancy shit way from Japan?"

"Stop touchin' stuff!" I told her. "You ain't gotta pick up every damn thing you see!"

"I know you ain't getting your ass up on your shoulders." Bunni walked into my room wearing a tiny yellow bikini with no straps on the top. Her hips were brown and curvy and her stomach was flat as hell. "I was just looking at the shit. It ain't like a soap dish is gonna break they damn bank!"

I was hot. Bunni was my girl, but she couldn't stay on track for shit.

"Look, try to act right when we go back out there, okay? I already told you these people are different and this ain't Harlem. And no, they ain't got no quarter-waters or no damn suey sauce neither! If we're gonna get that bank then we gotta play the role, so act right!"

Her hand flew to her hip. "Act *right*? I already told you I don't give a damn what these people think about me! Shit, I'm Bunni Baines ere'day, baby, and I ain't tryna be nobody else! Plus, they already know you from the projects, Mink. You ain't gotta put on no front and act like you come from money, because everybody can already tell that your ass don't!"

That shit hurt. I had gotten in the mirror and practiced talking proper for three whole days before we came down here! I had a very important role to play right now! If Bunni wanted that reward money, and if I was gonna get a shot at that

hundred grand, then I needed to at least impress Selah Dominion and make myself acceptable enough to be her daughter.

"Cool, Bunni," I said quietly. "Just don't forget why we
down here, okay? If they smell game on us then this whole shit
is gonna be over."

CHAPTER 17

"That chick Mink is a damn liar," Pilar told her cousin Barron as they left Carla and Ray chatting and slipped away toward the outdoor Jacuzzi. "A goddamn liar."

"Oh, I'm on her," Barron said and slid his hand around her tight waist as they walked down the stone pathway. "She's not fooling anybody."

Pilar pouted. "And what's up with that ugly white wig? That must be a New York thing." Pilar was hatin', but deep inside she had already admitted that Mink's shit was cold. Ghetto and funky, but still ice-cold.

"Those bitches from up north are so damn trifling. I just can't believe she brought her gold-digging ass down here dressed like some half-baked video hoe."

Barron nodded. He couldn't believe some of the stuff he had seen today either. Like how tiny Mink's waistline looked compared to her wide hips, and those big titties and that sexy explosion of plump, graphically-shaped ass she had on her.

"Yeah, she's trash," he said, "but it's crazy how much she looks like Sable. Even after all these years I can still remember those pretty eyes."

"Yeah, from the picture they do favor a little bit," Pilar admitted, "but the more I think about it the less sense it makes. Some little ghetto hustler drops out of the sky right before Sable's twenty-first birthday, and just in time to pick up her inheritance check? So where the hell was she all these years when your mother was looking for her? And what took her so long to show up?"

"She's fake," Barron said. "She slipped through the cracks, but she's fake."

"I just don't buy that shit," Pilar said, keeping her little rant going. "It's all about the dollars with her, Bump. This girl is on some shit and she's looking for a payout. The only thing she has going for her is that she happens to look a little bit like Sable, and she's a natural-born liar."

"Oh, I'm on her ass." Barron nodded as they stopped beside the enormous twenty-person Jacuzzi and sat down on a lounge bench. Pilar reached into a covered basket and sorted through the bottles until she found the one she wanted. She handed it to Barron, and his hands felt real good as he rubbed sunblock all over her back and down her hips and thighs.

Barron massaged the lotion into Pilar's toned, golden flesh as he thought about Mink. Her posing ass couldn't have shown up at a worse time. With his mother starting to drink again, his father in the hospital, and the board of directors readying for a vote, shit was shaky all around.

"So what happens if she does end up being your sister and your father dies?" Pilar asked. "Does that mean she gets to collect three hundred thousand a year too?"

Fuck yeah, Barron thought. If Viceroy died or his doctors declared him permanently incapacitated, then the terms of the trust fund would kick in and the door to the Dominion safe would pop right open.

"Yeah. She would get it. But remember, she's gotta pass a DNA test first, and that shit just ain't gonna happen."

"But," Pilar insisted as a jealous heat washed over her, "if it *did* happen, then Mink would automatically be on the board at Dominion Oil. That bitch would get a shareholder's vote!"

Barron couldn't even think about that. If his father died, then control of Dominion Oil would be in his hands. But that kind of power was only on paper because real control was in the board's vote, and without those extra ballots, the stockholders could vote him out and take everything his father had worked his ass off to build.

"Yeah, that's right," he admitted coldly. Mink was gonna have to get gone. The last thing he needed right now was her fake-ass throwing chaos in the mix. Barron was faced with a damned if he did, damned if he didn't type of situation. And no matter how it played out there was a double-edged sword stuck up his ass and the cut was gonna run real deep.

"I don't like Mink," Pillar said, and twisted around quickly. She caught Barron off guard as she pressed her lips to his and darted her hot tongue into his mouth.

"Yo, c'mon, now, Pilar." Barron pulled away slightly. "What I tell you about all that?"

Pilar laughed, then slipped her hand up the leg of his swimming trunks and squeezed the head of his dick. Barron scooted backward on the lounge bench and almost tipped them both over on the ground.

"Girl, cut that shit out!" he said as she grinned and reached for his meat again. This time she didn't have to reach far because his erection was rock hard, and the swollen cap at the head was pointing down toward his knees.

"You know you like it," Pilar teased as Barron jumped up from the chair. His wood was pumping with blood as he walked around in a circle and tried to shake it off.

Pilar laughed again. "You okay? You want me to kiss it and make it feel better?"

"Kiss what and make it better?"

Both of their heads swung around when they heard Carla's

voice, and the moment Barron locked eyes with his fiancée, he whirled around and jumped into the monster-sized Jacuzzi and hid his hard dick.

"You know, Ray is sitting by the pool all by himself," Carla told Pilar coldly, and she didn't sound anything like her usual goody-goody white girl self. "How about you go up there kiss something on your own man and make it feel better."

CHAPTER 18

The Fourth of July barbeque had been a banga even though the two grimy New Yorkers had tried to crash their shit. Barron couldn't help noticing how fast Mink and Bunni had clicked up with his father's family from Houston. They were drinking and laughing like old project friends, and as the night wore on the females got tipsy and started line dancing and shaking their asses to the beat. Mink had been right up front leading the charge, and the way she moved that racked-up body it was obvious that she was a professional.

Barron had hung out with his cousins and put back a few too many drinks himself, and when the clean-up crew pulled out of the driveway, he grabbed Carla's hand and they went upstairs toward his large, private suite.

Carla had just ran back downstairs to get her cell phone charger from the kitchen, and Barron was in his custom-designed bathroom taking a shower when he heard the door creak open.

"Carla?"

"Hell no. Forget Carla's ass!"

Barron rubbed his fist across the steamed glass and saw his cousin Pilar standing there with a big smile on her face.

"Pilar!" he yelled and backed into a deep corner of the large, marble-tiled stall. "What you doing up in here? Your ass can't knock? Carla's gonna be back in a minute and I'm taking a shower!"

Pilar giggled. "Chill the hell out, Barron. I've seen that thing already. We used to take baths together when we were little, remember?"

"We were kids, Pilar. That's what little kids do."

"Well tell me now"—she grinned as she pulled her silk shirt over her head and unzipped her matching skirt—"has it grown any? We can splash around in the bathtub like we used to if you want. If I remember right you had a little red water gun you used to like to squirt between my legs. And you liked to make doggie balls too."

Pillar slid the shower door open and stepped naked into the wet stall.

For a moment neither one of them moved. Barron was covered in soap and holding his dick. His breath caught in his throat as he stared at her caramel skin and round, perfect breasts with the inch-long nipples.

"Yo, P," he said as his eyes roamed over her flat stomach, tiny waist, and the gentle curve of her hips. Her neatly-manicured pubic hair was reddish-brown and curly, and it matched the color of the hair on her head.

"C'mon, now. You know we can't be up in here together," Barron said thickly.

"Why not?" Pilar whispered as her fingers slid between her legs and she inserted her middle finger deeply into her slit. "I want you, Bump, and I know you want me. What's so wrong with that?"

"We're family, Pilar. We're cousins."

"Step-cousins," she corrected him as she moved closer with her finger pumping. "You were adopted, Barron and you've always known that."

They stood toe-to-toe, and using her free hand, Pilar took
Barron's soapy fingers off his dick and replaced them with her
own. "We don't have a drop of family blood running through
our veins," she reminded him as she masturbated herself and
pumped and stroked his meat from the base to the crown of
his slippery head. "Not one fuckin' drop."

Barron moaned as she pulled her fingers out of her pussy
and cupped his balls. She leaned against him and urged him to
stand under the rainfall spray. Their lips met as the water
drenched them and washed his soap, and his willpower, right
down the drain.

Pilar ran her thumb across the head of his thick dick, then
jacked him slowly with both hands. He slipped his tongue
deeper into her mouth then pulled out and nibbled on her
lips. He cupped her fluffy ass and pulled her closer, and his entire body shivered as her hard nipples pressed against his chest.

"Pilar," Barron broke their kiss and tried one last time to
back away.

"Shhh . . ." She moved with him, pushing him down on
the shower's bench as she got on her knees between his legs.
Pilar swept her hands all over his hard, brown body. She
rubbed his arms, his stomach, and his well-shaped, muscular
thighs. She had been dreaming about fucking him for the
longest and her pussy leaked with excitement at the thought
of finally getting what that bitch Carla damn sure didn't de-
serve.

Barron gripped her shoulders and pushed her back. She
shrugged him off and raised her lips for another kiss. He
couldn't help it. He scooted forward and grabbed her neck,
and his tongue dove frantically into the warmth of her mouth
again. His hands found her juicy breasts and he squeezed their
softness and rubbed the tips of his fingers all over her nipples.
He sucked her bottom lip and ran his tongue over her teeth.

Pilar broke their contact this time. She sat back slightly and
took his wood in her hands again. She traced the rim of the

head with her thumb. Barron's dick was about eight inches long and harder than a boulder. It was black and pretty, and the top was smooth and perfectly formed.

With the sexy sound of rainfalls behind her, Pilar bent her head and swooped down on his dick. She throated every bit she could, then used that special little trick she knew that allowed her to lengthen her neck and gobble up that last pulsating inch.

She pressed her nose into his pubic hair as she slurped and sucked like crazy, squeezing her cheeks real tight and then letting them collapse around his throbbing shaft. Barron was all hers now. His knees had fallen apart and his legs were shaking. His hands were all in her wet hair, palming her head like a basketball as he thrust his hips and banged his pipe down her throat, moaning and trembling like this was the best damn dick sucking he'd ever had in his life.

Pilar could feel his balls clenching as she coaxed his nut out of him. His muscles trembled as he squeezed her body between his legs. His hip pumps got shorter and more frantic. His dick swelled two times harder and felt like it was about to explode in her mouth, and then somebody pounded on the bathroom door and both of them froze.

"Barron?" Carla called out in her singsong voice. "You still in there, baby?"

Barron jumped up and dashed like he was back on the football field. Sliding the shower door open, he snatched Pilar's clothes off the floor and hugged them to his chest.

"Barron? Did you hear me? Are you okay?"

He cursed as Pilar knocked the clothes from his hand and reached for his balls again. "Umm, yeah," he said weakly. Pilar bent down and raked her teeth across the head of his dick and it jerked in her hot mouth. "I'm still in here."

"Well hurry up and get out, baby. I've got something for you."

"Okay, in a minute. Let me rinse off and I'll be right out."

"You need a little help in there?" Carla laughed. She undid the knot at the back of her neck and pulled her sundress down over her pale breasts.

Barron's dick strained and he tried to stop himself from panting. Pilar gripped him in her hands and jacked his dick while she licked all over the head like it was a lollypop.

"No! I mean, nah, I'm good, baby. Don't come in."

Please don't come in . . .

"I'll soap your back for you," Carla teased as she let her sundress drop to the floor and wriggled out of her panties.

"For real, don't . . . I'm about to get out."

She giggled. "Here I *come . . .*"

Barron pushed Pilar into the corner of the stall and kicked her soggy clothes behind her. He grabbed his towel and covered himself, then cut off the water and slid the shower door open just wide enough to step out.

Carla smiled. "You should have waited for me. I was just about to jump in."

Barron coughed, then copped an attitude. "I told you I was getting out, didn't I?" He tried to brush past her but she reached out and pulled the towel from his waist.

"Were you getting out or getting it on?" Carla giggled at the sight of his long, stiff erection and his obvious heavy breathing. "How many times do I have to tell you that you don't have to masturbate in the shower, Barron? I know it makes you last longer for me, but I kinda like getting that first quick one from you. It makes the second one that much better."

Hiding in the corner of the shower, Pilar frowned.

Barron swallowed hard as Carla took his throbbing dick in her hand.

"Not now, baby," he said as she dropped to her knees and nibbled on his shaft with her soft pink lips.

"Carla." Barron tried to push her away. "This isn't the right time for that. C'mon now . . ." A moan escaped his lips as she growled and slobbed him down, tonguing his dick with long licks from the base to the head just the way he liked it.

Pilar heard Barron's protests and the unmistakable sound of slurping lips, and her eyes got big. *What the fuck is that bitch doing out there? I know she ain't sucking his dick!*

Barron arched his back and shivered as his dick got nice and wet again. That was one thing he could say about Carla. As sweet and ladylike as she was, she was a fuckin' slut in the sheets. She got down on the get-down, fucking and sucking like there was no tomorrow, and once she got him in her mouth it was a wrap.

"Ahhh, goddamn," Barron groaned. Carla was doing his top to death, and the thought of Pilar hiding in the shower and of having two different women sucking his dick less than two minutes apart totally blew his fucking mind.

Ahhh? Pilar thought as she listened to the sounds coming out of his mouth. *Goddamn?* What the fuck was up with that? She was soaking wet and shivering in the goddamn shower and he was out there moaning *ahhh* and *goddamn?*

Barron grabbed a fistful of Carla's silky blond hair and wound it around his hand. Holding the back of her head, he waxed her up and down his dick and got deep down in that neck pussy just the way he liked it. She reached back and gripped his ass and gave his muscular cheeks a deep massage, and when she bit down on his sweet spot oh so gently, that was all she wrote.

"Oh, shit!" Barron yelled as he straight up fucked her in her mouth. The hot friction sensations had his dick tingling down to the bone, and a vision of Pilar's luscious brown nipples popped into his mind. "Yeah! I'm coming! I'm coming! I'm . . ." He clutched the back of Carla's head and pushed his rock-hard dick straight down her throat. "Ah shit!" Barron whimpered as his love muscle jerked in a staccato rhythm and deposited a load of hot sperm deep in her esophagus. "I'm *coming!*"

Stuck hiding in the shower stall, Pilar straight up fumed. Her cute and costly outfit had gotten all fucked up and she'd gotten her damn hair wet while this fool got his top done. She was two seconds away from coming up out of that shower and fucking both of their heads up! Bump and his goddamn white girls! That chick Carla had to go!

CHAPTER 19

Pilar was on one as she stormed through the chilly mansion in her wet clothes and hurried back to her suite. She couldn't believe Barron had let that bitch suck him off while she was right there in the goddamn bathroom! And then she'd had to huddle in the damn shower for another thirty minutes while Carla took a bath and soaked her ass right there in the room with her!

Pilar sloshed into her suite with her perm plastered to her head and her dry-clean-only gear all fucked up. Her fiancé, Ray, was watching CNN, and when she walked in he looked up and jumped to his feet.

"Damn! What happened, baby? Did you go back outside and fall in the pool or something?"

"Yeah," Pilar said stiffly. She was so freakin' cold her lips were blue and her teeth were chattering. "I fell in the fuckin' pool."

She sniffled as Ray helped her pull off her wet clothes and murmured soft, comforting words. "It's okay," Ray soothed her as his big, clumsy hands stroked her back. "You're freezing, girl. Let me run you a hot bath."

Pilar accepted Ray's royal treatment as he helped her into the deep claw-foot tub that her aunt had gotten specially installed in her suite. As Selah's only niece, Pilar had always been spoiled like a daughter, and her suite at the mansion was just as grand as everyone else's.

The hot, bubbly water relaxed Pilar enough so she could gather her thoughts and plan her next move. She soaked for thirty minutes and then stood up and allowed Ray to pat her firm body dry with one of the European King of Cotton bath towels that Viceroy had sent home when he was on a business trip in London.

She stretched out on her stomach and Ray's hands felt strong on her back and legs as he massaged handfuls of lavender bedtime oil into her skin. His fat little fingers played the piano on her neck, across her shoulders, and straight down the middle of her spine. Pilar moaned just a little bit as he kneaded the top of her booty cheeks and sent chills vibrating deep in the crack of her ass.

She pressed her face deeper into the pillow. The last thing she wanted to think about was hairy-ass Ray with his big belly and jiggly man-tits, so she squeezed her eyes shut and imagined it was Barron back there making her pussy get nice and wet.

She could still taste his dick on her lips and remembered how that big black thing had jerked deliciously in her hands. Ray was slathering a whole handful of oil on her round ass. Pilar squeezed her cheeks when she felt a little bit drip down into her crack.

Ray's thumbs massaged the sensitive area right around her starfish. She could hear him breathing hard as he spread her cheeks open and gently kissed her down there. His beard was scratchy, but Pilar liked it. She thought about how Barron's lips might have felt on her if she'd had a chance to get him the way she wanted to.

She yelped as Ray slid his hand under her body and lifted

her hips in the air. She balanced a little bit on both knees and gripped the sheets in her fists when his tongue slithered into her from behind. It was long and firm, and he knew how to make it stiff and put his bomb head game down on her.

"Uh-uh-uh-uh!" Pilar cried out and humped rhythmically as Ray fucked her with his meaty tongue. It felt so hot and good sliding in and out of her pussy that she forgot how much she couldn't stand his ass, and she slid her knees apart and opened herself up even wider so she could ride that shit a little harder.

Pilar reached between her legs and rubbed her clit. She crushed it between her pointer and middle finger and squeezed it to the beat that Ray's soft tongue had going in her wetness. She squealed out loud when he abandoned her hole and swirled around her clit and licked her sticky fingers. He stroked downward and stabbed into her wetness again, then withdrew quickly and attacked her asshole, licking it gently and causing her pussy to spasm in her hand.

"Eat it!" she demanded, screaming into the pillow. "Eat it, dammit, eat it!"

She was up on her knees all the way now. Ray held her cheeks open wide as he dipped his face lower and sucked her clit like it was a sweet, swollen cherry. Pilar rose up on all fours and threw her head back. She grunted twice, then came right in his mouth, squirting her sweet juice all over his magnificent tongue.

"Wow!" she panted and collapsed flat on her face. Ray started planting small, gentle kisses on her ass and she knocked him away with a rude bump of her hip.

"Can we make love tonight?" Ray's hand was in his lap as he spoke in a gentle, hopeful voice.

Pilar came up on her elbows and glared at him over her shoulder in annoyance.

"No, Ray! I'm not in the mood for sex. I'm too tired. Maybe another time."

CHAPTER 20

I loved all my new hood uncles, aunts, and cousins! We stayed up talking shit and dancing and listening to Dane and Jock spit lyrics for half the night. Them jawns could put some beer and liquor away, and after a while the waiters just left the damn bottles out on the tables so we could go for ours. The cousins were real chill, and I was glad they were staying the night at the mansion. Selah told me the whole family was flying down to Houston tomorrow to see Viceroy, and she invited me and Bunni to go too.

Bunni called herself falling into Dane's lap and sitting her ass there for a few minutes, and when she got up everybody laughed 'cause his dick was hard and sticking straight out in front of him.

I got kinda tipsy and accidently walked into the pool. Them Houston niggas had been feeling my slinky red bikini, and about ten of them crazy fools jumped in to rescue me. I cracked up when one of the cousins from Brooklyn came outta the pool styling my dripping-wet white wig and doing an imitation of me switching my ass.

When the night was finally over I took a shower then

climbed in that big old bed and slept like I was stretched out on cotton balls. Bunni was snoring real loud and ugly in her room, but I was too comfortable to get up and close my door.

The satin sheets felt like heaven against my skin, and I smiled as I dug my face all in the plush pillow. This was the type of life I had always dreamed of. A family that had whips, mansions, and enough gwap to make all my dreams come true. I fell asleep thinking about the white Maybach I'd seen in the driveway, imagining that it was all mine.

"Mink. *Mink!* Wake up. We about to break out for Houston, girl. Which one of these do you think I should wear?"

It seemed like I had just blinked, and suddenly Bunni was standing over me telling me to get up.

"Mink!"

I opened one eye. I wasn't shit in the mornings, and Bunni knew it. She was standing next to my bed butt-ass naked and holding up two pairs of jeans. Her stomach was flat as hell, and her titties looked like two chocolate tennis balls.

"Mink! Which ones, I said? The yellow ones or the pink ones?"

I groaned and turned over. "Can you just get ya lil ugly coochie outta my face, man? I mean, damn! Can you just do that for me? I mean, that just ain't nothing I wanna see first thing in the morning, okay?"

She sucked her teeth. "Which ones, dammit?"

"The yellow ones," I grumbled.

"Those got pockets on the ass though. My booty looks better with nothing on the back."

"The red ones then."

"They're pink, okay? Pink!"

I was half-hungover and mad that I had to get up, but I knew me and Bunni had work to do. It was Saturday, and we were all gonna fly down to Houston in the Dominions' private jet so we could visit Selah's husband at the hospital. He was still in a coma, but he kept going in and out. I wasn't really tryna go see nobody in the hospital, but I needed to take advantage of every opportunity to get closer to Selah.

Bunni had gotten up way earlier than me. She'd already been on her laptop working on Mr. Pain Slut, who was now using the nickname Jed Clamp It, and she said my DNA test was practically in the bag.

"Oh it better be," I warned her and swept my glance around the room. "Or we can kiss all this here shit good-bye!"

I washed my hair in the shower and rubbed some conditioner on the ends. I was gonna cool it on the wigs for today because I wanted Selah to see a softer side of me. I squeezed the water out of my hair with a towel so it could air-dry and get all curly. I put on just a little mascara and some lipstick and left the rest of my face alone. I was going for the sweet, innocent look, not my regular wild and freaky self.

"You wearing a dress?" Bunni walked in again without knocking and smirked.

"Yep." I had slipped into a soft, peach-colored crocheted mini-dress that was simple but sexy. It had a body-glove under it in a slightly darker shade that hugged my curves just enough to keep it tasteful. "I want the Dominions to think I got some class," I told her. "Besides, we gonna be up in a hospital full of sick people. I ain't tryna give no old man a heart attack."

"Maybe you not," Bunni twirled around and checked out her heart-shaped, super-booty in the mirror. "But I am."

CHAPTER 21

Dane checked Mink and Bunni out as they came down the winding grand staircase the next morning. They looked like a pair of ghetto princesses with curves in all the right places. They reminded him of all the fly chicks he fucked with in the dorms at college. He had been born into money, but that didn't mean he didn't have a nose for the hood life. He had fought his father tooth and nail for the right to go to a historically black university, but college was just a front for his real grind. Dane was a rapper, a balla, a lover, and a lyrical monster, and he kept his ear close to the urban life. He was well-respected in the trenches and well-loved in all the hottest nightclubs. Known as Danger on the streets, when Dane stepped up to the mic nothing but pure fiyah spewed from his lips, and he was living proof that you didn't have to live in grime to have grime in your heart.

"Wussup?" He kissed Mink and Bunni on their cheeks. Just looking at them made him slip into Danger mode. Their gear was fresh and their faces were gorgeous, but despite all that, the odor of the ghetto still came off these babes in big fat waves.

"Hey shawty." He grinned at Bunni. "You killin' them red dreds, ma. That's how they rock them up in Harlem, huh?"

"Yeah." Bunni reached up and touched her hair. "We got all kinds of braid and twist shops around our way. Yours are real nice too. You should put some color on your tips or something. Where do you get yours twisted?"

Dane wasn't about to admit that he had an old lady come to the crib once a week and hook him up. He was one of them bougie-ass rappers. Instead of going to a shop, he dished off some dough and had a stylist come in and shampoo, condition, and twist his shit up right in the comfort of his own home.

"A friend of mine has her own shop," he lied. "She hooks me up."

"Well introduce me to her!" Bunni said. "'Cause I'ma need somebody down here to give me a re-do in about two weeks."

"Two weeks?" Barron had walked up behind them. "I thought you two were flying back to New York right after Mink gets her DNA test done on Monday? At least that's the story y'all told my mother, right?"

Both Dominion brothers busted the look on Mink's pretty face and Dane laughed inside as she scrambled to come up with a good one.

"*I'm* going back to New York on Monday," she corrected Barron. "Bunni has friends in Texas. She's gonna be down here for two weeks visiting them."

"Oh, yeah?" Barron turned to Bunni and hit her again real smooth. "What part of Texas are your friends from?"

Bunni looked shook, and Barron could tell she didn't know Dallas from Dickweed.

"Umm . . . I think they live in Houston."

Barron smirked. This chick was slow. Houston was probably the only other city in Texas that she'd ever heard of.

"Oh, that's cool," he spit real slick. "I'll send somebody upstairs to grab your bags. Since we're flying down to Houston today we can drop you off at your friend's house and save you another trip."

"Yo, raise up, Bump." Dane got in between them. Barron had a way of riding shit into the ground, which was one of the reasons Dane was stuck in the fucked up position he was in right now. "It's all good, dude. Leave the ladies alone. They'll let us know when they're ready to bounce."

Dane was actually glad Mink had showed up when she did, and he wanted her to stick around for a while so she could take all the attention off of him and his legal problems. Yeah, he lived large while he was under his father's roof, but he'd already gotten his hundred-grand inheritance and his ass was dead broke. He was going into his sixth year in a four-year college, and he'd spent the past two semesters smoking as much weed and fuckin' as many dorm chickens as he could slide his dick in.

But somebody had gotten mad jealous and busted on him to the administration. He was running out of money and fighting a sexual assault charge at the same time, and if that last piece of information got out in the open it could mess up his stake in the family's trust fund.

Especially if Barron found out. If their father didn't come out of his coma real soon, then Barron could end up in charge of the Dominions' millions, and Dane just didn't trust Barron, the brother who had never done a damn thing wrong in his entire life, to look out for him.

"Be cool," Dane told his brother, and Barron backed off slightly, then came at Mink from another direction.

"Hey Mink, do you remember when we were little and Uncle Suge bought us a baby goat named Blackie?"

Mink shrugged. "I think so . . . yeah, I kinda do remember that. . . ."

"I don't know how because he bought us a pony named Whitey."

"Oh well. I don't remember no damn pony at all. But then again I don't remember your ass neither."

"Shit, I don't remember a pony *or* a goddamn goat," Dane said. "So what you saying, man? I ain't ya brother?"

Barron dapped Dane out and slapped him on the back.

"Hell yeah you're my brother, man. And you know that dawg." He turned and busted on Mink. "But this chick ain't my sister."

Mink opened her mouth to bite him, but Dane interrupted and squashed it.

"Ay, chill with all that shit, Bump." Dane put one arm around Mink and the other arm around Bunni. "Check it out. Me and the ladies are gonna take a quick walk out back. We'll meet y'all out front in a few minutes."

CHAPTER 22

Dane took me and Bunni down by the pond, and the three of us sat out there and got lifted. He had some fat-ass trees and I could tell by the first toke that he had gotten his hands on some real good yay.

We stayed back there laughing and talkin' shit with him for about twenty minutes, and when all the weed was smoked up we walked around the front of the house where everybody was about to load up on the private jet. They had moved it out from under the awning, and I stood there looking at that huge cream-colored piece of luxury with dollar signs flashing in my eyes.

"Sweet ain't it?"

Jock was standing behind me. He had smoked more weed than a little bit last night by the pool, and I had busted him sneaking one of Fallon's hot-in-the-ass girlfriends in the pool house and closing the door behind them.

"Sweet as *hell*," I said. The words *Diva Dominion* were written in large script letters on the side of the jet. There were two pilots dressed in fancy uniforms. One stood at the bottom of the steps welcoming everybody as they got on, and the other one was posted up at the top of the steps looking seriously focused.

"It's a Boeing Business Jet. My mother's. Her Gulfstream was too small to handle all of us at one time, so my father got rid of it and bought her this one last year. C'mon. It's time to roll."

This shit seemed so unreal. Like I was wide-awake in somebody else's dream. I followed behind Jock, and the pilot kinda bowed a little bit like I was royalty or some shit. I stepped on the plane and the smell of money rushed straight up my nose. Everything was done up in cream-colored leather and dark wood trim. There were plush, inward-facing rows of seats in the front of the plane, and in the back there was a semi-circular setting with stuffed reclining chairs and ottomans.

Me and Bunni breezed past the front seats so we could go sit in the circle with some of the cousins we'd partied with the night before, but Selah called me back, and while Bunni got to go chill with Dane and them, I was forced to sit up front with her and that crazy-ass Barron.

She patted the empty seat between them and I sat down and crossed my legs. I looked at Selah and smiled. I was diggin' Mami's style and I could tell she had some Brooklyn in her. Her hair was pulled back in a neat ponytail, and she had on a chic little skirt suit that made her look sharp and sexy at the same time.

She smiled back at me as I put on my seat belt, but that dude Barron was acting all grumpy like he had a pickle stuck up his ass or something. Nigga was fly though. I had to give it to him. He was styling Armani gear all the way, and he even had on a pair of thirty-eight-thousand-dollar Amedeo Testoni shoes on his big-ass feet.

"So, Mink." He got in my ass and started giving me the bizz before the pilot could even sit down in his little compartment. "It's been a minute since I've hung out in New York,

but everybody knows it's a bad-ass city. I hear they've reno-
vated a lot of brownstones in Harlem. Did your family get a
chance to jump on any of those while they were hot?"

"Nah." I kept my voice light. "We never had that kinda
money. I already told you my whole family lives in the projects. Grant, Taft, Manhattanville . . . we're all over the hood."

"Oh, so you come from a big family, huh? How many sis-
ters and brothers do you have?"

"None, actually. It was just me. All my aunts had six or
seven kids each though, so I grew up with a whole lotta
cousins, but my moms only had one child. Me."

"How old were you when you found out you were adopted?"

I sighed like I was tired of his shit and spit out all the bullshit I had memorized and already told him. "I didn't really
know until I was eighteen. I needed my birth certificate and
my mother couldn't come up with one. I finally pushed her . . .
and that's when she told me."

"Told you what?"

"That I was adopted!"

"But last night you said you knew from the time you were
a little girl that you were adopted!"

"I said I knew from the time I was a little girl that I was *different*. I didn't know what made me different, though, I just
knew I was."

"Uh-huh. So what about your father? You never asked
him any questions?"

"Barron. I already told you. My mother was a single parent. When I was little she told me my father was up in
heaven."

"What high school did you go to?"

"We got put outta our apartments a lot, so I went to a lot
of different schools in the city."

"I bet it was hard on you when your mother died. She
must have been a real alky, huh? So where is she buried?"

"Barron!" Selah frowned and shook her head. "Come on

now. That's enough! Everybody wants to get to know more about Mink, but I know I raised you better than that! Enough with the endless questions! There'll be time for all that later. Right now your father needs our positive energy, so let's try to focus on that."

That yay I'd smoked with Bunni and Dane had my eyelids heavy. I knew it would piss Barron the fuck off, so I scooted slightly to my right and put my head down on Selah's shoulder, and I fell asleep with her patting my hand.

About thirty minutes later I opened my eyes and saw we were landing on a small airfield in Houston. Our entourage was ready to roll out, and I looked toward the back of the plane for Bunni. Her ass was laughing and clowning with Jock and Dane like they'd had a good old time back there. I figured they had probably guzzled some good liq the whole way down here, while I was trapped up front drinking apple juice with Barron's high-strung ass.

Fallon, Carla, Ray, and Pilar had ridden in the back of the jet too, and Pilar stood up with her gear looking crisp and every hair on her head was laid.

There were four sparkling limos waiting for us when we got off the small plane, and Selah made sure I got in the first one with her and Barron. We drove to the hospital and pulled into a private, restricted-access parking area. A representative from the hospital administration was waiting for us, and as soon as our limo driver opened the back door, the rep came over and shook Selah's hand and practically kissed her feet. His glasses kept sliding off his nose as he threw his fake love down on all the family, and when we went inside and I saw a plaque of Viceroy on the wall, I knew the Dominions must have donated some mega-ass bucks to this joint.

The rep led us to a private wing of the hospital where Viceroy was being kept. Everybody in our little posse walked behind him all quiet and dignified, and I couldn't help comparing the way these rich folks acted to the way my hood family had clowned up at the hospital when my mother had almost drowned. I mean, they had gone straight bonkers up in that mug. When the doctors came and told us she was in a coma and she might have some brain damage, my aunts and cousins had started acting so ill that somebody called security. And when two little scrawny-ass play guards came to put us out, my uncle Bushwick had taken both of their lil light asses down to the ground and fucked them up.

But I could tell there would be none of that going down up in this hospital today. These people had a completely different flow game than what I was used to. Selah and her crew was dressed to impress, and you could smell the money coming off of them, even from a distance.

We went into a real big conference room where three doctors were waiting to give us an update on Viceroy's condition. From what I could tell, they were saying not a whole lot had changed. Viceroy was still drifting in and out of consciousness, and even though today seemed to be a good day for him, they really couldn't predict what kind of condition he would be in tomorrow, so the only thing the family could do was wait and see what happened.

I could tell how much the whole family loved Viceroy because everybody took the news bad. It kinda reminded me of how I felt when the doctors told us they didn't have no crystal ball and couldn't see into my mother's future neither.

"That's okay," Selah said. She had a brave look on her face as she tried to comfort everybody except herself. "We're not giving up no matter what! Everybody just stay positive and keep praying! Our prayers are already working whether we can see the results or not!"

Only three people were allowed to go into Viceroy's room at one time.

"Barron, you and Mink come in with me," Selah directed us. I busted a twisted look on Pilar's face as Selah reached for my hand, and I sashayed real close to Barron's so-called "cou-sin" so she could suck up my fumes as I passed by.

But something came down over me when I stepped into Viceroy's hospital room. I felt some kinda way, the way I always felt whenever I went to visit my mother. Her little room wasn't even half the size of this one, but it held the same smell of the sick and the dying.

I dragged my feet behind Barron as we went toward his father's bed. Viceroy was laid out flat with the top of his head wrapped up in bandages. A long, clear tube ran outta his mouth, and one of his eyes was swollen up like a boiled egg.

I felt kinda grimy for stepping in on their private moment. Hell yeah, I had come down here so I could get my hands on this man's moolah, but I didn't know I was gonna have to be going up in no hospitals and shit.

"Viceroy." Selah sat on the edge of the bed and rubbed his hand. "Wake up, Viceroy. I brought somebody to see you, baby." She called his name over and over, and then finally his one good eye slowly opened.

"We're all here," Selah said. "And everybody loves you."

My feet were stuck in place but my eyes were glued to the man in the bed. I couldn't tell a whole lot about him other than he was a long-legged dude who had been fucked up real bad.

Selah motioned for Barron to come closer, and he stepped up and greeted his father with real love. He talked to Viceroy like the man could hear him, and it was the first time I'd seen a side of Barron that wasn't cold and on guard.

It was my turn to talk to Viceroy next, and all Mizz Mink wanted to do was break for the door. Selah reached for my hand, and I forced myself to focus on that hundred-grand jack-pot as I reluctantly moved toward the bed.

"I brought a special visitor with me today," Selah said as she drew me closer to her. I stared down at Viceroy's one good eyeball, and I knew for damn sure that he was staring at me too.

"Viceroy," Selah said after a deep sigh. "I think we might have found our daughter."

It seemed like every machine in that joint stopped beeping. Viceroy's good eye got real big and the expression in it totally changed. I heard the machines in the background click on again, and the one that was recording his heartbeat started kicking all outta whack. Selah took Viceroy's reaction for excitement, but something in that one eye told me the man in the bed was seeing straight through me.

"I know!" Selah beamed and talked to him like they had a mental conversation going on. "Look at her! She's beautiful, isn't she! She looks exactly the same as she did when she was a little girl!"

Viceroy's blood pressure musta been off the chart. His body trembled on the bed and he clenched and unclenched his ashy lips around the tube in his mouth.

Him and Selah seemed like they was communicating.

"I know!" she shouted again real loud. "I know! It's Sable, isn't it? It's really her!"

I couldn't take that shit no more.

The look in that rich man's eyeball freaked me out. I broke away from Selah and jetted for the door. I rushed past all the family waiting outside and ran into the bathroom and started splashing cold water all over my face.

I was staring at my trifling self in the mirror when Bunni walked in.

"Umm . . . what the hell was all that about? You came flyin' up outta there like somebody was chasin' you with a knife. Girl please don't tell me your ass is getting soft!"

"Chill, Bunni!" I snapped. "Ain't shit soft about me. I just don't like hospitals that's all, and you should already know why."

"Yeah, uh-huh. Right." She peered at me like she was tryna read my mind. "So what the hell just happened in that damn room?"

I shrugged and played it off. "Nothing happened. The daddy was laying in the bed all tubed up."

"So why you come bustin' outta there like a damn crack house was being raided then? You catchin' feelings for these people or something? Girl, you got my left titty itchin'. I'ma need your brain to stay real focused on the money, okay? That's the only reason we came down here in the first place, remember?"

"Bunni." I patted my face dry, then smoothed some gloss on my lips and acted like I was schooling her on the finer points of the con game. "I don't know about that itchin' titty of yours, but I ain't got but one thing on my brain, and that's getting paid. That lady in there really *wants* me to be her daughter, and when I was little I woulda gave almost anything to have a family like this. But we're talking real life, okay? So I'ma need you to concentrate on getting next to that big pussy-ass nigga at the lab, and you let me handle all the family shit. Cool?"

CHAPTER 23

Bunni went with Pilar, Fallon, and Carla downstairs to the snack bar, and I was sitting in the hospital waiting room watching TV with some of the little kids.

"The results are in," Maury said as a hush fell over the crowded studio. The jump-off sitting on the stage laughed and looked like she just knew what the fuck she knew.

"Please, please, please, please!" a young dude sitting across from her with cute cornrows in his hair whispered as he stared down Maury's throat like he was praying the right words would pop outta Maury's mouth. Another guy wearing a fitted and some baggy jeans sat next to him and he was getting tested too. A picture of a sleeping baby girl came on the screen, and mug shots of both of the could-be daddies was posted up on either side of her.

"In the case of two-month-old baby Taiquanapaula . . . Taiquan, you are . . . but wait!" Maury faked us, going for the stall. *"Taiquan, if you are the father of this precious little girl, are you planning to take care of her?"*

"Hell yeah!" he lied. *"I'ma man-up and handle minez!"*

Maury turned to the trifling-ass baby mama who sat there

in a halter with a muffin top spilling over her belt. *"If he is your baby's father, do you still want to be with him?"*

Dummy hunched her shoulders.

"Okay, in the case of two-month-old baby Taiquanapaula . . . Taiquan, you are NOT the father!"

Dude jumped outta his chair and leaped off the stage. He started happy dancing all in the aisles and dapping dudes in the crowd like crazy. *"I TOLD you! I TOLD you! That baby don't look nothing like me! That baby got chubby cheeks and my face is real skinny! Yeah! Yeah! Yeah! I TOLD you!"*

"But wait, we have a second test," Maury said as he calmed the crowd down. *"We have a second test!"*

This time, Baby-Mama-Jump-off squinched her eyes closed and crossed her fingers as she waited for the second bomb to drop.

Maury turned to the other dude, who was now looking scared as fuck, and continued. *"In the case of baby Taiquanapaula . . . Paul . . . you are NOT the father!"*

Mami fell dead outta her chair. She rolled over on her stomach and started kicking her feet and banging her head and fists on the floor.

Paul jumped off the stage too. Him and Taiquan started doing the Kid 'n Play foot dance as the crowd chanted, *"Do that shit! Do that shit! Yeah! Do that shit! Do that shit!"*

"Them boys got lucky, didn't they?"

I looked up and saw a tall hunk of black dude who had come into the room. He looked like a gangsta cowboy. He had on a spotless white Stetson, some starched black jeans, and a real sharp white shirt with black lanyard trim.

"Yeah, they did," I laughed. "Baby-mama-drama all day long."

"You got any kids?"

I gave him the look. "Do baby boogers go with my dress?"

He laughed and sat down next to me. His skin was real smooth, and his mustache was jet-black and sharply trimmed.

He was a fine-ass old head. I took him to be about thirty-five, and not only was he tall as hell, he was built real yummy and he looked like he could rope a bull.

He nodded at me. "How you doing today?"

I side-eyed him. "I'm good."

"You looking good too, little lady. Are you sure none of these are your kids?"

Before I could answer, one of the little boys from Houston ran over and jumped up in his lap.

"Hey Uncle Suge!"

"Aw, hell, Terrence!" He tossed the little boy up and started tickling him. "You one of *our* kids!"

Terrence wiggled out of his lap and came over to me.

"I'm hungry, Mink. Are we gonna leave soon?"

"Yep, it won't be much longer, babe. As soon as everybody gets back we're gonna go get something to eat."

"Mink?" Ol' boy gave me a look. "You're *Mink*?" He pulled off his shades and checked me out real good. "The long-lost daughter from New York?" He grinned and held out his hand. "Well I'll be damned. Nice to meet you. I'm Suge." He looked sexier than a mutha as he grilled me up and down. "Your . . . um . . . uncle."

"Mink LaRue," I said, busting the hungry look in his eye. "And yeah, Mister." I smirked, just a teasin' and a flirtin' with his ass. "I have heard some *stuff* about you!"

"Like what?"

"Like you're Viceroy's crazy-ass brother who just loves to gamble and chase tail!"

He laughed, showing off a nice set of even white teeth. "Is that the kinda shit they be telling people about me?"

"Uh-huh!" I said, nodding my head.

His sexy eyes skimmed across my thighs.

"Well I guess I'm guilty 'cause they sure as hell ain't lying!"

He crossed his leg at the knee and I stared at the spiky-looking things sticking out all over his boots and the emblem of a Texas longhorn that ran up the front.

"Wild Alligator," he said, nodding at his feet. "They snap hard and stroke deep, just like me. You like 'em?"

"Yeah," I admitted. "I mean, you ain't gonna catch no brotha runnin' around New York in those, that's for sure. They're nice, though. They look expensive."

He chuckled. "Baby doll, everything good in the whole wide world costs money, and men like me don't mind spending it." He put his arm around the back of my chair and I caught a whiff of his cologne. *Goddamn*. Clive Christian No. 1 for Men. And he wasn't slumming with the cheap perfume spray that you could get for under a grand, neither. Nah, Unc was rolling in that Pure Splash, baby! Twenty-one hundred smacks a bottle!

"Damn." He shook his head and chuckled again as he appreciated me with his eyes. "You probably about the prettiest thang I've seen all week and you could end up being my niece. Ain't that some shit? You're a beautiful girl, Mink LaRue. Real fine. Welcome to Texas, baby doll. I'm glad you're here, but I hope like hell we ain't related."

CHAPTER 24

Barron walked out of the hospital room with his mother wrapped in his arms and his brothers Jock and Dane by his side. The image of their father as a tough, invincible hard-hitter was the only one they'd ever known, and seeing him in such a weakened condition was an emotional blow to all of them.

"Take Mama back to the conference room," Barron directed his youngest brother. "We're leaving in ten minutes so make sure everybody starts heading back to the limos."

Barron walked down the hall feeling the weight of the Dominion name on his shoulders. Viceroy looked much worse than he did the last time he saw him, and his doctors seemed to be stuck in a cycle of let's wait and see.

He was heading toward the visitors' waiting room when he saw something that fucked him up and turned him on at the same time. Mink was sitting in a chair with her shapely legs crossed and her firm breasts staring right at him. Her waist was so tiny and her hips looked so damn lush and round that for a moment Barron wished his face could be the seat of her chair.

She had a big grin on her mug as she carried on a conversation with the skirt-chasing nigga who sat beside her with his eyes glued to her amazing chest.

Suge. His slick, scaly ass had his arm wrapped around Mink's chair, and his lying lips were steadily moving as he leaned toward Mink and laid his old-ass rap down in her ear.

Grimy muthafuckas! Barron cursed as he watched their little encounter play out. Mink uncrossed her sexy legs, then threw her head back and laughed and crossed them back again. Barron didn't need to hear what they were saying to figure out that his father's younger brother was scoping for some pussy. He took three long steps and busted through the door, and both of them looked up in surprise.

"W'sup, Suge. You slummin' through today? What? You came to see if Daddy was dead yet?"

"Hey what's up, B?" Suge rose up from his chair to give his nephew some dap.

"Nah, don't get up," Barron told him. "You look real comfortable sitting there, man. You ain't gotta move for me. I just thought you mighta came around here to check on your big brother, you dig? You know, the guy who brings in all the money in this family and slides you that sweet lil paycheck every week. The man who's laying down the hall with shrapnel in his head? Yeah, that dude. Your *brother.*"

Ignoring Barron, Suge leaned toward Mink with a grin on his face. "It was real nice talking to you, baby doll." He touched her hand, then his eyes got smoky and the I-wanna-fuck-you look crept up in them. "I'ma holla at you again, okay? Real soon. I promise."

He stood up and walked over to his nephew. Barron was just as tall as his uncle, but he wasn't quite as thick and solid.

"You all right, Lil Bump?" Suge asked, and slapped him hard on the shoulder. "If you ever need somebody to talk to or . . . you know . . . somebody to teach you how to handle these . . . uh"—he glanced hungrily at Mink's legs and grinned again—"type of thangs . . . you just holla at your old uncle Suge, ya hear?"

He was walking out the door when he turned and said over his shoulder, "By the way, nephew. How's that sweet little Carla doing?"

Barron felt his jaw tighten and ice glinted from his eyes.

Suge chuckled. "Uh-huh. I thought so. You be sure to tell her old Uncle Suge sends her a whole lotta love."

Superior "Suge" Dominion had always been a down-ass nigga. He'd been the go-to guy in the Dominion clan since he was seventeen years old, and in the early days of Dominion Oil, while his older brother Viceroy had been busy cutting deals on the corporate ladder, Suge had been cutting ass in the trenches as his right-hand man.

At six feet five and packing a good two-fifty in pure muscle, Suge was real good at crackin' heads and throwing his weight around. Whether it was stranglin' niggas or pumping heat, all Viceroy had to do was say the word and Suge would put a cat down in the dirt real quick, no questions asked.

The Dominion brothers had grown up poor as shit in the slums of Houston. They were twelve years apart because Suge had been one of those late-in-life babies. Fearless in the streets and wild with the ladies, he quickly became a ruthless, street-hustling problem, and since their father was in and out of prison and their mother was too old and too worn out to keep after him, Viceroy had taken him under his wing and son'd him.

Making millions had always been on Viceroy's agenda, but amassing a fortune without going grimy was damn-near impossible. And that's where Suge had come in. When Viceroy needed to keep his image clean in the corporate world, he entrusted his baby brother to get down-right brutal with his competition and anybody else who came between him and his dough.

Suge's official title at Dominion Oil was some bullshit like "executive assistant," and while he didn't actually clock a nine-to-five for the three hundred and fifty grand his brother paid him every year, he was worth ten times that amount because he put in *work*.

Suge was the only living person Viceroy completely trusted, and he became his big brother's loyal homeboy, his handyman, and his quicker-cleaner-upper. The Dominion boys had a love thang going on between them. Viceroy dad-died Suge from his heart, and he had no problem telling people that if he woke up one morning and didn't have but one wrinkled dollar left to his name, his little brother would still be good for fifty cents.

And right now, all the money in the world couldn't replace Viceroy, and Suge had a hard time believing his brother was down the hall laying on what could have been his death-bed.

With one last glance at Mink, Suge gave his oldest nephew a cold nod, then took his time walking out of the waiting room. With Viceroy down, Lil Bump was feeling himself, but if he jumped out like that again he was liable to get his gangsta tested.

Suge was halfway down the hall and he could still feel Barron's eyes heating up his back like the young'un wanted to do something. He was tempted to go back in that waiting room and toss him up in the air, but he knew what his nephew's problem was. Back when Barron was a junior in college he had brought a big-titty white girl home with him for a week-end barbeque.

Suge's horse had won real big on the track that morning and he'd been drinking and celebrating at the Dominion Es-tate all day. He had jumped in the pool for a little swim, then passed out drunk in an easy chair in the pool house. When he woke up, he was surprised to find Barron's young white honey standing next to him in her wet bathing suit and staring down at his dick. They'd been flirting with each other all day, and half-sleep and still half-drunk, Suge had reached for her hand and put it in his lap.

The girl pounced on him, and Suge had had her down on her knees about to jam his big dick down her throat when Barron walked into the pool house naked calling her name and holding his wet swim trunks in his hand.

A drunk tongue can be a deal killer, and Suge's tongue was full of liquor as he looked at his naked nephew's rock-hard dick, then looked down at the pulsating beast the white girl was gripping in both her fists and laughed, "Damn, boy! That shit ain't grew none since you was two!"

Suge had meant it as a joke, but Barron had gotten swole and wanted to fight him.

"Oh this your girl, Lil Bump?" Suge hollered as he weaved and ducked the garbage can full of beer bottles that his nephew was hurling at him. "You got *feelings* for this bitch? Then what you bring her sweet ass around me for then?"

Barron had never talked about what went down again, but he had never forgiven Suge either. The water had been cold between them for years, and even though Suge had apologized to keep shit smooth in the family, what he'd done had fucked with Barron's pride, and it stood to reason the boy was gonna go for his one day and try to get some back.

Suge entered his brother's hospital room and stood quietly by his bedside. Viceroy was a big, strong man, and Suge knew if there was any way he could have gotten up outta that bed and stood on his own feet, he would have.

But even if he didn't, Suge was gonna keep doing what he did, regardless. He'd stay down for Selah and the kids, and he'd be there for Barron too, whether his nephew wanted him to or not. But Suge was smart enough to know what kind of dirty love he could expect from Lil Bump in return. When Viceroy was gone he knew Barron was gonna take his legs out and cut him off from the company. He'd kick Suge off the payroll and strip him outta his paid position, but there was one thing that young pup couldn't touch, and that was Suge's vote and his stockholder shares in Dominion Oil.

Viceroy had made sure his baby brother would always eat cake. Suge's vote could be worth millions, and for the past twenty years, whichever way Viceroy's vote had swung, his baby brother's vote had followed, no questions asked.

But Barron couldn't get that kind of loyalty outta Suge, and if Viceroy wasn't around to run Dominion Oil, then Suge would be a rich nigga and a free agent, and just like every other shareholder on the board of directors, his vote would be up for grabs by the highest bidder on the block.

CHAPTER 25

We rolled up outta the hospital in our four fly limos and went to meet Selah's brother Digger at a steak house that one of Viceroy's friends owned. Selah seemed to be in a good mood after seeing her husband, but Barron had a case of the ass and his grill was on ice the whole way there.

Uncle Digger was standing at the door talking to Pilar's man Ray when we walked up. Ray looked even shorter and rounder today, and even though he had a cute baby face, he had one of those jacked-up hairlines with bald spots on both sides. Pilar was walking up ahead of me, and I cracked up as she barely slowed down long enough for her man to kiss her on the cheek, then kept it moving right on past him.

The manager had closed off the entire back half of the restaurant just for us. There was a huge round table for the grown folks, and the kids were sitting at a smaller table right next to us. I sat down next to Barron's squeeze Carla, and I was real surprised when a few minutes later Uncle Suge showed up too.

"Hey son." He picked a little boy up outta the chair right beside me. "Uncle Suge got some grown folks' business to take care of. Go sit at the kids table, you hear?"

My stomach was still tossed up from all the beer I had drank at the barbeque the night before, and since I didn't want none of that Texas critter-shit Bunni and them was ordering off the menu, I just got me some fries and a glass of sweet tea.

Our food came out about fifteen minutes later. "I'm a meat man," Suge told me as he cut into a huge piece of steak. He sat with his legs open and his massive thigh was pressed all up against mine. He nodded toward the naked, shriveled up chicken breast on Barron's plate. "Not every man can handle a big piece of meat, you know. You gotta have some nuts if you're gonna break off in a solid hunk of beef like this."

I busted the look on Barron's face and giggled my ass off! I had already picked up on how he was busy scoping on me and ignoring his damn fiancée, who was sitting right next to me. Shit, he wasn't tryna hide the fact that he didn't like me and he thought I was fake, but he couldn't keep his damn eyes off me neither!

Fallon had on a pair of headphones and was holding her iPhone in her hand, while Bunni had a little battle going on between Dane and Ray. She was sitting in between them and her head swung back and forth as both of them tried to talk her to death.

I ate my fries and tried to get into the white chick, Carla. She had a country accent but she seemed real cool.

"So how long you and Barron been kickin' it?" I probed her.

"Oh, ever since college." She grinned. "He was the star of the football team and I was a cheerleader. He used to stare at me so hard he would almost fumble the ball!"

I almost bust out laughing. She mighta wanted to jump up and do a couple of cartwheels and splits 'cause that nigga sure wasn't lookin' at her ass no *more*!

The restaurant was cool like a mug, and after I picked over

my food I crossed my arms and shivered as I broke out in chill bumps.

"You cold?" Suge asked. He leaned over and rubbed his big, rough hands up and down both my arms and sent shivers tingling through my whole body. "Hold up. You got a tag sticking outta ya shirt," he said, and the next thing I knew I felt him fumbling at the back of my dress. He tucked my tag in, but then his hand slid down my back and rubbed against my bare skin. His big fingers swept my back from left to right, then back to the left again, rubbing lower and lower on each pass.

"Suge!" Selah busted him. She shook her head like, *Get ya damn hands off her*, then she smiled and tried to play it off. "It's good to see that everyone is enjoying Sab—I mean Mink's visit. She fits right in with us as a family, and I'm so proud of y'all for accepting her with so much love after missing her for all these years."

Yeah, I thought as Uncle Suge scooted back in his chair. He stretched his long legs out and let his eyes roam over me. There was *some* acceptance in the Dominion family. I glanced over at Barron and his fuck-cousin Pilar. The look on both of their faces made it real damn clear that not everybody was feeling me, because neither one of those two schemers believed a word I said.

When it came time for us to leave Uncle Digger made a real big show about picking up the tab. There were a lot of us sitting at the table, and the kids had played around in their food and wasted most of it. He whipped out his platinum card and flirted with the waitress a little bit, and then lit a cigar and sat back in his chair and crossed his arms over his jiggly belly. I was shocked when the waitress came back a few minutes later and handed him back his card and whispered something to him.

Everybody else was still talking and chillin', but my nosy New York eyeballs were halfway down his throat. He sat up straight for a second, then laughed and went back in his wallet. He took out another credit card and gave it to her, then shrugged and put the first one back in his wallet.

That shit went down twice.

Digger got his wallet out again, and I busted the look of shame in his eyes even though he tried to play it off with a grin. I also busted the look his daughter Pilar shot him. Not only was she embarrassed as hell, that chick was pissed off too.

The next person who came over to the table musta been the manager. By this time Barron had peeped game too, so he was ready for her. Before Digger could pull out another one of his maxed-out credit cards, Barron stood up and said something to the manager that I couldn't hear. She nodded and walked off, and a few minutes later the waitress was back looking shaky in the face.

Uncle Digger and Barron took her off to the side, and her manager just stood there while they had some icy words with her. That chick held her head down like she was about to cry, and then she started untying her apron as she walked toward the kitchen doors.

I didn't say a word as I peeped all the drama going down, but Uncle Suge leaned over and whispered, "That nigga's broke," in my ear, and confirmed exactly what I had been thinking.

Uncle Digger was all smiles as he came back to the table.

"That little lady ran my card up all wrong. They gave her the rest of the day off, and I guarantee you she'll be looking for a new job tomorrow."

Suddenly all the cards fell in place and I knew exactly why Pilar was so desperate to hook a paid nigga like Barron, even if he was her damn cousin. Her daddy's shit was slidin', and she saw her little rich-girl lifestyle going down the drain.

Hmph. I crossed my legs and gave Uncle Suge a big uh-huh look. Carla better watch her damn man, and Ray was gonna need to find himself some brand-new trim. Because if it went down the way Pilar planned for it to go, the only chick who was gonna walk down a damn aisle with Barron was *her*.

CHAPTER 26

Dane wanted to take me and Bunni to a nightclub when we got back to Dallas. I was all the way cool with that. My nerves were shot-out after just two days of being around Barron's tight ass, and besides, it was "Operation Hook 'Em" time, and since we were scheming to get as many family members in our corner as possible, this would be a real good opportunity for me to try and get closer to Dane.

I couldn't wait to get my mood lifted. Dane said the place we were going to was one of the hottest and hardest night-clubs in the city, and hard and hot was just what I needed.

The club was on a busy city street, and sweet whips and rugged SUVs were parked along every inch of the curb. They had one of those red velvet ropes to control the lines, but Dane had mad pull and high-level VIP access. We walked up in there like we were ballin' baby, ballin'. All eyes were on us and I loved drawing that kinda spotlight attention. I actually roasted under that kinda shine, and cutting in front of all the waiting nobodies got me to missing my thug nigga Gutta because he commanded that kinda respect too.

Dane was on his Danger grind tonight. He had left his little college boy act back at the house, and all the groupies and sucka nigs greeted him with love.

"These cats are gonna adore y'all asses up in here," Dane said and grabbed my hand as he led me through the swarm. I nudged Bunni and we pranced through the crowd setting fire to some eyeballs as we followed Dane toward the VIP lounge.

These Texas niggas had never seen nothing quite like me before. I was Mink Minajin' them from head to toe. My bright-red wig was a perfect set-off for my tight cherry-red freak 'em dress that glittered with silvery sequins. My big legs looked delicious in my bright-red fishnet stockings, and I moved like a hot demon in my six-inch red booties. We had smoked some chronic on the way over that had me feeling Nicki-ish all down in my bones. Not only was I looking like her, I had her confidence, her idiotic way of taking shit to the visual extreme, and most of all I had her sexy swagger and fuck-me strut.

I gave them niggas exactly what they was lookin' for as me and Bunni swung our hips and did the fresh pussy stroll. We were deep in the heart of Texas, but I noticed something for sure. A sucka nigga in the South wasn't no different than a sucka nigga up north. There was envy and haterade in a whole lotta lame boyz' eyes as Dane walked past with me and Bunni on his heels.

We hit the VIP lounge like we had paid the rent on it. There were ballas out the ass chillin' in a restricted-access area, and they were glossed out in platinum, diamonds, and other kinds of shine.

I glanced around real quick to check out the competition. Honeys of all different sizes and shapes had their goodies on display. They stood around poppin' gum, flossing weave, and gyrating booty out the ass. I gave up a few props where they were due. A couple of chicks had some decent game going, but most of them were amateurs who needed to get their weight up.

Dane led us over to the biggest booth in the house. Three high-rollers were chillin' with mad magnums of Krug and puffin' on expensive cigars. The one in the middle was fine as hell, and I could tell he was large in the game. He had a cute-ass chick sitting beside him, and she was dripping so much ice there shoulda been platinum puddles all around her feet.

"Wus good!" The big dude stood up when he saw Dane coming and dapped him out. He was tall and thick. He put me in the mind of Rick Ross, but everything about him was solid and well put together.

My eyes was wide open. I had a thang for big, powerful niggas. I dug the hell outta them ax-swinging, lumber-jack-lookin' gigantic dudes like Gutta, and this balla here was definitely all that.

"Yo, whattup, Siddiq. I got a couple of new honeys with me tonight so shit is all good."

Dane turned to me. "Mink, Bunni, this my manz, Siddiq. He's a business owner here in the city and he's official, nah'mean?"

Siddiq reached for my hand, and when I gave it to him he kissed it. I caught a whiff of his breath. It smelled just like he'd been hittin' that nasty purple drank.

"New York? That's word?"

I smiled and nodded.

"Yo, I'm ya man Siddiq from Brooklyn, baby! The Ville. Never ran, never will! What y'all know about that there type a' shit?"

I glanced sideways at Bunni and we tried not to crack the fuck up! Brooklyn was a big, bad-ass borough and we had pulled a hustle on damn-near every corner of its streets. Downtown Brooklyn was ripe for our particular grind, in fact, we had gotten so good with our light-finger dip game that the police started spotting us before we could spot them, and we had given up our lucrative Fulton Street hustle and relocated to places like Flatbush Avenue or even Pitkin, which was dead smack in Siddiq's hood.

"Oh, we know a little bit about Brooklyn," I said, grinning mysteriously. "It's one of our favorite towns."

"Yo, word?" He elbowed his little cutie and nudged her outta the way. "Get up Stanka and let my homegirl sit down. Yo—what's your name again, luv? Binky?"

"Mink," I stated. "And this is my friend Bunni. She's from New York too."

"Okay, Mink and Bunni! Y'all bring ya fine asses over here! You come over here, Bunni." His eyes shifted toward the dude on his left and that nigga jumped up like somebody had pressed an eject button under his seat. "And Mink, you sit over here where Stanka was just at."

His head swiveled around on his big-ass neck. "Yo, Stanka," he said to his icy chick who was standing there lookin' sho nuff stank. "Go chill over there with Bean and nem 'til I holla at you, dig?" He pointed toward a nearby table where a couple of dun duns sat waiting at his beck and call. Stanka shot me some hate, then ran off like a well-trained little monkey.

Siddiq looked toward the bar and a big-titty waitress appeared outta nowhere. She was wearing booty shorts and a low-cut bra, and I wondered how the hell she was walking around in them ten-inch heels and carrying all them drinks at the same time.

"Glasses for the ladies," Siddiq told her. "And another magnum too."

He tossed the liquid in his glass down his throat and turned back to me. "Ain't no party like a New York party, so what brings you two dolls down to Texas?" he said, grilling me with those sexy eyes and giving me and Bunni his full attention.

"A wedding," I lied real quick. "Bunni's friend is getting married down here so we came to show her some love. What about you?" I turned the convo around real slick-like. "You got that mad Brooklyn swagger all over you, pa. What you got going on in the Triple D?"

"Business," he said and puffed his blunt. "I'm a record producer, ya dig?"

I smirked and killed my champagne. Ol' boy looked certified, but I'd heard that record producer shit too many times to
be impressed. Besides, I knew a slanga when I saw one. With
all that shine and adornment his ass had to be real deep in the
drug game.

"Yeah, I produce for Black Dungeon." Siddiq kept talking
as he passed me the blunt. The sweet smell of cush felt good
sliding up my nose. "And I handle Two-Play and Earth Life in
my stable. Rap is fadin', man. There's a lotta biters out there
and everybody's shit is starting to sound the same. I came
down here last year to find me some fresh new talent to shake
up the game. That's how I got hooked up with ya boy, Danger.
I caught him spittin' one night and his flow game was nice and
original like that."

We sat in the booth getting toasted up. This kinda shit was
right up my alley. Low-level nigs kept coming over to pay
Dane and Siddiq their respect, and me and Bunni racked up so
many hater looks that I stopped counting.

All this attention made me miss those days when I used to
reign on Gutta's arm as the queen of the club set. My boo had
carried so much weight that dudes envied him and chickens
went to bed every night praying they would wake up hatched
as me.

I was vibing live, but something wasn't smooth across the
room. My street intuition was always on point, and I peeped
the temperature as soon as it changed. There were some rival
camps posted up in the VIP lounge, and some unspoken shit
was going down. Every posse that entered the joint either
turned right and came over to show love to Siddiq, or they
headed left and swung over to a booth where a real buff, light-
skinned dude sat chillin' in a money-green shirt and a matching team fitted.

After hanging in cutthroat New York City clubs night after night with Gutta, I could spot a turf clash going on even from a distance, and there was definitely no love lost between the two sets up in here tonight.

The music was crashing and Bunni had been steady dancing in her seat.

"What's up with these niggas?" she yelled. "What? Niggas don't dance down here in Syrup City?"

I got embarrassed. "That's Houston! We're back in *Dallas*, Bunni!"

"I don't give a damn where we at!" she said and got up outta her seat. "Ain't none of this shit *New York*!"

"Yo, Bunni—" Dane tried to call her back, but she had already slid outta the booth and started snapping her fingers and popping her ass. She pranced toward the dance floor like she was about to get loose, but then she turned left until she was standing right in front of the rival camp.

The dude in all the green was eyeing her, and Bunni did like any natural-born slicksta would do. She zeroed in on his ass like a bullet on a target. She got in a wide-legged stance that made her hips and ass look crucial, and even though I couldn't see her from the front, I knew that deep split in her na-na was driving niggas wild.

Dude in the green came up outta his booth and got up in Bunni's face. He cupped her left ass-cheek in one big hand and threw his rap down in her ear. Bunni tossed her head back and I could tell she liked that shit. My girl was the type who needed it rough and raw, and she would test a dude's heart in a minute. If a playa didn't push up on her with more swagger than she was bringing, then Bunni didn't want shit to do with him. Even from where I was sitting I could tell that this dude had approached her exactly the way she wanted him to, and she was loving his game.

"Yo, Danger," Siddiq growled real low as he grilled the

click Bunni was busy entertaining. "Tell that bitch to get back over here. She fuckin' around on the wrong side of the street."

I didn't say a word as Dane got up and went to get Bunni, but I damn sure wasn't surprised at what happened next. Static jumped off. You know, the kind you expect when dangerous nigs found a reason to go at each other's throats. All it took was for Dane to put his hand on Bunni's shoulder. That green T-shirt nigga straight bit my play-brother. He bounced Dane in the chest and then his entire set swarmed.

"Oh, shit!" I hollered as Dane went down under a hail of killer blows.

I got outta that booth way before Big-Man Siddiq did, and I was praying no shots popped off before I could pull Bunni's ass out from the bottom of the pile.

But Siddiq was traveling real deep. A football team full of niggas came from every corner of the room and converged on green T-shirt's crew. Niggas was cracking champagne bottles over heads and going in hard.

"Bunni!" I screamed like she was gonna hear me over a room full of wildin' beasts. "Bunni!"

I wanted to dive into the middle of the mob to search for her, but I knew them fools would crush me too. My cute little red dress wouldn't be nothing but a greasy doo-rag by the time they got finished with me. Besides, we had been around more club fights than a little bit, and Bunni knew the drill. When niggas got to fighting, whether they were swinging, slashing, or shooting, the rule was always the same.

Stop, drop, and roll.

Damn right. If you were in range of the whoop-ass, then you stopped whatever it was you were doing, you dropped down to the floor where most dudes weren't tryna be, and then you rolled your ass away from the fight and outta the kill zone.

I was jumping up and down on the edge of the crowd and looking for her when I got snatched from behind.

"Girl, bring ya ass on!" It was Bunni. I whirled around and thanked God my girl was okay.

"I thought you was caught up in the middle of all that shit!" I hollered as we held on to each other and dipped for the door.

"*Sheeeiiittt*," Bunni said. More niggas was rushing into the VIP lounge and blocking our exit. "Bitch I know how to stop, drop, and roll!"

Since so many dudes was running toward the door on the right, me and Bunni skirted around a long table and tried to get to the exit door from the left side. We were almost there when Stanka and a few of her friends called themselves stepping to us.

She wilded out on Bunni first. "Look what the fuck you did, stupid-ass! You shouldn'ta took your ass over there in the first place! If you don't know the rules then stay in ya fuckin' lane!"

"Kiss my ass!" Bunni yelled. "You need to check ya self!"

"Nah." Stank One pointed toward Bunni's crotch. "What you need to do is fix that nasty-lookin' pussy you got! Look like you got a lil dick-swanging going on! Go get you a mini-pad and hide that camel toe, *okay?*"

Bunni just laughed in her face. "Bitch, is you crazy? This cookie ain't for you to crumble. It's for ya fuckin' *man's* lips only!"

I don't know who swung first but them two got to scrapping. Hair was flying everywhere but it wasn't Bunni's 'cause it was long and silky. Ol' girl was swinging haymakers, but Bunni was patient and she clutched her up Harlem-style. She charged in and got Stanka in a headlock, then twisted her scrawny-ass neck and pounded her with a flurry of devastating lefts.

"Kick that bitch ass!" Stanka's crew was shouting. "Fuck her ass up!"

I had never been a fighter but I wasn't no runner neither. Just let one of those tricks think about getting in it! There would be a whole lotta ass showing tonight because I was damn sure gonna jump in too!

But a catfight ended up being the last thing we had to worry about, because just when one of Stanka's friends looked like she wanted to take a swing, gunfire boomed in the VIP lounge and everybody froze. And then niggas scattered everywhere!

My Harlem instincts kicked in and I dove under the nearest table. But Stanka had already beat me there, and we started scrapping and scrambling tryna get to the best position—in the back!

"Move, bitch!"

"*You* fuckin' move! I was here first!"

I had been at plenty of parties before where somebody started shooting outta the blue, and I knew the safest place was behind somebody else. I put my head down and dug my way in behind Stanka. I used my shoulders, my elbows, and my knees, and by the time the bullets stopped popping off I had dug my way to the back and Stanka was curled up in front of me like a human shield.

The music had stopped and it was city-morgue quiet up in that bitch. I didn't know where Bunni and Dane was, but all them niggas who had been beefing and fighting was probably deep up under tables too.

"All right!" a dude's voice boomed. "Nobody move, and nobody gets fuckin' blasted! I want everybody's shit! Everybody's! My manz are coming around and don't think they won't blast ya ass! Take off ya shit! *All of it!* Ya shine, ya ice, ya cake, I'ma need you to give all that up, ya heard? Get up off that shit right fuckin' *NOW!*"

I peeked over Stanka's shoulder and I couldn't believe what I saw. I had only been hit by a club lick one time in my entire life, and that had been in a greasy lil hole up in the South Bronx.

But there were at least ten dudes down on this lick and they were moving fast. They wore black hoodies and ski masks and carried AK-47s. I knew they had locked shit down out in the main club area too, because after all those shots didn't nobody come to see about us, and they moved with confidence as they went around the room filling up pillowcases with other people's loot.

"A'ight, now! I want every nigga in here to come outta ya kicks and ya pants! Come up outta that shit! All I wanna see is holey socks and dirty drawers! Move, muh'fuckas! Give up that shine, then strip outta ya shit!"

Still clutching the back of Stanka's dress, I peeked out and watched as niggas gave up their tools and their jewels, then stepped outta their sneakers and let their pants hit the floor. Two guys pushed up on Big Man Siddiq, who was still sitting in the same spot I had left him in. The shorter dude smashed Siddiq dead in the grill, and a spray of blood splashed on the mirror behind him.

"Get the fuck up, you thick-neck muh'fucka! What? You think everybody else getting stuck up in this bitch except you?"

Siddiq rose to his feet. After all that Brooklyn rah-rah shit he had talked his ass looked scared as hell. He took off the ring I had admired, and his Rolex too. He lightened up the load around his neck and then emptied his pockets into the pillowcase and tossed a nice-sized package of cocaine in there as well. He dropped his pants, but he was so big he had to sit back down to get his kicks off. Dude standing over him was getting impatient, and he came down hard on the back of Siddiq's dome with his AK, and Siddiq pitched over face-first on the floor.

"What you do that for?" Stanka sounded off in front of me, and I was just about to pinch that ass and tell her to shut the hell up when a pair of black Uggs entered my picture and the armed robber who was wearing them demanded our shit.

"C'mon now, ladies. Y'all asses ain't invisible. Come out from under that table and fill up my goody bag."

Stanka got up first, and then I uncurled myself and crawled out on my hands and knees. I stood up beside her, and dude checked us out side to side. "Damn! Both of y'all big-titty bitches is fine! Maybe we can hook up in a threesome when I'm done robbing ya asses!"

We both gave him the stupid face, and he laughed.

"Take off all that shit, my honeys. The earrings, the brace-lets, all that. Give up the cell phones too."

Stanka was wearing way more expensive shit than I was, and she came up outta her jewels real reluctantly. I moved real slow too. Hell, I wasn't even tryna drop my shine in his funky, wrinkled laundry bag. I pretended like I was fumbling with my earrings as I turned my diamond ring around and cupped the stone in my palm, tryna hide it. But Stanka's ass was check-ing me out. She had already given up her shit and she knew I was tryna be slick. Her eyes was bouncing all over me, and the way she was smirking and bucking her eyes toward my hand, ol' boy figured it out too.

"Yo, lemme get that ring you got on ya finger, shawty," he said. "Toss it on in the bag. My bitch loves stuff like that."

I wanted to beat Stanka's stank little ass! She musta been down with the lick! She didn't have to bust on me like that!

When they were done collecting all our possessions they backed outta the lounge with their gats aimed and ready to spray. Every dude in the room was caught out there in his drawers with no firepower and no cell phones.

I looked for Bunni and saw her standing next to Dane looking mad as hell. She had been stripped down too. Her dangling earrings and thick gold choker were gone. I turned to say something slick to Stanka, but she was gone. I cursed real loud. I didn't know where Siddiq got his lil gutta chicks from but I had a feeling Ms. Stanka was definitely down with his competition.

"You okay?" I rushed over to Dane and touched his cheek. A noogie was rising up under his eye where he had gotten the shit knocked outta him. "Me and Bunni tried to pull them niggas offa you!" I lied hotly. "We jumped on some backs and got us some punches in, for real!"

Bunni flowed with me. "Damn right! I pounced on that nigga in the green shirt! I drilled him right in the eyeball. I bet his ass is gonna be seeing two of every damn thing for the rest of the night!"

Dane put his arm around both of us as he walked toward the door in his drawers.

"Thanks, y'all. But if something like that ever pops off again don't worry about me, just hit the door. Niggas is crazy out here and they'll ambush a female in a minute. I can handle mine, and I wouldn't want neither one of y'all to get hurt over me."

"Awww," Bunni said and we both slid our arms around him.

"I can tell you got good hands, but that was too many niggas for any one dude to be handling! Besides, ain't no way I could run away and leave you in no fight, Dane," I said, like I was insulted he would even think such a thing. "I'm a ride or die, big brother. Especially for my fam!"

He was straight up touched.

"You're a real cool sister, Mink," he said, and kissed the top of my head. "It's gonna be good having somebody like you in the family."

Got him! I thought as I cut my slick eyes at Bunni.

She shot me a *hell yeah* grin, and then that crazy fool reached behind Dane's back and grabbed the underside of my arm and pinched the shit outta me.

CHAPTER 27

We got up and went to church on Sunday morning. Bunni didn't wanna go and neither did I, but Selah made it clear that every damn body under her roof would be riding out to the house of the Lord.

I looked all through my gear until I found something decent to wear. I didn't know if Bunni had ever been inside a church in her life, but something told me she didn't get those skin-tight Donna Karan riding pants off no rack of Holy Ghost clothes.

Selah took us to a mega-church where I could tell at first glance the preacher was a grifter who had him a helluva hustle going down. The joint was gigantic. It ran about three blocks wide and two blocks deep. There were more luxury cars in the massive parking lot than a little bit. Beemers, Mercedes, Lexus, Jaguars, you name it—if it cost over fifty grand, it was there. I tried to figure out how much dough flowed into those collection plates every week and my head started pounding at the sheer absurdity of the numbers.

I felt like I had just walked into Madison Square Garden. I had never been inside a church so big before. When I was little the only time my grandmother got the Spirit was when she was tipsy, and then she would drag us down to one of those real small storefront joints and foam at the mouth and speak in tongues until she passed out drunk in the pews.

Rich-people church was a lot like the club. Everybody had a role to play, and you could tell a person's stats just by where they sat. The con-man preacher posted-up on the stage with his little sanctified posse, and the members who contributed the most cream to his pot got front-row seats in the VIP areas. All the regular folks, the jump-offs, the come-ups, and the posers, sat up in the bleachers.

I fell asleep almost as soon as the sermon started, and I didn't wake up again until the choir got to singing. The first thing I noticed was that Bunni was gone, and the next thing I noticed was the size of the collection plates. Those joints were monster-sized buckets and folks were tossing dollars down in them until they started just overflowing all over the place.

I whispered to Selah that I was going to the bathroom, then I held my pointer finger up in the air and got the hell up outta there. I walked right past the bathroom and snuck outside looking for Bunni, and I wasn't surprised to find her outside chillin' with Jock. That young boy was a little pussy freak. He was sniffing deep in my girl's ass too. I had heard him tell one of his little high school friends that he was gonna run his dick up in Bunni's gap before she went back to New York.

"Your little brother is gonna treat us to the movies tonight." Bunni nudged me and laughed. Jock was looking at Bunni like he wanted to go swimming in her pussy, and the boy damn-near had drool running down his little chin.

I shook my head. "I thought we was gonna go buy some new cell phones and then hang out with Dane and his friends?"

"*First* we're gonna go buy some new phones, and *then* we're gonna go to the movies with Jock." Bunni pinched him on his cheek. "And after that we'll go hang out with Dane. Okay?"

"Cool. I'm down for that." I elbowed Jock. "Hey, lil brother. What you got good for the head?"

Jock took us around to the side of the church and we stood huddled between some parked cars. "Y'all want some 'ludes?" he offered us. "Or maybe a little X?"

"I'll take some of that X." Bunni was ready to jump all on it, but I checked her real quick.

"Fool, we still got a whole lot more church to go! You do *not* wanna be trapped next to no Holy Ghost choir and tripping at the same time. Just give us some weed," I told Jock. "We can save the X and shit for when we get to the movies tonight."

Later, when church finally let out and we got back to the mansion, I warned Bunni not to fuck with Jock's head. I knew this was all just a grimy little game for me and her, but dudes always got bent over Bunni, and I knew how much she liked twistin' up their noodles. Jock was too young to be going through all that.

"Just leave him alone, Bunni," I told her. "He's so fresh off Selah's titty his breath still smells like milk. If you're gonna fuck with anybody, then get with Dane. That dude is fine as fuck and he's fully grown."

"But Dane's ass is broke." Bunni rolled her eyes and looked real devilish. "Jock ain't even come into his inheritance money yet."

"Just leave him alone," I said again, and even though I got Bunni to swear off the boy with her mouth, when we got to the movies that night I noticed her promise didn't stop her from letting Jock drape his arm over her shoulder and rub his long skinny fingers all over her two-inch nipples.

CHAPTER 28

"C'mon nigga, *push* this bitch!" Jock's boy Dre hollered from the backseat of the SUV as they whipped down the streets of Fort Worth.

Jock was already going eighty in a thirty-mile-per-hour zone, and he stomped the gas pedal even harder as he jumped on the highway and headed south toward the Dominion Estate.

They were fucked up on some E and had just picked up a fine white chick from a group home in the heart of the city. Sean and Dre were chillin' with her in the back-seat, while Jock and Glenn rode up front blasting music and passing a blunt back and forth between them.

The four of them had been on their group home grind for a minute now, and they loved flossin' Jock's 2012 Lincoln MKT in front of a bunch of hot ghetto chicks who were practically living on their own. Whether they were prowling around in Dallas or Fort Worth, there were tons of state-run residential houses out there where ten to fifteen teenaged chicks lived together until they graduated from high school and got turned loose by the government.

Yeah, the girls had a counselor and a curfew, but so what. Rules didn't mean a damn thing to most of these honeys, and as soon as the state-paid baby-sitter turned her head they climbed outta the window and jumped into whatever whip was waiting at the curb.

The white girl they were partying with tonight was riding solo. There were usually enough out-the-window chicks to go around for all of them, but there had been two other whips parked outside the group house tonight. The honeys they usually banged it up with had giggled and walked right past Jock's ride as they jumped in some other nigga's car.

The white girl had come straight at them though, and it wasn't until Jock got a good look at her in his rearview mirror did he realize he'd seen her before. Her name was Gina. She was cute and had a real nice body, and best of all she was down for the ride.

Jock kept peeping her as she slurped down beer and Henny with his boyz. She laughed a lot and sucked on the blunt he'd passed back there like it was a big brown dick. Less than thirty minutes after picking her up they were chillin' in the Dominions' pool house and getting lifted. The coffee table looked like a buffet line. There were pills in all shapes, sizes, and colors spread all over that bitch, and no matter what it took to get your head nice, between Jock and his boyz they had copped plenty of it.

"You know I've been here before," Gina said as she glanced around the large room then sat down on the sofa between him and Dre. "It was around Christmas."

"Uh-huh." Jock knew. He remembered seeing her with Barron's girlfriend, Carla. She mentored all kinds of kids from disadvantaged backgrounds, and she had brought Gina out to their Christmas dinner last year.

Jock leaned back on the sofa next to Gina and turned on his laptop. He logged into one of those hot webcam chat rooms and they smoked some Ls, popped some E and some xanies, and drank a few rum and Cokes while watching complete strangers fuck live on-screen.

Gina really got into that shit. She gripped Jock's thigh with one hand and popped xanies like they were gumdrops with the other one.

"Yo, this shit right here is all me," Jock told his boys as he put his arm around Gina and claimed her for himself. He slid closer to her on the sofa and she grinned, then picked up two more oval tablets from the table and washed them down with Dre's beer.

"You better watch that shit," Jock warned her. "That ain't no candy you eating, baby. Those are one-point-zeros. The good shit, you feel me?"

Jock put his hand on top of hers and immediately she took his cue. She slid her fingers over his rocked up crotch and squeezed him through his pants. He pulled her to him and covered her thin pink lips with his. Their tongues darted everywhere, and the acrid taste of pills and the slightly sour taste of beer filled Jock's mouth. He ran his hand up her bare arm and let it trail over her breast. She moaned as he fingered her nipples, and Jock's dick grew about two more inches in the confines of his pants.

"Let's go in the other room," he whispered. He stood up and held his hand out to her, and she took it. They walked past his boyz who were still getting lit and watching the action on the webcam.

In the darkness of the bedroom there were no need for words. All Jock wanted was some wet pussy, and he knew all Gina wanted was the drugs he was dishing off and the two hundred dollars he was gonna slide her when they were through.

They stripped down naked and got ready to mash it up. Gina was out of her clothes first, and she jumped on Jock's bone like a playful little doggie. Jock wrapped it up and let her have it. At eighteen, he had more cum in his balls than a little bit, and he banged Gina up with nothing but getting his nut off on his mind. It took him a minute to realize that she was just laying there beneath him not doing shit. She wasn't wiggling her ass or moaning or clenching her pussy muscles down on him or nothing.

Fuck it, he thought as he pounded into her real deep and got his. This wasn't no damn romance. For two hundred dollars she shoulda been sucking all on his dick and getting him ready for round two, but he could tell the chick was pretty fucked up, and he lost his load after less than five minutes anyway.

Jock rolled over. He was embarrassed for cumming so quick, and he didn't wanna go back out in the living room with his boys so soon, but now that his joint was soft he had no desire to be up under the strange chick neither. She lay there with her legs wide open and breathing real deep, and once or twice she reached over and rubbed his wilted dick halfheartedly, then snored a little bit.

Jock forced himself to lay beside her for as long as he could.

"Yo, get dressed," he told her after a few more minutes. He felt around on the floor for her clothes and then handed them to her as she struggled to sit up.

"You finished already?" she slurred like she hadn't even realized it was over. She pushed her long blond hair out of her face and started putting her shirt on backward.

They walked into the living room together, and Gina plopped down on the couch next to Dre and reached for the blunt he was smoking.

"Where's Sean and Glenn?" Jock asked.

"They left," Dre said and went back to a conversation he was having with two naked white chicks on a Skype video chat. "Yo, man," Dre told Jock, "call that old fat lady who keeps burning up your kitchen and tell her to bring us something to eat." He laughed. "This chronic got me, man. I need me some fuckin' hot wings."

"Who, Katie? Hell nah, man." Jock looked around at the mess in the room. "Do you see all this shit up in here? Man, I ain't waking her old ass up so she can smell this yay and have Bump getting in our asses."

"Fuck your corporate-ass brother," Dre yapped, even though his father was a millionaire financial analyst and as corporate as they came. He licked his lips as the two white chicks started kissing and touching each other on the screen. "Ga'-head, J! Barron don't scare nobody. For real. I'm starving! Go in that big-ass house and get us something to eat, man!"

"A'ight, cool," Jock said and nodded at Gina, who was now leaning on Dre's shoulder and killing his blunt, "but don't forget we gotta ride back to Dallas and take her home."

Jock jogged around the swimming pool and down the path that led to the main house. After punching in his pass code, he pushed through the side door and jetted into the large, spotless kitchen. He slipped into a bathroom on the other side of the wall and took a quick shit. When he was done he reached under the counter and got a washcloth and wiped his dick and balls with some hot, soapy water.

Back in the kitchen he found a tray of lunch meat in the fridge and took a bag of rolls from the breadbox. He got a bunch of mayo and mustard packs from a basket in the pantry, then put all that shit on a big serving tray and headed out the door.

Jock had only been gone for about ten minutes, but by the time he got back to the pool house it was already too late.

"Help me!" Dre screamed the moment his boy pushed through the door. "Come get this stupid bitch!"

Gina was slumped over on the sofa. The two white girls Dre was Skyping with were making worried noises as Dre shook the girl violently and tried to wake her up.

"What the fuck did you do?" Jock dropped the tray and

jetted over to the sofa. Foam was coming out of Gina's mouth and her eyes were rolling back in her head.

"I didn't do *shit!*" Dre hollered.

The white girls watching on the screen were busy saying stuff like, "Oh my God, is she okay?" and "Maybe you should call an ambulance!"

"Man, what the hell did you give her, Dre?"

"I swear, man. As soon as you walked out the door this crazy broad scooped up about twenty tabs and throated them shits! Ask them!" He pointed at the girls on the computer monitor. "She said something stupid like, 'See ya on the other side' and then she just started *eating*, man! How was I supposed to know her ass was suicidal?"

"Oh shit!" Jock said as he slapped Gina's cheeks over and over and called out her name real loud. "I knew something was off about her ass!"

"Gina!" He grabbed a handful of her hair and held her up-right. Then he used his thumb and forefinger to try to hold her eyelids open so he could see if her pupils were dilated. His hands were shaking and sweating so bad he poked her dead in the eyeball a couple of times, but on the third or fourth try he was able to peer into her fishy gray eyes.

"Oh shit! Wake up, Gina!" Her head lolled from side to side as he shook her and tried to get her to respond. "Gina! Wake up, dammit. Open your eyes, girl. Wake the hell up!"

"Do you think she's dead?" one of the chicks on the video chat asked real loud.

Jock had been thinking the same fuckin' thing, and his first instinct was to throw the laptop across the room and get up out of the chat completely. But then he realized that these chicks had already seen Gina, and they could see and identify him and Dre too. If this crazy white girl really was dead, then all roads would lead directly to his pool house door.

"Nah," Jock chuckled a little bit even though his gut was gripped with panic and sweat had broken out all over him.

"She's straight, everybody. Just relax, y'all. She ain't dead. Hell nah, she ain't dead."

Almost right on cue, Gina arched her back and groaned. Her eyes flew open, and her body lurched as she spewed hot, stinking vomit all over the coffee table full of drugs.

"See?" Jock shouted happily as Gina upchucked beer and stomach sludge and the Skype girls made *eww, vomit* noises. "I told y'all she wasn't dead! I told y'all!"

"Yay! She's alive!" Dre hollered. "Now let's get this crazy bitch up outta here!"

Jock reached down and flipped the laptop closed and cut off the Skype connection, but as soon as he turned back to Gina he knew the shit wasn't done hitting the fan just yet.

She had slumped over again. She wasn't throwing up no more, but now she wasn't breathing either. Jock shook the shit out of her and slapped her cheeks a few more times too. He ran over to the small freezer and him and Dre took turns sticking ice cubes down her panties and in her bra, and they even rubbed them all over her neck, face, and wrists, but they got nothing out of the girl. Nothing. Not only wasn't she breathing, but it felt like her body was starting to get kinda cool under their hands, and it hit Jock like a roadside bomb when he realized the girl really, really, really was dead.

Him and Dre spent almost an hour trying to come up with a lie that would keep them both out of jail. "I don't understand it," Jock just kept saying. He felt so bad for the fuckin' girl, but he just couldn't get his head around what she had done. "What would make a chick do something like that? And why would she wanna go out right here in front of us? Fuck! We're in trouble, man. We're in *trouble*."

"But we didn't do nothing," Dre insisted. "Didn't nobody force-feed that girl nothing. She swallowed all that shit on her own. At least you fucked her, man. I didn't even get none."

"Shut up, Dre! It don't matter who the fuck did what!"

Jock barked. He had closed Gina's staring gray eyes and covered her up with the sheet they had just fucked on, and her body lay on the sofa getting colder by the minute. "They can still tie her to us, man. Not only did the chicks at the group home see her getting in my Lincoln, but Sean and Glenn and them two white girls on Skype saw her here with us too."

"Man," Dre mumbled, "I ain't going to jail because of no dumb-ass girl. Nobody made her do shit, my dude. They can't hang this on us."

Jock wasn't planning on going to jail behind no girl either. He had no idea how many different kinds of pills Gina might have had mixed with all that beer and liquor, and he felt real sick knowing he had just busted off with the chick and now she was gone. But like Dre had said. Nobody had made her do shit.

"Look dawg," Dre stood up after a while. "What you gonna do about this, man? I gotta get up outta here in a minute, yo. I need to get back to the crib."

Jock stared at his boy. They had been tight since the elementary days, and while Dre had always been one of those typical whining-ass rich kids, Jock couldn't believe his boy was gonna leave him out there like this.

"So what? You just gonna leave me hanging, dude? What? I'm supposed to get rid of a dead fuckin' body all by myself?"

Dre shrugged. "I don't know what you gonna do, man. But I know this. That chick was alive the last time those two girls I was Skyping with saw her. She was sitting up and tossing vomit everywhere, yo. And that's the last thing I remember about her. I got outta here right after that, and when I left the broad was still breathing. That's my story. You need to come up with yours."

Jock jumped to his feet as Dre walked outta the pool house. His whole body was shaking as he rushed to follow his boy outside.

"Yo, Dre!" he hollered as his friend walked toward his car and got inside. "Dre! You just gonna leave me like that, man? Yo, we got a situation here, nigga! You was down for the ride. I ain't going down by myself, Dre! If they get me they getting your ass too!"

Jock watched Dre take off in his car, but just as his boy pulled out of the driveway, another ride pulled in.

"Oh shit," Jock muttered under his breath when he saw who it was.

Dane jumped out of his Hummer, and Mink and Bunni were right behind him.

"Hey Jock!" Bunni hollered like she was tipsy. "You ready to rock?" She bust out laughing and started walking toward him with Mink and Dane right behind her.

"Nah!" Jock tried to wave them off. There was no way in fuck he could let them get close to the pool house. "Y'all go ahead inside. I gotta get something! I'll meet you in the house in a second!"

"What you doing, man?" Dane hollered at him from the other side of the pool. "I thought Bump told you to stay outta there at night, dude?"

"I . . . I . . . I think I left something in there!" Jock hollered. "Yo, man, y'all go check on Katie for me real quick! She's burning the shit outta something in the kitchen!"

He ran back inside the pool house and locked the door. The sheet-covered body on the sofa seemed to take up all the space in the room, and Jock felt like he was walking through a bad dream. The last thing he wanted was for his young life to be linked with this chick's crazy death, and he couldn't stop the tears that slipped from his eyes as he tried to figure out what to do.

What Jock needed right now was a clean-up man. A closer. Somebody who could make all this shit go away like it had never even happened. There was only one dude he could think of who could take care of something so fuckin' crucial. This guy was known for wiping up a lotta messy shit in the past, and if anybody could clean up this kind of doo-doo, Jock knew this man could.

He picked up his cell phone and made a quick call. He spoke a few words to the man on the other end of the line, and then he unlocked the door and sat on the floor and waited for his uncle Suge to arrive.

CHAPTER 29

When we got back from partying with his friends, Dane said he wanted me and Bunni to come check out his space. He stayed in a dope-ass apartment over the ten-car garage during the summer when he wasn't at school and living in the dorms, and it was pimped the hell out up there.

Bunni oohed and aahed, all impressed as he showed us around, but I played cool with it like I saw quality shit every day. Brother Dane was a pussy hound, and his crib was a bad-ass little fuck den. There were two large bedrooms, two full bathrooms, a living room, a loft, and a full-sized kitchen that was stocked with food. Papi had a stripper pole in his loft, and a sex swing hanging from the ceiling too. Pictures of half-naked chicks were everywhere and in all kinds of poses, and with all that ass tooted up everywhere I didn't know how he could sleep at night. I busted Bunni eyeballing that stripper pole and licking her lips, and I stuck my finger into her back pocket and yanked her ass up outta there.

Dane told us he played music at a lot of college parties, and he had all kinds of DJ equipment to show for it. Turntables, bass speakers, tweeters, bottoms, all that. He was into cuts like "Tony Montana" and "I'm on One," and he was blasting the beat to "Maybe She Will" by Lil Wayne while he threw his own rap down over it.

We kicked off our shoes and I climbed up on his huge loft bed. I sat cross-legged on his prime cashmere blanket and wiggled my toes. Dane went to the kitchen and came back with three cold Heinekens, and then he sparked up two blunts and passed one to me and the other one to Bunni.

"So, whattup. Y'all missing New York yet or is Texas starting to feel like home?"

I grinned. I was digging Dane. Outta everybody we had met so far, him and Jock had been the only two who seemed to accept my bullshit story straight off the bat.

"Yeah, I kinda miss Harlem. You ever been there?"

He nodded. "Yeah. I was there when my sister Sable—when you, I mean—was kidnapped."

I did a puff-puff pass and was about to change the subject, but Bunni jumped right on it.

"So you remember the day that Sable got snatched, huh?"

"Nah, not really. I just know I was there. I was almost five, Sable was three, and Bump was around seven or eight. He remembers it, though. That dude remembers everything. And now . . . Mink is here . . . right on time for Sable's twenty-first birthday."

"Uh-huh." I played it off. "And this year I'm gonna eat my birthday cake with my fam!"

Dane laughed. "Hell yeah, and you're gonna pocket a hundred grand too."

"It's not all about the money, Dane," I lied. "It's about getting what's yours in life and knowing who you are."

"That's cool. But did you know about all the other money you can get from the family trust?"

"What *other* money?"

Dane shrugged. "Bump is prolly gon' go gorilla 'cause I told you, but fuck it, if you're Sable then you've got a right to know. There's a three-hundred-grand annuity waiting for all of us if my father dies or if he can't go back to work as head of his company."

"Annuity? What's that?"

"It's a cash payment you get every year. Pops set it up in a trust for all his kids. It's like life insurance, but you get an annual payment, and the government doesn't get their hands on it and tax the shit out of it."

Bunni was on it even quicker than I was. "Hold up. So if your father dies all y'all muthafuckas get three hunnerd g's every goddamn *year*?"

Dane nodded. "Yeah. I mean, he set it up so that, you know, there's a lot that goes into it and a lot you gotta do to get it, but basically, yeah. If he dies or if he's declared incompetent to deal with his own affairs, we get it."

Bunni jumped up and started dancing, and I took an extra-long puff on the blunt.

"So what do you have to do to get it?" I threw the question out there real casually, but every nerve in my body was tingling.

"Look, my pops was a straight-up G back in the day, and when he made it big in oil he knew he was gonna have to polish up his image and reinvent his legacy, nah'mean? So he changed his ways and started living the clean life. He vowed all his children were gonna live that way too. If they wanted to get his damn money, that is."

"But what do you have to *do*?" I insisted.

Dane laughed and looked at the blunt in his hand. "Definitely not the kinda shit I've been out there doing, that's what's up. For real though, Pops just wanted us to do all the normal stuff. Graduate from high school and go to college"—he nodded toward the spliff Bunni was rolling—"stay away from drugs, make sure we didn't get arrested or do nothing stupid that would shine a bad light on our family name. You know. He wanted us to live right."

I listened to that yang, but I knew my ass was straight dis-qualified. I had never graduated from anywhere. I mean, I had enough credits to walk across the stage with my high school class, but them mugs had refused to let me because me and two other girls had got busted running a scheme with the booster club funds.

And I damn sure had me a nice little arrest record. In every freakin' borough in the city of New York! I glanced down at the blunt Dane had passed me . . . stay away from the head bangaz? That shit was completely out!

Dane threw on a cut by Reem Raw and his sound filled the room.

Bunni grabbed Dane up in the collar and took him into the loft to show him a few of her pole tricks. I went with them, but instead of dancing I stood there watching Bunni and mentally digging around in my bag of lies. Three hundred free g's a year would keep me and my girl both laced real lovely. Nah, I wasn't grimy enough to get down on my knees and pray for Viceroy to check outta here, but if his banged-up ass happened to kick the bucket, I was damn sure gonna be on line with all the rest of his kids, holding out my greedy little hand.

I left Bunni chillin' in Dane's crib. She was demonstrating some of her hot moves on the sex swing, and it didn't take me long to realize that three was a crowd. I went back to my suite and logged onto Facebook, and I was just about to check my inbox messages when I heard a car pull up outside my window.

I went over and opened the curtains, then broke out in a big-ass grin when I saw who it was. Uncle Suge's big silver truck was right out back, and I figured he had pulled up under my window so Selah and Barron wouldn't bust him coming to see me.

I ran in the bathroom and sloshed some Listerine around
in my mouth, then checked my nose for boogers and grabbed
my slim Gucci purse and wrapped the strap around my wrist.

I tipped down the spiral staircase and dipped out the door
right off the kitchen, but when I got outside Uncle Suge wasn't
parked under my window no more. His truck was right next
to the pool house now, and I swore all out a snake was gonna
get me as I ran across the grass to the other side of the pool.

I could tell shit was funky before I even got all the way
over there. The back passenger door of the truck was wide
open, and I couldn't believe it when Uncle Suge and Jock
came outta the pool house carrying a limp white chick.

Uncle Suge had her under her arms, and Jock was holding
her right under her knees. She looked like she was toasted up,
and since I was an underage drinker my damn self, I wasn't
about to throw up no shots just 'cause the liq had knocked
mami out.

"What the hell was *she* drinking?" I joked as I walked up
on them outta the darkness. "Whatever it was, I want me
some!"

Jock jumped so bad he let go of the girl's legs and the bottom half of her body swung down and hit the ground like she
was out cold.

"Oh, that bitch is wasted," I giggled, but then I saw the
look on their faces.

Uncle Suge looked deadly, but Jock was scared as hell. He
was sweating bullets and his eyes were real red and mad big.
"Damn!" he screamed on me. "I thought I told y'all to go in
the house!" He looked wild in the face. Crazy. Like a dust head
who was freaking the hell out.

"Who you screamin' at?" My hand shot up on my hip as
Harlem jumped right outta me. "I ain't one of ya little freaky
friends, baby boy! You better know it!"

"Go back in the house, Mink," Uncle Suge said quietly as
he hoisted the girl up under her arms again. She looked like

dead weight from where I was standing, and when I moved up on them a little bit and peeped in her mug, she looked straight up *dead*!

"What the hell happened to her?" I had never seen a white person who looked like this before.

"She's straight," Uncle Suge said. They pushed the girl into the backseat of the truck and shut the door, then Uncle Suge went around to the driver's side and got in.

I ran over there and stood on my toes at his window. "Is she dead?"

"Nah. She's gonna be all right. Go back in the house. Both of y'all. I got this."

Me and Jock just stood there as the truck rolled across the grass and drove off into the night.

"What the hell happened to her?"

Jock shrugged. "She just got carried away, Mink. A lotta people do. Can we just not talk about this? Can you just forget you even saw her?"

"Oh, I can do whatever I wanna do," I told him, thinking fast. "But I tell you what. If you want me to keep my mouth closed then you better watch how you talk to me and start acting like I'm ya damn sister!"

CHAPTER 30

It had been a wild and crazy weekend, and when the sun came up Monday morning me and Bunni were both ready to get it poppin'. We left the house at six-thirty, even though the lab didn't open up until eight. Bunni said we needed to get there early, way before the staff arrived, and I was cool with that.

Barron gave us a driver who couldn't speak no English, and neither one of us could understand a lick of Spanish. He looked fresh and sharp for it to be so early in the morning, though, and I could see he took his job real serious.

"Go all the way around." Bunni pointed and ordered him as he pulled up in front of the two-story building. "They make the workers park in the back, and that's where we need to be."

I was nervous like a mutha, but I had mad faith in my girl, though. I could always put my money on Bunni to come through with anything she set out to do, and in all these years she hadn't let me down not one time yet.

"Okay, you got everything you need, right?" I asked even though I had watched her pack up her scary-ass torture kit the night before.

She nodded. "Yep, I got my dick clamp and my male

chastity device, my anal drill, my spiked whip, and my steel cuffs. Chillax, Mink. I'm set. For real yo, the only thing you really need in this game is enough heart to hurt one of these freaky fools," she said. "If you can get past pinching a nigga's balls and slappin' his dick around, you straight."

Bunni took her kit and got outta the limo. I felt like I was watching my kid go off with her lunch box on the first day of school. She never even looked back as she hurried over to the empty building and stood behind some high bushes.

I watched outta the limo's window for about fifteen minutes before a car pulled into the lot. Bunni had told me Kelvin Merchant was the one who opened up the clinic in the mornings, and when the doors on the old cream cheese–colored Lex with gray guts swung open, I wasn't surprised to see a fat, yellow dumpling roll out.

He looked just like he had looked in the picture we'd seen on the Internet. Big and bald. His shirt was hiked up in the back and his ass crack was about ten inches long. He reached back inside the car and got a briefcase, then he pulled his T-shirt down in the back and slammed the door.

"*Okaaaay*," I muttered under my breath as he waddled toward the building. The future of our hundred grand was riding on this nigga right here! If Bunni had never worked her mash game before I needed her to get it on right now!

Dude was right up on the door when Bunni stepped outta the bushes. She leaned into him real quick like she was saying something. He froze for a quick second, and then he went ahead and stuck his key in the lock. I almost hollered as he pushed the door open and Bunni pranced inside before him. Her head was all up in the air and she high-stepped up in that bitch like she was da Queen of England!

I was fiendish as I watched both the door and the dashboard clock. When ten minutes had passed and Bunni still hadn't come out, I started wondering. After twenty minutes I was worrying, and ten minutes later my ass was ready to wild the fuck out. It was five minutes to eight, and according to the Web site the lab opened up at eight a.m. sharp.

My instincts told me that something musta gone wrong up in there, or Bunni woulda been back by now. Maybe dude's Facebook profile was a front. Maybe instead of submitting to pain, he was the psycho type who liked to dish that shit out! I pictured his big brawny ass with his meaty hands around Bunni's throat, and I snatched off my earrings and slid my pocketknife outta my Coach bag.

My breath caught in my throat as another car pulled into the parking lot. It was a beige Mitsubishi, and an older white lady got out and started walking real fast toward the back door.

That was it. I was going inside, and if I had to shave some meat offa Kelvin's big sucka ass, then I was gonna cut that nigga all the way down to the bone.

"I'll be right back," I told our silent driver. I met his eyes in the rearview mirror and held up my palm like stop! "Stay right here. Don't go nowhere, you understand?"

I opened my door to get out, just as the door opened on the other side and Bunni jumped in.

"*Woooo hoooo!* We did it! We did it! Drive around to the parking lot!" She shooed the driver and pointed her finger. "Go 'head, drive over there!"

I slammed my door shut and looked at her to see if she was hurt. She was crackin' the fuck up!

"What took you so damn long?" I blasted her as the limo pulled off. She was scooched down in the seat giggling like hell, and when she sat up her clothes were on her all crooked and twisted.

"That shit was *fun!*" She grinned and clapped her hands like a lil kid. "I wanna do it again, Mink! I wanna do that shit again!"

"You almost got *caught*, Bunni! I saw a white lady bust up in the back door!"

"I know, stupid. That's why I busted out through the front."

"Your ass didn't go in there to play, goddammit! We got big bank riding on those DNA results, remember? You was supposed to convince that fool to hook us up!"

"God*damn*, Mink," she said like she was done with my annoying ass. "Go sit down somewhere with all that, okay? I know what I went in there to do, and I did it. I *worked*," she said looking at me like I was stupid as hell, "and then I played."

"So what did dude say? Is he gonna put in work for us?"

"Oh," Bunni smirked and waved her hand. "We got all that important shit outta the way first. I'm a professional, baby. You know it's always about business before pleasure with me. Trust me, I left that pain slut in PAIN!"

"Okay, okay, so you handled that bizz, so now I can go inside and let them take my DNA right?"

"Mink! Calm the hell down! Yes, go 'head and take your ass inside. Your ass could show up with the DNA of a ninety-year-old rabbit, and your shit would still come back a perfect match for Sable Dominion."

"Are you sure dude is really down, Bunni?"

"Yes! He said for me to bring you in so you could take the damn test!"

"And what did he say after that?"

"He didn't say *shit* after that, Mink! Hell, the nigga couldn't talk!"

"Why not?"

Bunni giggled. "'*Cause*, stupid. He had my whole ass in his mouth!"

CHAPTER 31

Barron stood in his father's office holding several sheets of paper and staring at a portrait of his parents that had been taken more than a year before he was born. When Barron was growing up, Viceroy had schooled him on the ways of cunning men, and instilled in him the street instincts that had kept him afloat in an ocean full of hungry, cutthroat sharks.

He would never admit it, but his father's health and the problems at Dominion Oil weren't the only things messing with his head. He'd been having some real fucked up dreams about Mink almost every night, and they were so damn real that his dick was getting hard and his body was actually responding like she was right there in his bed, and even when he was wide-awake, he just couldn't get that gorgeous face or that bomb-ass figure of hers off his mind.

And if Mink was on *his* mind and he didn't even like the bitch, then Barron knew damn well there were countless other men who stared at her banging, tantalizing hips and felt the exact same way. One of the first things he did after they came back from seeing Viceroy in Houston was go to Craigslist and look up escort services under New York City's sex ads. It had taken him a couple of minutes, but eventually he'd come across the kind of Web site he was searching for.

There were all kinds of pictures of Mink plastered up. She was dressed like a sexy little slut and showcasing that hot stripper's body as she advertised her quick-sheet services as hot naked massages.

Barron looked down at the papers in his hand. He had printed them off the Web site, and they were his written proof that the natural-born liar who was trying to slide her hand into the Dominions' trust fund was just another gold digger looking to score some easy cash.

He had done a little bit more searching, and nothing he found on this chick came as a surprise. Mink was pure trash. She had crawled up out of some New York City gutter looking to take advantage of Selah in her time of grief, and it fucked Barron up that a poser like her had managed to get past their front door, let alone eat off his father's table and sleep under his roof.

Barron had also scanned the sex ads on Web sites for other areas of New York City to see what he could dig up on Mink. Brooklyn, Queens, Manhattan, the Bronx, and Staten Island. This chick had been running game in every borough of the city. This was the exact type of scandalous shit that Viceroy had been worried about. The Dominions had an image to protect, and even if Mink did somehow turn out to be Sable, as much dirt as she had done, her grimy ass wouldn't be getting a penny out of the family trust fund.

Barron couldn't wait to snatch the cover off her little hustle and show his mother what he'd found. Mink was about to be exposed, and with a dick-bricking body like hers Barron hoped she could sell enough pussy to get back to New York City real quick, because her free, fun-filled Texas vacation was about to be over.

★　★　★

It was supposed to be a family vacation, but her husband had gone to work every day since they arrived, and once again the kids were going stir-crazy from being trapped inside the hotel room. She'd gotten them dressed and called down to the front desk for a taxi, and when it showed up she piled her babies inside and rode downtown to the small office her husband maintained in New York City.

She had expected to see a beautiful, familiar face when they got off the creaky elevator in the drafty building in the Financial District, but the receptionist's desk was abandoned. Her seven-year-old was anxious to see his father, but by now the two babies had fallen fast asleep. They walked through the empty waiting room and started down the narrow, carpeted hallway to her husband's office.

The door was open a crack. She pushed against it gently and then froze, struggling to understand the sight that greeted them.

The girl was naked and on her knees. Her beautiful skin glowed with youth, and her light brown hair cascaded down her back. Her figure was slender, yet shapely, and she had almost the exact same ass as the woman who stood there watching her.

Her husband was standing near his desk. His silk underwear and pinstriped trousers were on the floor around his feet, and the 9 mm he always carried with him was strapped to his left ankle.

She watched quietly as he held on to his desk with one hand and palmed the head of the girl who was sucking his dick with the other.

"Yeah," he panted and pounded his hips as the nineteen-year-old girl stroked him with both hands and jutted her neck back and forth on his shaft. Her lips smacked wetly as she slurped and sucked and tried to cram every inch of him down her throat.

Her husband responded by throwing his head back in pleasure. His handsome mouth went slack as he muttered thickly, "Suck it, baby. That's right. Suck it. Suck it all the way down to the bone."

It was her seven-year-old son who made their presence known.

"Daddy?"

The frantic thrusting slowed at first, then ground to a stop as her husband patted the top of the girl's head and pulled himself from her dripping mouth.

"Selah. Baby . . . ," he whispered as he called her name.

The young girl jumped to her feet leaving her lover's shrinking dick exposed. Her lips were wet and swollen. A glistening trail of cum dribbled down her chin, and she wiped it away with the back of her hand.

"I'm so sorry . . ." The beautiful young girl who the woman had loved and sacrificed for stood shaking with shame as she covered her mouth with one hand and reached out for her older sister with the other. "It didn't mean anything. I swear. I was just trying to help, that's all. He needed it. He needed it."

The woman gathered her children and fled without saying a word. She rode back downstairs on the squeaky elevator and headed straight to the nearest liquor store. Dazed, she wandered the streets of Manhattan until she came upon a park, and while her two younger children played on the slide, she opened her bottle and tried to wash those horrible images of her husband's dick sliding in and out of her sister's mouth from her mind.

It took her an hour to drain the bottle, and she was in pretty bad shape when she stood up and summoned her children. Her vision blurred as she pushed her baby's stroller across the busy city streets. She staggered and got swept along in the crowd as they walked, her heart hardening and becoming vengeful. The betrayal hurt even worse than the cheating, she realized, and she was going to pay Viceroy back one day, she promised herself. Pay him back with his worst fucking enemy.

The well-dressed woman was totally plastered when she stumbled into a Duane Reade store leaving her three small children waiting outside. She was only in there for a couple of minutes. Two, maybe three. But that was long enough. Because when she came back out again, one of her children was gone.

"But what does any of this matter?" Selah asked. Her hand shook as she sipped a martini, and she looked tired and distraught. Barron had walked in on her while she was taking a nap on the sofa in the study. She had been gripped in the clutches of a familiar nightmare, and right away she'd gone over to the bar to fix herself a stiff drink.

Selah took a brief glance at the provocative sex ads her son had printed out, then shrugged her shoulders and took another sip of her drink. "I'm sorry, Barron. Identity theft is going on everywhere these days, and even if it really is Mink in these pictures, I don't care about any of it. I just don't think it matters."

"Damn right it matters, Ma!" Barron was shocked. "You know the terms of the trust fund better than I do. Look at those pictures! This chick probably has a rap sheet longer than a red carpet. I bet there isn't one dirty corner in the entire city of New York that this broad hasn't worked. She's a stripper, Ma. And a so-called "escort" if you dig what I'm saying. She's a con artist and a pickpocket too!"

"But what does her lifestyle matter if she's your *sister*, Barron? Anything that girl has done, and anything she may have had to become just to *survive* out there on those streets, it was my fault and not hers! If I hadn't lost Sable . . . if she had grown up safe and protected right here with us, she would have lived a different life! None of this shit would be an issue because she would have had opportunities to make better decisions, Barron! It just doesn't *matter*!"

Selah put her drink down and stood up. She walked over to her oldest son and put her head on his arm.

"I love you, Barron. I love you from the bottom of my heart, and I'm so sorry about what happened that day. Not just about what happened to Sable, but about what happened to you too. But I have to tell you, if Mink really is my daughter . . . if she is your sister, then nothing you've shown me will mean a damn thing. We're still going to love her, we'll still respect her, and most of all, we'll *accept* her. Okay, baby? Okay?"

Barron looked at Selah for a long time, then nodded. He loved his mother and he would do almost anything to keep a smile on her face. But Selah was blinded, and he wasn't feeling her on this one. Mink was a fraud. That chick had a whole bunch of grime on her, and even if she did turn out to be Sable, when it came to the Dominion fortune Barron was going to make sure she stayed her shiesty ass on the outside looking in.

CHAPTER 32

I had been all up in everybody else's grill, but I hadn't really gotten a chance to see what stank Miss Fallon's trip was. I'd left my DNA at the lab, and then me and Bunni had come back to the mansion to celebrate with a few drinks by the pool. Bunni messed around and chugged down one too many peach Cîrocs, so I left her out there sleepin' it off and went to check my little play-sister out.

Fallon was a beautiful young chick, but I could tell she had issues. The girl was just stupid strange. Ever since we came back from Houston she'd been walking around with the somebody-took-a-shit-on-me look plastered to her mug.

I wandered around the mansion like I was casing the joint until I came up on a door that had a big KEEP OUT sign taped to it. Loud music was playing on the other side, some type of rock shit, and since I already knew where Jock's room was I took this one to be Fallon's.

I hollered her name again and nigga-knocked on the door. "Hey, Fallon! Open the door girl. You in there?"

She opened the door a crack and I swear to God she looked like one of those crazy people on 42nd Street who stand on the corner tryna convince everybody that the world was about to end.

"What's wrong?" I blurted out. I already knew she didn't like my ass, but she looked so busted the question just came flyin' outta my mouth. She didn't look a damn thing like the fly little beauty queen who had tooted up her ass for me to kiss on the first day I met her. Instead, she was wearing a white one-piece shirt dress that looked real off-brand and dingy, and her hair was looking right ratchet. "Damn girl," I said tryna peek past her and into her room, "you good up in here?"

"Yeah, I'm cool," she said standing in the door crack like she wasn't about to open it no wider. "What do you want?"

"I came to check you out," I said and ignored the twisted look on her face. "I wanna come in for a few."

She let me in, but her room gave me the creeps from the gate. It was painted in rectangular sections of dull gray, purple, and black, and there were all kinds of Goth symbols and pictures of tombstones, vampires, and werewolves stuck up on every wall.

"Damn!" I said before I could catch myself. "What the hell is all this shit about? You must be one of those *Vampire Diaries* fans, or you on some real *Twilight* shit. All this scariness don't give you nightmares when you close your eyes at night?"

Her expression never changed.

"What you tryna say?"

I waved my arms around like, *Look at all this shit!*

"You know, the dark stuff. That other-world scene. The kinda drama that goes down in all those headless-monster horror movies."

She rolled her eyes. "If you don't like what I'm into then you don't have to come up in my room. Besides, it's not like this all the time. I paint and redecorate a lot."

"But you do beauty pageants and all that kinda stuff, right?

I woulda thought you'd have a whole bunch of trophies and tiaras and stuff like that laying around. You know, some real fly, girly-girl shit."

She gave me a bored little shrug and shook her head. "I don't compete in pageants anymore. I put all that kinda stuff in the storage shed out back."

Her bedroom was really huge, and she had it set up like a little apartment. Her king-sized bed was even nicer than the ones me and Bunni had in our guest rooms. It had a gorgeous canopy rack up top, and some thick, ugly black curtains were draped over the bed that woulda gave me nightmares for real. There was a marble counter with a sink, a small refrigerator, and a microwave over in the corner, a bomb sitting area with a big-screen TV mounted to the wall, and a big silver disco ball hung from the ceiling right over the metallic leather couch.

I sat down, and she walked over to her iPod and killed the rock music, then picked up the remote and clicked on the TV. She acted like I wasn't even there as she started flipping through the channels, so I busted open a big bag of Funyuns that were on her coffee table and went at 'em.

"So what's good, little sister?" I said and crunched on the crispy-salty onion rings. "How they do it in your world?"

She cut her eyes at me and smirked. "Not like they do it in yours."

I probed her. "Lemme guess. You got man trouble, right? Your lil boyfriend actin' bogus or something?"

"Please. Don't come up in here playing the big-sister role, okay? I been doing just fine all these years without one."

"Why?" I straight up challenged that ass. "'Cause you had Pilar as your sister? You ain't gotta worry, Fallon. I didn't come here to change nothing around or to make no waves. You been the baby girl in this family for your whole life, and trust me, I'm not tryna steal your shine."

She laughed. "Nah, you're just trying to steal a little money, right? If you can get your hands on some of Sable's cash, then everything'll be straight, huh?"

I was gonna have some problems with this grown-ass lil chick. I could tell Pilar was all up in her head just as deep as she was in Barron's, and it was gonna be real hard to run game on Fallon and get her on my side.

"You're a real nice-looking girl, Fallon," I said, buttering her up because I was pretty sure she got that compliment damn-near every day. "You got a lotta female friends?"

"Uh-*uh*. Hell no," she said, shaking her head real quick. "Are you crazy?"

I laughed. "Me neither! I ain't never rolled with a bunch of girls. For some reason a lot of chicks just don't be feelin' me like that." And that was the truth. Sometimes females took one look at me and started hatin' for no reason at all. The way we did each other was just crazy like that.

She nodded. "Even some of my friends who I thought were cool are turning out to be undercover haters," she admitted. Then she folded one leg under her butt and asked me, "What's it like to live in New York? I mean, I've seen it on television and all that, but what's it like to walk down the streets?"

"You've never been to New York?" I was surprised. In my mind everybody in the whole world was up on New York.

"No." She shook her head. "I've never been allowed to go. Sable got kidnapped there remember? After that, my mother got all paranoid. When I was born she swore I would never step foot in that city. And I haven't."

I nodded and checked myself. I don't know how the hell I kept forgetting that these people had really lost the person I was pretending to be.

"Well, New York is live," I told her. "I mean, I was raised in the projects and it can get real grimy in some areas, but overall, the City That Never Sleeps is always alive and full of action. It's hot."

"You must feel so free there. I mean, everybody is different but it's okay to be different in New York, isn't it?"

I cracked up. "Baby, different ain't the word. We got some real freaks walking around on our streets. There are nutcases all over the city, and no matter how strange and kooky somebody is, a New Yorker has always seen somebody worse. Don't a damn thing surprise us."

Fallon sighed. "But people are accepted in New York, right? Everybody gets to be whoever they really are, don't they?"

I had to think about that one. "I wouldn't say all that, but for the most part people are tolerated up to a point. It's like, 'go 'head and do ya thing, just don't do it over here on me.' That's the kinda attitude a New Yorker rolls with. Fuck around, lay around. Don't start none, won't be none. You know what I mean?"

Fallon nodded. "I think so. But I'm gonna go see for myself as soon as I turn eighteen."

I started to say something stupid like, *Even though your mother told you not to go?* But then I caught myself. I had never paid no mind to a damn thing that came outta my mother's mouth. If she told me not to do something I took my little fast ass out there and did it twice. Sometimes I did it three times in a row. Shit, Mizz Mink wasn't qualified to be advising a chick like Fallon on *nothing.*

I didn't stay too long in her room, and she seemed kinda relieved when I stood up and said I was about to go. I was walking out when a picture sitting on a little table caught my eye. I reached out to pick it up, but Fallon beat me to it and slammed it face-down.

"*Ohhhh!* Whattup with that? I can't see your picture?"

"For what? You don't know anybody in it."

"It looked like a cool picture." I played her. "I just wanted to see it."

She handed it to me real slow, and as soon as I looked at it I knew how she was rollin'. It was a picture of Fallon and her stud boo. This broad looked way older than eighteen. Hell, she looked damn-near my mama's age. She had a shaved head and tats all up and down her flabby arms, and she was nibbling on Fallon's ear like she was a dude for real.

"So this your man, huh?"

If she was expecting me to be shocked shitless she was outta luck. I saw so much of this on a daily in New York that it didn't press me out at all.

"Yeah, that's Fredericka. Freddie. My best friend."

"Y'all look happy, so why you didn't want me to see her?"

I could tell by the way she sighed that I was in there with her. We were talking about something that *she* wanted to talk about, and she'd let her little defenses down.

"Well, we ain't really as happy as we look. I mean, we love each other, but we're just into different things."

"Different things like what?"

"Well, Freddie's into the club scene, and I'm basically not. She likes all the fancy cars and the jewelry and all that, and I don't really care about all that. I'm really big on drawing, and all Freddie wants me to do is dance."

My ears got big. "Dance? Dance how? Dance where?"

She muttered under her breath, "At the strip club." She shocked the shit outta me. That mess came outta her mouth so low that for a second I thought I was hearing things.

"Come again? You said Freddie wants you to dance in strip clubs?" I couldn't believe this shit!

"Yeah"—she nodded real quick—"but only for private sessions. She doesn't want me to do it for the money. She just likes to watch."

Aw, hell. Freddie had some freak in her bald-headed ass! I was a strip club connoisseur, and I knew exactly what time it was. Freddie was the type who liked threesomes. She got off on watching Fallon strip for dudes, then she jumped in the mix so the two of them could put Fallon in a sandwich and take turns eating her young ass.

"Look Fallon," I said, and I really, really, *really* tried hard to just say what I had to say without coming across like I was preachin' to her. "Stripping ain't the worst thing you can do, but it ain't no legitimate grind neither. Your family gives you everything you need so it's not like you gotta hump the pole so you can eat and pay your bills. Freddie might be a female, but she's strollin' you the same way a dude would. If watching chicks strip is her thing, then let her buy some chips and rent herself a pole freak. You shouldn't be letting no man *or* no stud trick you off like that."

She waved all that noise away. "It's not that serious, Mink. I only do it every now and then, and it's not like we have sex every single time."

"Cool," I said as I headed out the door. I recognized the "don't tell me shit" look in her eyes. I used to give it to my moms on the regular.

"Do you, baby girl. But Freddie-boo needs to get her own damn grind, and whenever y'all get together to do whatever it is y'all do, I hope you make sure everybody in the room is wrapped up extra-tight."

It was real late that night when I saw Fallon again. I had just got outta the shower and slipped on a white satin night-gown that Peaches had boosted for me when somebody knocked on my door.

I opened it up and was surprised to see Fallon standing there in the same raggedy dress she had on earlier.

"It was cool of you to come to my room today," she said, and the left side of her face almost cracked a little smile. "I just wanted you to know that I'm not stupid, Mink, and that I do have plans for my life."

"Cool, little sistah," I told her. "That's what's up girl. Having plans for your future is real smart."

I touched her on the shoulder as she turned to leave, and then I walked her all the way back to her room.

CHAPTER 33

Barron was standing in the alcove outside his mother's suite when he saw his problem coming out of Fallon's room. She stopped to peer out of a large picture window, and he almost stopped breathing when she raised her arms in the air and stretched like a cat under the glow of the moonlight.

Mink had on a sheer white nightgown, and from where he stood she looked naked as hell underneath. Every one of her vicious curves was outlined in detailed perfection. Her hips were three times as wide as her tiny waist, and her toned, shapely thighs tapered down to perfect calves and slim ankles.

He had already told her to stay away from his mother's wing of the house. But Mink was sneaky and hardheaded and she was starting to fuck with him. She raised her arms again and arched her back. The swell of her ass poked her gown out in the back, and when she shifted her weight to her hip Barron felt that shit all down in his nut sack.

A door closed in the hall behind him and Barron jumped.

Whirling around, he strode back down the hall and headed toward his own suite where Carla lay on the sofa pretending to watch television. Walking right past her, he grabbed a two-hundred-dollar bottle of lotion and went into the bathroom and sat down on the closed toilet. Unbuckling his pants, he extracted his hard dick and squeezed the head. He could have popped one off just from the sight of Mink's hips alone, instead he rubbed the scented lotion in his palm and slathered it up and down his rigid shaft. With the memory of Mink's half-naked flesh sending spiraling heat through his body and his mind, Barron closed his eyes, bit back his shame, and fucked the shit outta his palm.

CHAPTER 34

Lil Mama I can see it in ya eyes we can ride if you ready to roll . . .

Ch-ch-ch-ch-Chere!

I got the Caddie double-parked outside we can slide if you ready to go . . .

Ch-ch-ch-ch-Chere!

The way she grind, pop it back, make it wind, got my mind going outta control . . .

Sauuuucy!

Otha bitches they don't wanna see you shine, she get by 'em when she's droppin' it low . . .

It was only Thursday night but we was ridin' dirty in Dane's custom Hummer while Reem Raw's "Break It Down" blasted all out the windows. We had Jock with us, and he was taking us to Dallas so he could hook up with one of his lil rich, drug-head friends who had some X and some real good weed.

All of us was already toasted up to the max, and I didn't know how Dane was even driving between the white lines. We pulled into a gas station to get some Black & Milds and some gum for Dane, and I spotted that bitch Stanka as soon as I jumped out the whip.

I thought about the jewelry I had lost that night at the club, and how this trick had hipped the dude pulling the lick that I was tryna hide the ring Gutta had slid on me. Stanka had dipped before I could get at her that night, but seeing her ass again brought all my Harlem rolling up outta me.

"Hey, Stanka! Ya *stank bitch*! Remember me?"

She was getting in a sweet red Lexus with a couple of other chicks, and when she saw me that heffa had the nerve to put her hands on her hips and let her neck roll.

"Bitch who is you? Huh? Who is *you* for me to be re-membering? Kiss my ass! You ain't no damn body to be re-membering!"

With Bunni on my heels I dashed over to her car and got up in her grill. "Oh, I can give you something to remember me by. You can believe that shit!"

That tricked dropped everything in her hands. Her bag, her keys, her bottle of soda went rolling, and in a flash she was posted up and ready to fight.

"Well, bring it, bitch!" She balled up her fists and got in her lil Tyson stance. "Bring it!"

I brought it all right. I did a Mayweather on her ass. I clocked her in the mouth before the words were off her lips good. We started *thumpin'* out there in that parking lot! She was country-strong and I was Harlem-hood. We got it in with her girls screaming and cursing for her, and Bunni screaming and cursing for me. She snatched off my curly lavender wig and I yanked her entire shirt over her head. Ms. Stanka was bare-breastin' under her tank, and them big titties was bounc-ing everywhere.

She tried to pull my hair and I got her in a yoke and started banging her face. She bit me on my side, and I slung her down to the ground, and that's when her crew jumped in and we all went down together.

Bunni got in there too, and it was North against South as we scrapped and rolled on that dirty gravel. It was all about the punch, bite, kick, scratch game with us, and me and Bunni fought like we was getting a check at the end of the match.

But on the real though, we ended up getting a whole lot more than what our asses was looking for. An all-girl scrap in Harlem didn't hardly attract no attention unless somebody got shot or stabbed. But it looked like every cop in Dallas rained down on us at that gas station, and the next thing I knew all of us were in handcuffs and getting a ride down to the precinct.

Me, Bunni, Stanka, *and* her two friends all looked a hot-ass mess under the bright lights in that station house. They had even brought Dane and Jock down to the lockup too.

"I had some fuckin' where to go!" Stanka yelled at me as they led her past me in her inside-out shirt. "Your dumb ass ain't even worth all of this!"

I had left my Gucci purse back in Dane's whip when I jumped out to get at Stanka, and I didn't have a piece of ID on me. So when they asked me for my name, I thought for a split second and then said the first thing that came to my mind.

"Sable Dominion," I told the cop, knowing damn well the Dominion name carried a lotta weight down this way. "I'm Sable Dominion, and the two guys you brought in with me are my brothers Grayson and Dane."

The cop looked at me like I was crazy. He thought me and Bunni were a couple of tricks that Jock and Dane had picked up off the stroll for the night. He told me I was gonna have to call somebody from the Dominion family who was sober and over twenty-one and who could come down to the station and get all four of our drunk asses out.

Immediately I thought about Barron and how he would probably tell them cops to throw my ass under a cell and let me dig a tunnel straight to China. But then I thought for another moment and came up with the perfect Dominion.

"My uncle can come down here and get us," I told the cop. "Call him up. His name is Suge Dominion."

★ ★ ★

Uncle Suge came and got us out. Every time I saw that nigga, he was dipped in shine and styling a fresh Stetson and some dead-animal-skin boots, and if he knew I was a faker he sure as hell didn't seem to give a damn. He had never acted pressed over whether I was Sable or not. But he *had* let me know without a doubt that adopted niece or not, he was feeling my ass.

And don't think I wasn't feeling him too. Suge was the type of big-money dude who had ten gallons of swag comin' outta his left nut. He moved like a lion. Chest out, sturdy legs, muscles everywhere, hungry as fuck and lookin' for trouble!

"Thanks for coming to get us, Uncle Suge," I said, tryna sound all sweet and shit. I was sitting up front, and there were crazy sparks flying between us as he drove us home. He had bust up in the police station like he was the damn sheriff or something, and I couldn't help wondering if he could throw his weight around where it really counted the most.

Suge had the perfect truck for a big man. One of those Ford joints that looked like it could fit about fifty cows in the back. We got up in that baby and immediately his manly scent went up my nose and got my thong all wet. His ride was rugged on the outside but boss on the inside. Plush leather seats, sleek controls, bamming stereo system, and lots of room on the front bench seat in case a sistah wanted to stretch out and get straight!

When we pulled up outside the mansion Uncle Suge put his hand on my arm, telling me to wait and let everybody else get out. Bunni walked into the house holding hands with Dane, and I knew my play-brother was gonna get all in that pussy tonight.

"I'm glad you called me," Uncle Suge said.

"I'm glad you came," I said, then grinned and bit my lower lip in a real sexy way. "Thanks again."

"Nah, baby." He reached over and pulled me close to him and I wanted to lick his neck and taste his cologne. "You ain't gotta thank me. But you *can* kiss me."

He didn't have to tell me twice. His mouth felt delicious as he thrust his long tongue down my throat and squeezed my titty in his big, rough hand. I moaned and lip-humped his tongue like it was a dick, and my hand shot down into his lap and put a choke hold on that thang I was looking for.

They said everything was bigger in Texas, and from what I was squeezing they had that shit right. Suge's wood was stiff like a baseball bat, and I was tryna zip his pants down so I could get next to some skin when he stopped me cold and started laughing real loud.

"You ain't had enough fighting for one night, huh? Girl you ain't ready for none of this." He reached across me and opened my door. "Gone, Miss Sexy. Get yourself on in that house before you run up on something you can't handle. I ain't going nowhere, and you ain't either. I'll catch up with you another time. In fact, I'll pick you up for lunch tomorrow."

My crotch was moist and I didn't appreciate his ass teasin' me like that and then putting me out, but I liked it. I couldn't remember when the last time a dude had passed up an opportunity to stick his fingers in my drawers, and I didn't know exactly what to say to that, so I just did like he said and bounced.

CHAPTER 35

Barron opened the door to his suite and stopped dead in his tracks.

Mink was curled up like a kitten in his pillows. She was dressed in all white: a white wig, a short white negligee, a white garter belt and stockings, and a pair of white spiked pumps. She had a big red lollipop clutched in her fist and she winked her eye at him and gave it a real big lick.

"C'mon now, Mink." He stepped into the room and slammed the door behind him. "What the hell are you doing in here?"

She grinned and motioned for him to come closer.

Barron could smell the candy she was licking. He could smell something else too, and that sweet scent made his mouth water.

"Mink!" His dick jumped in his drawers as her name left his mouth. She turned over onto her stomach and pointed her feet in the air and crossed her slender ankles. "Get up outta here!"

He was barking but he couldn't help looking. Mink's white thong peeked from between her cheeks and her plump ass was rounder than round. It was all flesh too. Big and firm, and without a single stretch-mark, pimple, or blemish on it.

"I'm gonna fuck you, B-Boy." She looked over her shoulder and giggled as she rubbed the lollypop all over her sticky red lips. "I'm gonna fuck the shit outta you."

She rolled over onto her back and lifted her legs in the air. She parted her thick thighs and exposed her moist slit. Mink licked her finger, then slipped it between her lower lips and inserted it deep into her vagina. Still sucking her lollipop, she masturbated herself until her whole hand was slick with juice.

Barron covered his crotch with his hands. His dick was so hard it ached in his pants. Sweat broke out on his nose and his collar got tight. He couldn't take his eyes off her fingers as they pulled on her clit and dove deep into the folds of her dripping slit.

"Wanna lick?" she teased him as she rubbed her red lollipop between her pussy lips.

His breath caught in his throat as she inserted the candy in her cream-filled hole and coated it with her tangy juices.

"Here," she whispered, offering it to him seductively. "Come and get it."

Barron was by her side before he knew his feet were moving. He opened his mouth and accepted the sweet treat she held out to him. Her slippery cum dripped from the bright red candy, and his tongue shot out to catch every drop.

"*Mink . . .*" He was crazed as she rubbed the lollipop all over his lips. Her scent and the delicious taste of her pussy just drove him wild. His tongue was everywhere as he slurped and suckled from the candy. He was smacking and moaning and gulping that coochie-flavored treat like a starving man, and Mink giggled in his ear and called out his name, "Oooh, Barron! Taste me, Barron, taste me! Ahhh, yes! Lick this pussy! Barron! Barron! Barr—"

"*Barron!*" Carla screamed and slapped him in the face. "Barron! Wake up! What's wrong? Are you okay?"

Barron opened his eyes in total confusion. His dick was rock hard and the unmistakable taste of pussy was on his tongue. Carla was leaning over him looking worried as hell. Her hair hung down and flopped in her eyes, and she reached out and smacked the shit outta him again.

"Wake *up!*" she shrieked. "I thought you were having a damn seizure! You were moaning and licking your lips . . . The way you were carrying on I was afraid you were going to swallow your tongue!"

Barron sat up and swung his legs over the side of the bed. His wood was flat up against his stomach and harder than it had been in years. He couldn't believe what the fuck he had been doing in his sleep. Whose pussy he had been desperately trying to get a taste of.

"Barron," Carla said behind him. He was trying so hard to hold on to the last bits of his erotic dream that he had forgotten she was even in the room. "I asked you if you were okay?"

"I'm fine." He stood up and walked into the bathroom. He turned on the shower and stepped inside, then worked a bar of soap in his hand until his palm was full of lather. Closing his eyes, he touched himself and stroked his meat with warm sudsy bubbles as he recalled the memories of his dream.

That bitch was in his head. She was all *in* his head. He knew it was wrong to wanna fuck Mink, but she had turned him on and he couldn't help himself. He didn't even like her. But that didn't stop him from shuddering and spurting a load as he remembered the way her sweet brown pussy had looked as she played in it, how hot it had smelled when she opened her legs, and most of all how good it had tasted as he rubbed it on his tongue.

CHAPTER 36

"So we have a deal, then?"

Digger Ducane stood up and accepted the hand that was being extended to him.

"Absolutely." His returned the firm grip of Rodney Ruddman, president of Ruddman Energy and chief competitor of Dominion Oil.

"I can't thank you enough for this opportunity, Mr. Ruddman. I'll need just a couple of weeks to tie things up at Dominion Oil, and then I'll be ready to take over your new in-house fleet."

The grin on Rodney Ruddman's greasy face disappeared. He was a stocky, cigar-smoking businessman. Not much to look at. But if ever there was a crafty, conniving, gutter-crawling snake, then Rodney was it.

"Hold on now, Digger," he said and toked on his expensive cigar. "I just made you a junior partner in Ruddman Oil. A company man. You're not telling me you need to take two weeks off to go work for my competition, now are you?"

Digger back-pedaled real quick. "No, I'm not talking about working for them, sir. I'm an independent contractor for

DO, not an employee. I just need a little time to close out some accounts and tie up a few loose ends. That's all."

Ruddman sat back in his oversized office chair and crossed his fat arms. "You know, Digger, when you brought me your business proposal I thought you were committed to moving up the ladder and making some real financial gains. I know Viceroy is your blood family, and he's in a bad way right now. Mrs. Ruddman and I pray for him every night. But, perhaps I was wrong to offer you this position, and maybe this isn't a good time for you to make such a critical move. You may not be ready to jump in with the caliber of power players we have here at Ruddman Energy. How about we reconsider the offer and discuss it again at another time?"

Digger almost shit on himself. A junior partnership at Ruddman Energy was exactly what he needed to get his money right, and he wasn't about to let this once-in-a-lifetime opportunity get away from him.

Small businesses were drying up in record numbers all over the damn country. With the high interest rates at the bank and more than half of his credit line being cut, Digger's private transport fleet was going down faster than a two-dollar whore.

Contracting his tank cars out to Dominion Oil was no longer a profitable enough business venture. He needed corporate backing, the kind that Ruddman Energy could provide, and the security of having a large, regular paycheck coming in each and every week grew more and more attractive as his reserve funds dried up.

"No, another time won't be necessary," Digger assured him, and he was relieved to see the light come back into the man's shifty little eyes. "You're right. There's nothing really pressing that I need to tie up at Dominion Oil. In fact, there's no reason for me to go back to their headquarters at all. I can be here by seven sharp tomorrow morning. Six-forty-five if you'd like me to come in early."

Digger knew he was about to shit on a twenty-five-year relationship with Viceroy Dominion, but his back was against the wall, and right now he had no other choice but to get under the covers and make some real nasty moves with his brother-in-law's competition.

"Digger, *nooo*," Selah wailed as she stormed into her brother's kitchen holding the business section of the *Dallas Morning News*. She tossed the paper right down in his plate of grits, and the headline stared up at him in bold, accusing letters.

DIGGER DUCANE JOINS RUDDMAN ENERGY AS CONGLOMERATE'S NEWEST PARTNER

"Please tell me you didn't. I know goddamn well you didn't!"

"Yes, I did, Selah! What the hell did you expect from me?"

"I expected your ass to be *loyal*, that's what! To show some goddamn appreciation for the man who dragged your ass out of that Brooklyn gutter and made you a millionaire! Viceroy did more for you than Ruddman *ever* will. He's the one who got you started in this business! Look at how he set you up!"

"Oh, he set me up all right. He set my ass up to fall! Open your damn eyes, Selah! Times are changing. The economy is fucked up all over the world! You ain't never paid a bill in your life, little sister. You sit up there in that big-ass mansion and you don't even have to think about money because everything is handed to you. Well ain't nobody handing me *shit*! I gotta get out there and get mine!"

Selah's eyes narrowed. "By biting the hand that fed you all these years? How low-down is that, Digger? Viceroy would have given you the shirt off his back if he knew you needed it, and you know that. If you were in trouble then he should have been the first person you turned to, not that toad-looking freak Ruddman! Not him! He's Viceroy's *worst enemy*! You could have gone to *anybody* except him!"

"Is that right? Then tell me why after more than twenty

goddamn years your husband has never offered me a seat on the company board, huh? Every damn Dominion on this side of Houston sits on that board and has a voting share of the stock. When the money comes rolling in, every last one of y'all feast. But what about me and Pilar, huh? She's your *blood*, Selah, and I can't even buy my baby a goddamn pair of shoes without my fucking credit card melting!"

Selah's eyes narrowed. She was calm as she stared at her brother quietly. "Okay. Do whatever you have to do, Digger. But I'm gonna need you to remember something that I'm sure you've probably already forgotten."

"Yeah?" her brother said flippantly as he tossed the newspaper out of his plate. "What's that?"

"Viceroy isn't dead yet."

CHAPTER 37

Uncle Suge came to pick me up for lunch the next day just like he promised, and I couldn't wait to take another ride in his monster truck. Bunni had spent the night up in Dane's little pussy palace, and when I went up there to get her she told me she was still tired and to come back later.

I had thrown on some sexy gear and waited for Suge to show up, and now that he was here I was ready to hit the streets with him and see what his shit-talkin' ass was all about.

His truck was beast! I felt like I was jumping up on a damn bronco when I tried to get up in that thing, and I almost twisted my ankle tryna look cute in my purple Prada heels.

"Careful," he said and gripped my elbow to steady me. I grabbed a hold of his beefy shoulder and his muscle was so hard I felt like I was rock climbing. He helped me slide inside, and then he ran his eyes from my shoes all the way up to my hair, pausing to check out the way my legs looked beneath my purple Prada flare skirt.

I sat there and posed for his fine ass. Bouncing tits, smooth legs, hot coochie, and sweet perfume, I was a prime purple package and I knew it. I had ditched my Glama-Glo wigs for the soft, curly look of my own hair, and everything about my body and my gear was just perfect.

"So where we going?" I asked as he peeled up outta the driveway so fast he left half of his tires on the ground. This nigga was wild. Big, swagged out, and sexy as fuck. He rode with one hand at the top of the steering wheel and the other one propped up on his door. I couldn't help but notice how his thigh muscle flexed when he stomped down on the gas. All that power turned me on, and he coulda been taking me to a snake farm and I still woulda wanted to go.

"We're going to the races," he said. He gave me a slick glance, then chuckled. "I gotta see a man about a horse."

I'd seen a couple of pit bulls chasing behind each other, and I'd even watched the kids on my block race bikes up and down the sidewalk in the summer, but I had never been to a horse race before and I was cool with that.

We jammed some old-school R & B while we rode, and Suge surprised me when he started singing along to a slow cut. His voice was deep as hell, and all that bass he was pushing had my nipples hard and my panties wet!

He cooled me right off, though, when he started talking about money.

Now, don't get me wrong. Cash was my favorite subject, and I could smell a dollar bill tucked away in the deepest corner of a nigga's wallet. But I didn't wanna be that stuck-up chaser named Sable today. I was having too much fun being Mink.

"You know Barron's riding your ass, right?"

I gave him the side-eye to see if he was tryna be funny, but he was still chewing on his toothpick and his expression hadn't changed.

"Yeah, I know. But I'm not worried about that dude. I can't help it if he doesn't like me."

"Oh, I think he likes you," Uncle Suge chuckled. "He likes the hell outta you. But he definitely doesn't trust you."

"That's cool," I laughed too. "'Cause I don't trust his ass neither."

"You know, if for some reason my brother doesn't make it Lil Bump is gonna try to cut you off, right? That nigga is crazy over that trust fund. Three hundred grand every year is a lotta money to get up off of for a man like him. He ain't gonna hand it over just like that. His pride and his ego just ain't gonna let him."

"But if my DNA test—" I blurted out, and then caught myself. "*When* my DNA test results come back proving I'm Sable, then the money is mine, right?"

"Not if Barron can find a way to stop you from getting it. He's about to have full control over at Dominion Oil, and that means he's gonna be in charge of the trust fund too. All he has to do is get a little dirt on you and bring some bullshit charges up to the board. They'll review it, and if they feel like something you did violated the terms of the fund, you're out, baby girl. All the way out."

"But that shit ain't right!" I whined. "If the trust fund is for all the kids in the family then Barron shouldn't have that kind of power!"

"You wanna see power? Let me show you something." He glanced in his rearview mirror and his tires screeched as he cut across three lanes of traffic. I bounced all in my seat as he drove his big old truck up over the curb and into the grass and made a U-turn across the center lane of the highway.

"What's wrong? Why we going back?"

"We're gonna make a little detour baby. Uncle Suge's got something big he wants to show you."

★   ★   ★

We pulled up outside of a big mirrored-glass building that had the letters DO cut into a huge mound of pretty grass. The initials were also on a gigantic sculpture right outside the front doors, and a sparkling gold sign across the awning said DOMIN-ION OIL in shiny black letters.

A doorman in a blue uniform greeted Suge like he was the king of Texas or some shit. He was an old black dude, probably about sixty, but he perked up when he saw Suge coming and dapped him out like he was from the hood.

We walked inside a lobby where a huge picture of Viceroy took up a whole damn wall. There were two armed security guards posted up by one of those body scanners you see at the airport, and when they recognized Suge they snapped to attention like soldiers and started yes-sirring him half to death.

Suge showed them both some love, then he took my hand and led me around the security station and past a desk where a young white receptionist sat.

"Good afternoon, Mr. Dominion," she said, jumping to her feet and grinning all over herself.

"What's good, what's good." Suge smiled and motioned for her to sit back down. We rode a private elevator up to the fif-teenth floor, and it opened inside of a real big office with an-other reception desk and about a million cubicles sitting off behind it.

Suge moved like Black Jesus through that joint. White men in three-piece suits were breaking their necks to bow down to him, and I had to sneak a quick look at his feet to make sure that nigga wasn't walking on water.

He introduced me to everybody as a family member from outta town, and for the first time in my life I had a bunch of high-powered white people up in my face who weren't tryna put me in jail.

We walked up to an office that had a wood-carved name-plate on the door with real twenty-four-karat gold letters embedded in it.

"What in the hell . . . ," I whispered. I had never seen anything like it, and I couldn't stop myself from reaching out to trace the glittering letters with my pointer finger.

The nameplate said SUPERIOR DOMINION, and I gave Suge the crazy look.

"Superior?"

"Yeah," he laughed and pushed the double doors open. "That's me."

I felt like I was in a whole 'nother world when I stepped inside. Everything I'd seen in the building so far had been cold as ice, but Suge's spot was truly beast. It was a corner office, and both of the outside walls were completely made of blue-tinted glass. The floors were done up in some real shiny dark wood, and it was the exact same color as his desk.

He had a winter-white rug on the floor near a plush, cocoa-colored leather sofa, and that baby was so big and fluffy it had probably come off the backs of at least ten polar bears.

I closed my eyes and took a real deep breath.

"Yummm . . . ," I moaned happily. "I ain't *never* taking my ass back to New York! I can just *smell* the money up in here."

Suge laughed and put his arm around me. He pulled me close to him, and with my titties pressed against his chest, he slid his hands down my back and cupped my ass.

"Nah, that ain't no money you smellin' up in here, girl. What you're smelling is something people like us call *power*. Now you better find a way to make sure don't nothing come up outta your past to fuck up that trust fund for you, baby girl, 'cause trust me, Bump's office is ten times bigger than this."

★ ★ ★

We left the Dominion Oil headquarters and hit the race-track. Suge told me women were his bad-luck charm when-ever he got around horses, and he almost never brought a female with him when he went out to gamble. I told him I wasn't his ordinary chick, and that me and Lady Luck were tight like that.

The racetrack was a lotta fun, but it was hot as hell out there with all those stankin' horses. I loved animals but I wasn't used to the mess they made. The jockeys were walking a few stallions around in the grass getting them stretched out, and my lips got straight twisted every time a big pile of hot doody fell outta one of their asses.

I let Suge go through his little speech about how to calcu-late the odds on a horse bet, but that nigga must didn't know. Miss LaRue had grown up with a gambling daddy, and I'd spent more time in grimy little number holes than a little bit.

He wanted me to play it safe and go with a straight bet, but I shrugged him off and went with a place and a show. Suge had box seats reserved up in that baby, and I jumped up and down just like a white girl as we screamed for our horses to win. Neither one of my horses did a damn thing, but Suge bet big and he won big too. He treated me to lunch at the restaurant right there at the racetrack, and we ordered lobster and tossed back bubbling champagne like the big-timers we were.

I kinda hated for our day together to come to an end, and I wondered where Suge's woman was 'cause I knew a swole nigga like him sho nuff had one.

"You ready to head back?" he asked me, and I could tell by the way he said it that he was testing the waters and feeling me out.

I threw him a hot-pussy look and batted my fake eyelashes. "I'm ready for whatever you got."

He chuckled. "You think you can handle this here, little

girl? They don't grow 'em like this up in New York, baby. This is Texas, darling. Everythang down here is a whole lot bigger."

"Hmph," I spoke with mad confidence because I was sexually experienced and well trained in my craft. "The bigger the better Suge-Daddy. The bigger the better."

CHAPTER 38

Suge's crib looked just like him. Big, flamboyant, and a whole lotta fun. That fool had a whole cow head posted up on the wall, with beady eyes and horns and everything, and a big-ass stuffed alligator was chillaxin on the floor in front of his fireplace.

"*What the*— Is that shit real?" I nudged it with my toe.

"Hell yeah," he laughed. "Watch yourself though. You better hope don't nothing bite your fine ass up in here."

Suge was a Dominion so he knew how to live large. Everything in his living room was high-tech, and I spotted all kinds of expensive, quality shit. He went over to a bar that was surrounded by crazy lights and poured us some wine.

"Nah," I said. I got up from the sofa and switched my round ass over to him. "Pass the yak, big boy. Mizz Mink knows how to pour her own troubles."

I fixed me a triple shot of Rémy on the rocks and gulped it as I walked over to a huge floor-to-ceiling glass door. I could see some real nice patio furniture, a tennis court, and a huge swimming pool that was lit up with swirling lights in all different colors.

We sat on his sofa and smoked a little weed, and I leaned

over and kissed his cheeks, then his ears and his neck. I loosened three buttons on his shirt, then took his ebony nipple in my mouth and tugged on it with my teeth.

"Let's go upstairs so I can treat you right," he said and pulled me to my feet.

Suge had one of them glass staircases with no floor underneath it and no banisters, and my woozy ass felt like I was floating on air as he led me upstairs to his bedroom so we could really get loose.

"I didn't come here for no nonsense." I shook my finger at him when we walked inside his darkened room. "And I ain't drunk, neither, so don't think you gonna push up on me, okay?"

He scooped my ass up and tossed me into the middle of his extra-long king-sized bed, and I bounced like a kid and cracked the hell up with my legs all up in the air.

"You ain't gotta do nothing you don't wanna do." He lit a couple of candles and pushed a button, and some soft R & B came out of some hidden speakers.

I scooted up against his huge cherry headboard, and he kicked his boots off and sat down next to me with his feet stretched out on the bed.

He leaned his head back and I got closer to him and kissed down toward his stomach and rubbed my face all in his lap. I undid the rest of the buttons on his shirt and licked his tight belly, swiping my tongue up and down the jet-black tufts of hair that snaked down into his pants.

My fingers were skillful as I unbuckled his belt. I was inching his zipper down when he grabbed my wrist. I looked up at him and saw all that lust in his eyes. He was getting weak for me, and I knew he wanted to slide his dick straight down my throat.

"You know what you doing, Lil Mama LaRue?" he checked me.

Shiiit, I thought wickedly. I could show this nigga better than I could convince him.

He unbuttoned his pants and I stuck my tongue in his navel. I licked around the edges, then slipped lower until my lips touched the top edge of his pubic hair. He pulled the elastic of his boxers down low and freed his dick. I almost hollered as that thick Texas rattlesnake jumped out at me and stared at me from its one eye. It was so long and pretty that the only disappointment I had was that I hadn't got me none of it sooner.

I held it in my hands and it throbbed and gave off mad heat. I stroked it gently for a couple of seconds, then I attacked that thing like I was a mongoose and snake killing was my business.

I swooped my mouth down on it and wet it all up at once. I soaked that baby and marinated it with the hot juices in my mouth as I bobbed my head up and down with real long strokes.

Suge moaned as I throated that good wood. I took him down inch by inch, relaxing my neck pussy and wetting that thing up like I had a sprinkler system in the roof of my mouth.

I put down a damn-near flawless dick-lick game, and Suge cupped my ears and pounded up into my face as his thighs shook and he made all kinds of crazy fuck sounds and then smashed my head down deep in his lap and came real hard.

His hot cum hit way in the back of my throat, and I sucked and swallowed and sucked and swallowed until his dick got a little softer and he pulled himself from my mouth.

"That shit was good, baby," he said, wiping sweat from his forehead. "Damn, girl. Your lips. Your throat. The way you vibrated that tongue . . . it's your turn now baby."

Suge undressed me stitch by stitch. He wouldn't even let me help him. He admired my body the whole time he was taking my clothes off, and he growled a bunch of sexy compliments that blew my mind.

When he had me completely naked he just looked at me for a little while. My breasts, my stomach, my hips and thighs. His eyes roamed over me with appreciation and desire, and I loved the way that look made me feel.

He pressed his lips deep down on mine, and instead of that frantic tongue fight we'd had the last time we kissed, he took his time and moved a lot slower now. His fingertips rubbed my cheeks as he got to know my mouth in a real tender fashion, and I reached up and wrapped my arms around his neck like he was my lover for real.

He left my lips and kissed my throat, my collar-bone, and under my left armpit. Then he held my juicy titty in his hand and sucked it deeply into his mouth, moving real slow on me and creating a sensuous thrill that made me arch my back and cry out softly.

Suge sucked my titties like they were beautiful objects of art. He handled them gently and stroked them like he had never before held anything so precious in his big, rough hands.

He slid his fingers down my stomach and ran them through my pussy hairs. I spread my legs as juice leaked from my slit and dripped onto his bedspread. I reached down and massaged myself, then held my fingers up for him to lick one by one.

"I been wanting to taste you," he said swirling his tongue around on my middle finger. "So fuckin' *bad.*"

He grabbed my hips and pressed his nose into my pussy. He turned his head left and right and rubbed his face all in my stuff. His fingers dug into my booty cheeks as he lifted me toward his mouth, and when he finally put it on me, that man put it on me *just right.*

He almost swallowed my whole pussy with one gulp. He stretched his mouth open wide, then brought his lips together gently, licking and sucking everything that was between them.

He pressed down on the spot right above my mound, then

stuck his tongue deep inside me and ate me gently, darting his tongue all around down there with long, slow licks.

I reached up and grabbed the headboard, then wrapped my legs around his head and squeezed until I came. I rode his face as sparks of fire shot outta my center, and he hung with me the whole way.

Suge stood up and got all the way naked just like me. He put on a condom, then pulled the sheets back and got in the bed. He pulled me over until I was laying on top of him. Our groins were pressed together and my titties was smushed against his broad chest.

He drew my knees up until I was straddling him, and using his strong arms, he lifted me by the hips and until my snatch was hovering over his erection.

I reached between us and guided him into me. I wanted to scream as all that thickness slid up in me, and as soon as my body expanded I got to bumping up and down on that dick.

"You're so damn beautiful," Suge whispered, running his hands up from my hips to my armpits and thumbing my nipples. He fucked me with deep, thorough strokes. "So fuckin' sexy and beautiful."

I rode him hard, thrusting my hips back and forth and bouncing up and down. He grabbed my shoulders and pulled me forward until I was laying flat on top of him. He ran his hands up to my neck, then slid them down my back and gripped my whole ass in his palms.

Outta nowhere that nigga smacked me. Right on my left cheek. My ass jiggled and burned under his big hand, and I almost lost my nut right then and there.

"Ugh," he grunted and slapped me again. I moaned and squeezed his dick between my thighs and crushed my clit against his pole. He went for my left cheek the third time, and as he brought his hand down flat on my ass, he thrust his dick deep inside me and pushed his finger into the rim of my ass-hole.

I screamed and tightened my booty cheeks, and as his dick jerked inside of me, that was all she wrote. He fucked me hard in both my holes, and we exploded together as my sweet cream overflowed from my inner walls like burning hot lava.

We laid there hugging each other close and breathing hard. After a couple of minutes I rose up on my hands and looked at him with a big grin on my face.

"Ummm . . . I got a question," I said stupidly.

He laughed. "I got an answer."

"Okay. Tell me this. After all that nasty shit we just did, do I still have to call you 'Uncle' Suge?"

He laughed and cupped my sweaty ass and squeezed it tight.

"You can call me any damn thing you wanna call me, baby." He lifted his head and kissed my lips. "Just as long as you call me."

CHAPTER 39

Carla Hildegrand gave up that wet neck and marveled at the size of her fiancé's dick. It was true what they said about once you go black you never went back. Barron had the biggest, blackest, and sweetest dick she had ever tasted, and she couldn't imagine putting anything weak and pale into her mouth ever again.

She crouched down on the floor and dropped her lower jaw as he slid himself deeply into her mouth and thrust with long, swirling strokes. Carla vibrated her tonsils and massaged the base of his pole with her tongue, flattening it out and sweeping it sensually from side to side.

Small moans began to escape his throat, and knowing how much she pleased him turned her on even more. Carla rotated her body until her nose was pressed firmly against Barron's balls. The tiny hairs on his nut sack tickled her nostrils and almost made her sneeze.

She retracted herself and brought her lips up over his helmet-shaped crown, then licked his glistening shaft like it was a Popsicle. Chocolate was her favorite flavor, and she loved the way his pre-cum tasted sweet and salty and slippery on her tongue all at the same time.

Swirling back around again, Carla bobbed her head and slurped and sucked both of them into a hot frenzy. Giving Barron head was something she lived for, and he had once told her she should put dick-sucking down on her résumé because she had the best neck pussy in the entire state of Texas. She flip-flopped her tongue over the head of his dick in a series of figure eights. This part usually drove him wild, and he would grab handfuls of her hair and pound that hard dick into her mouth until the back of her throat caught fire.

But this time Barron didn't grab her hair. In fact, when she opened one eye and peered up at him, his arms were crossed in front of his chest, his face was turned away from her, and his eyes were squeezed shut real tight.

Carla never slowed her pace, but she was puzzled. She could tell Barron was highly turned on by what she was doing, but he seemed so far away, and there was a strange look of reluctance on his face. Carla doubled her efforts and Barron's body responded. His muscular thighs trembled and his stiff dick got longer and even harder.

"Yeah, suck this shit baby," he muttered and gyrated his hips to her powerful rhythm. Carla peeked at him again. He wasn't looking at her. He wasn't touching her. He wasn't even into her. The lower half of his body was still perched on the chair, but his upper half was turned as far away from her as he could get. And the words coming out of his mouth . . . he had never spoken this kind of ghetto fuck-talk to her before.

"Lick my fuckin' balls . . . slurp this dick. Yeah . . . wet it up, bitch. Keep it nice and juicy. Lemme get this nut. I'm 'bout to blow. Ooooh, yeah. Just like that, don't stunt. Stroke it. Tighten them lips. Squeeze my big black balls! Ohhhh, *SHIT*! Suck my nut! Swallow this fuckin' cum!"

He palmed her head and jammed her face down into his groin. She felt like she was suffocating but he held her there as he pumped three quick, hard thrusts and then erupted so deeply in her throat that she didn't even taste his seed as it slid down her throat.

Immediately he dropped his hands and let his head loll over onto his shoulder. There was none of the usual stroking or soft words of love that came from his lips. The only thing Carla heard was the sound of his breathing and the nagging realizations that had suddenly jumped into her head.

She was still on her knees as Barron pulled his slightly hard penis from her mouth. He swung his leg over her head and stood up. His naked body was covered in a sheen of sweat, and every muscle on his body looked coiled and perfectly formed.

"Barron," she called after him as he walked toward the bathroom.

"Hold up. I gotta take a piss."

Carla waited on her knees and listened as he urinated, flushed the toilet, and then turned on the shower. She was still right there waiting ten minutes later when he came out of the bathroom wrapped in a towel.

"I see the way you've been looking at her," Carla said softly. All kinds of thoughts had run through her mind while he was in the bathroom. She hated that these thoughts were in her head, but he was the one who had put them there. "I hear you calling out her name in your sleep."

Barron walked over to the dresser and picked up his deodorant. Raising his arms, he rubbed the canister into his pits before turning around.

"You still on that one? How many times do I have to explain the way we do things in our family?"

"Save it, Barron. There's no excuse for that kind of behavior in any family. None. You look at her the way a man is supposed to look at a woman! Like she's so fuckably delicious that she makes your mouth water! But with me . . . with me you can't even bear to open your eyes when I'm between your legs sucking your dick!"

"It's just a black thing, Carla. A black thing! I was black on the day you met me, and I'm going to be black on the day I die. Black families are just close like that. Especially ours. You know how my mother is. She loves my uncle Digger, so of course we all love Pilar. Yeah, we're close, but she's my cousin, Carla. My *cousin*. And I'm getting tired of having to explain that to you all the damn time! There is nothing going on between me and my cousin! *Nothing*!"

Carla met his steady gaze with a steely one of her own.

"Oh, I believe you," she said softly. "But I'm not talking about your cousin, Pilar, Barron. I'm talking about your sister. Mink."

CHAPTER 40

I was really startin' to feel Selah, but at the same time me and her crazy son Barron stayed going at it hard!

"So when are you heading back to New York, Mink?" He walked up and blasted on me outta nowhere. "There's a hood up in Harlem that's missing two sewer rats."

I had just left Selah's suite when he caught me off balance. I had gone up there to tell his moms good morning and to see how she was doing, and now this fool was following me all the way to the other side of the house and talking crazy shit.

"Kill that hater noise," I said and scratched my ass right in front of him as I walked into my suite. "I like Texas. I might not never go back to New York."

He stepped up on the side of me and put his finger in my face. "It's time for you to get up outta here, Mink. Y'all can't stay here any longer, okay? Not you, with your fake, scheming ass, and not your ghetto-ass, drinking-milk-straight-outta-the-carton sidekick either! Who the fuck does that anyway?"

"My *mother* said I can stay here as long as I want to," I said, irking the shit outta him. He got swole just like I knew he would.

"Yo! I'm not playing with you. Stay the fuck out of my

mother's room. I already told you not to go up in there funking her space up."

"You know what, Barron?" Bunni got up off the sofa and walked toward him with her bottom lip quivering. "You real disrespectful, you know that? I wish my brother Peaches was here. He'd knock you dead on ya ass for talking to Mink that way. Word."

Barron stepped up on her too. "Fuck you *and* your 'brother' Peaches! What? I'm supposed to be scared of him or something?"

"Oh, you need to be," I told him. "Just go 'head with all that, Barron. Matter fact, get gone from outta here. Mama says this is *my* suite, and I want your tight ass to get the fuck out of it."

That fool went beast. He bent over me and blasted down in my face.

"She is NOT YOUR FUCKING MOTHER!"

I blasted right back! "Get the fuck out my *face*!"

"Get me the fuck out your face!"

Without a word, Bunni snuck around and jumped on him from the back and I jumped on him from the front. We were two New York hoodrats on a mission as we swung and scratched and lit into his ass like he was the one tryna steal something from us.

"Cut that shit out!" he hollered as he tried to hold me off with one hand and Bunni off with the other one. We fought like two wolves in a pack. Bunni rushed him high and I rushed him low. He threw his hands up to grab Bunni and poked her right in the eyeball.

"*Owwwww!*" she screamed and grabbed her face.

He tried to pry me off his legs and his Rolex grazed my mug and busted my lip. Blood trickled down my chin and I let him go for a quick second, but when Bunni lunged at him and got back in the fight, I lunged again too.

We were all over that fool. We hung off his ass like toddlers, using our weight to drag him down so we could tackle him and fuck him up. He staggered backward and crashed into a dresser, but we held on to him and threw killer blows everywhere we could land them.

We were sweating like a muthafucka up in that room. All three of us. Barron knew better than to just come out and swing on us, but he did toss our asses. He picked Bunni up first and chucked her across the room and she landed hard on the couch. Then he lifted me up like I was just baby weight, and he tried to spike my ass down on the king-sized bed like I was a football.

"You are not my fuckin' sister, Mink," he spit, breathing real hard. We had ripped the buttons off his shirt and scratch-welts had popped up on both sides of his face. "I don't know *who* the fuck you are, but you sure as hell ain't Sable."

He turned to walk out the door and I couldn't help but get the last word in.

"Just watch, asshole! The DNA test ain't gonna lie, asshole!" I shouted. "The muthafuckin' DNA test ain't gonna lie!"

CHAPTER 41

Barron had just climbed behind the wheel of his Maybach when he saw a DHL van pull up in the driveway behind him. He watched in the rearview mirror as the driver hopped out and walked toward the front door carrying a large yellow and red envelope in his hand.

"Ay!" Barron opened his car door and called to him. "Lemme get that over here!"

His stomach clenched as soon as he saw the return address on the envelope. It was from Exclusively DNA, and his jaw stiffened as he touched it. He signed for the envelope and then waited until the courier got back inside his truck and took off.

Finally, Barron thought as he walked into the house. The results were in, and as soon as he broadcast that shit out loud those two scheming bitches from New York were gonna get tossed out the door. He felt a big weight lift off his chest. This shit was almost over. He'd have the maids go through those guest suites with a few gallons of bleach and wash all traces of that gutter trash from his father's house. Barron tucked the envelope containing Mink's DNA results under his arm, then he headed upstairs to his suite and locked his door.

Anticipation surged through him as he sliced into the envelope with a letter opener. As great as it would have been to find Sable and get that vote he needed on the company's board, the only thing Barron wanted right now was for Mink to get her ass out of all of their lives.

He slid the three pieces of paper from the envelope and let his eyes skim over the cover sheet.

"Oh, *hell* fuckin' no!" He almost crumpled when he read the summary statement and the conclusions of the test. Somebody was playing fuckin' games! There had to be some kind of mistake!

Barron skimmed over the other two sheets of paper and he couldn't believe what his eyes were reading. And he damn sure didn't want anybody else to believe it either. He could hear Mink's voice as she screamed all in his ear.

The DNA test ain't gonna lie, asshole! The muthafuckin' DNA test ain't gonna lie.

Well some damn body was gonna have to lie, Barron thought grimly. He stuck the papers back inside the envelope, then grabbed his keys and headed back outside to his car.

Two hours later Barron's wallet was lighter and his heart was too. It had cost him ten grand, but it was money well spent. A new DNA report was about to be generated at Exclusively DNA, and he'd be receiving a copy through courier mail in just a few days.

He had been in the right place at the right time to intercept that envelope, and he didn't know what the hell would have happened if somebody else had gotten their hands on that shit first. Just the thought that somebody might find out that Mink's DNA was a match and that she really was his sister Sable was scary.

That shit was scary as hell.

CHAPTER 42

But two nights later Selah called for a family dinner.

The servants had just set the plates on the table when Barron and Carla entered the elegant Dominion dining room. His mother was already there, and so were Dane, Jock, Fallon, and a few of their aunts and cousins from Houston.

Barron sat down in the chair that was right next to Viceroy's empty seat. The scratches on his face were just starting to heal. He looked up as Bunni and Mink walked into the room, closely followed by Pilar and her father, Digger.

Mink's bottom lip was split in the middle, and Bunni's right eye was red.

The kitchen staff overloaded the huge round table with pans of lasagna and bowls of salad. Glasses of ginger ale, sweet tea, wine, and ice water were set on trays. Selah Dominion stood up at her spot at the table, across from Viceroy's empty chair. Her skin was glowing, and her champagne glass was already half empty.

"Excuse me everyone," she said, ringing her glass with her salad fork. "I have an important announcement to make."

Lips started flapping as everybody looked clueless but interested, and Barron sat stiff in his seat as he stared closely at his mother with a questioning look on his face.

Selah refused to meet his eyes. Instead, she cleared her throat and said, "Thank you everybody for coming to dinner. I know we haven't been eating together all that much since Viceroy went in the hospital, but I have some news to share with you tonight, and I wanted everybody to hear it at the same time."

Selah looked around the table and met everyone's eyes.

"Eighteen years ago, in the blink of an eye, I lost my three-year-old daughter. "But today God blessed me with proof that no matter what happens in life we should never stop hoping or praying."

She reached under the table and picked up a small, beat-up looking baby doll with a yellow ducky for a face and black yarn for hair, then looked directly at Mink.

"After Sable was kidnapped I vowed I would sleep with this doll every night until my baby was safely back at home. Well, I received a fax from the DNA lab today, and the little girl I lost in New York all those years ago, my sweet three-year-old daughter Sable . . . well . . . the truth is right here in black and white."

Barron's heart almost stopped as Selah picked up a sheet of paper from the table and held it up high in the air. He recognized the logo even from where he was sitting.

"Mink, my darling. That beautiful little girl I lost all those years ago was you."

Tears were streaming down Selah's face now. The raw emotion took away her voice leaving her speechless, and all she could do was mouth the words, *I'm sorry. I'm so sorry.*

She pushed her chair back and walked over and took Mink in her arms and hugged on her like she was her long-lost daughter, finally found.

"Welcome home baby," she whispered, crying uncontrollably now as she waved the ugly doll she'd been sleeping with for eighteen years high in the air. "Welcome home!"

Everybody broke out clapping, and Jock stuck two fingers in his mouth and let off a loud, sharp whistle. Chairs were pushed back as the family swarmed on Mink to welcome her back into the Dominion fold. There were hugs and kisses and mad love for her everywhere.

Except on Barron's and Pilar's faces.

Barron jumped to his feet. "Nah, hold up!" he barked. "This is some *bullshit*!" Everybody froze. "Lemme see that piece of paper, Mama, because I don't believe this shit!"

Selah stared at him as she passed her son the form that had been faxed to her. "I understand how you feel, baby," she comforted him. "This comes as a big shock to all of us Barron, and nobody has ever felt worse about Sable being taken away than you. But sometimes God sees fit to grant us a miracle, son, and you're holding the proof right there in your hands."

"I still don't believe this shit!" Barron insisted. "I know it ain't true!"

"It *is* true, Barron," Selah laughed happily. "And it's the best damn thing that has ever happened to this family. Now let's eat, everybody!" Selah shouted and picked up her champagne glass. She turned that bad boy up to her lips and drained it. "Um . . . pour me another one, Barron. A big one this time. In fact, I want *everybody* to knock back some wine! My baby is home, and I'm celebrating tonight!"

CHAPTER 43

Being Sable didn't feel nothing like I thought it would. I had sat through that dinner with a brick in my stomach, and the only way I'd been able to stay in that room was by guzzling glass after glass of wine until I got dizzy.

Everybody agreed that they had never seen Selah so happy before. She came all outta her shell, and the way she throated that champagne showed me a hint of Brooklyn peeking through the mask she usually wore on her face.

Bunni was already talking about how she was gonna spend her twenty-five large reward money, but the thought of getting all that cash didn't even excite me like I had thought it would. Bunni told me to chill and said I was numb and in shock. She said my brain just needed a minute to process all those zeros that were about to be rollin' around in my bank account after that number one. But all throughout dinner I had sat there feeling like shit, and since I pulled ganks out the ass for a living, I figured my stomachache musta been from the wine.

I went back to my suite as soon as we were finished eating, and it was real late when one of the servants knocked on the door and gave me a note that said Selah wanted to see me. Bunni had gotten one of the drivers to take her across town so she could spend a few hours of pleasure with her pain slut, Kelvin, and I had already taken a shower and was stretched out across the bed still feeling sick.

"She wants me to come up there right now?"

The older black woman, whose name was Grace, nodded. "That's what she said, Miss Mink."

I put on my Prada bathrobe and slid my feet into the matching slippers. I didn't know what to expect outta my new mama, Selah, but I woulda never expected what she dropped on me when I walked into her suite.

"It was all my fault!" she blurted out almost as soon as I stepped into her extra-spacious room. This was my first time seeing her without her makeup on and she really scared the shit outta me. Forget all that soft shit she had sucked down at dinner. Mami was straight liquored up now. I could smell the vodka coming off her breath real strong. Her face looked mad bloated, and it was shining with sweat. The long hair that was always perfectly whipped had been pushed back off her forehead and hung in limp strands like she had sweated it out in the shower.

"I'm sorry, Sable." She grabbed me in a bear hug and held me close to her and cried big, rocking tears. "I swear I'm sorry. It was all my fault, baby. All my fault."

I let her hug me for a few seconds, and then I gently pulled away. This was all a big hustle to me, but it was some crucial, real-life stuff to her, and for some reason I was starting to feel guilty as fuck.

"It's okay. It wasn't your fault."

She clutched my hand and I let her lead me over to a huge black velour sofa on the other side of her room.

"I lost you, baby." There was crazy pain in her eyes as she stared deeply into mine. "*I lost you.*"

"I don't get it. How did you lose me? I thought I was kidnapped, so how could that be your fault?"

"It WAS my fault!" She gripped my hand and damn-near

yelled in my face. "I was DRUNK, okay? Drunk! I had just seen something terrible at your father's job, and I ran out of there and headed straight to a liquor store! I sat in a park and drank until I was ready to pass out, and then I pushed your little stroller down the block and went inside a drug store so I could get a bottle of mouthwash.

"I left Barron up front to watch you and Dane. I know I shouldn't have. He was just a kid, and not nearly old enough to watch two toddlers, but I was only going to rinse my mouth out and come right back. I couldn't have been gone for more than two minutes. Not even two minutes! But when I came back . . . you were gone. Barron was there, Dane was still there, and your little pink stroller and ducky-doll baby were still there . . . but *you* were gone."

Her whole face crumpled. She squinched her eyes closed and turned down her lips, and the wails just fell all outta her mouth.

I was all fucked up. I didn't know what the hell to do. I damn sure didn't know what to say. I felt bad for bringing this kinda pain into her life. I felt responsible for giving this real sweet lady so much false hope and for poking my sticky fingers inside all of her most painful spots.

"It's okay, Selah," I said as she put her head down and cried on my chest. "It wasn't your fault. You didn't do anything wrong. Please don't cry."

And then I said the words that I had been so freakin' unable to say to my real mother, another drunk woman who was laying up in a nursing home helpless and outta touch with reality.

"I forgive you," I said softly. I patted her hand and stroked her sweaty hair. "I forgive you."

I sat with her as she cried for a whole hour.

She felt so bad for being drunk when her baby was snatched. Just so damn guilty all down in her bones that twice I almost came outta my face and told her that I wasn't really

Sable. Twice I almost blurted out the truth and took back my lie. But I didn't.

"Will you sleep with me tonight?" she asked me. Her eyes were bloodshot and her bottom lip was doing the drunk chick's sag. "When you were a baby you used to sleep with me every chance you got because you couldn't stand your crib. You hated the bars. You just didn't like being fenced in. It used to drive Viceroy crazy, but I loved it."

She put her head on my shoulder and sighed.

"I haven't snuggled with my baby girl in almost eighteen years. Will you let me be your mommy tonight?"

I wanted to scream and get the fugg up outta there! I liked Selah. She was cool and I felt real sorry for ganking her. And for real, her room was plusher than any hotel I'd ever seen in my life, but nah, that didn't mean I wanted to sleep with her, okay?

But I did it. Her bed was so big it had to be custom made. It sat up on an elevated platform with a smoked marble base that was trimmed in gold. She pulled the sheets back and I took off my robe. We climbed into her bed together, and the cool satin sheets felt like a mother's love on my skin.

I had a bunch of cousins so I had slept with plenty of females before. When you come from a family full of trifling people it was rare to have a bed all to yourself. But I had never been held by a woman in my life, and I didn't really know how to take it when Selah scooted up behind me and put her arm around me. I lay there stiffer than a mutha as she touched my hair, then rubbed my arm. A few minutes later she was snoring softly in my ear with that raggedy little ugly ducky-doll baby clenched in her fist.

I don't know when I fell off, but I did. And I slept good too. Damn good. I woke up the next morning and the memories from last night crashed down on me. I lay there not knowing how in the hell I was supposed to feel. I mean, I was still on my game, and getting that dough was always at the top of my to-do list, but I had never even thought about how fucked up Sable's family was gonna feel behind me and Bunni's grimy mess.

I peeped over my shoulder. Selah had rolled over to the other side of the bed. She looked a lot younger than she had a few hours earlier. That sleep had worked some hella miracles on her during the night. Her face looked smooth and slack, like all the stress had left her body. She looked happy. Real content. And the ugly little ducky-doll that had comforted her while her baby was gone was still cuddled in her arms.

CHAPTER 44

"That grimy muthafucka!"

Barron had sent Carla home in a limo so he could spend the night wildin' out in his suite, and as soon as she was gone he grabbed a bottle of Crown Royal from his private stock and chugged that shit down like it was warm water.

There was no way in hell his mother should've gotten a copy of that DNA report. No way! He'd made a deal with the fat-headed dude who worked at the lab, and not only did that bastard cross him up by not sending him a negative report like he was supposed to, that fool had faxed a copy of the *real* report to Selah and blew Barron's whole shit up in the air!

Barron felt like he was still playing college football. Rage and aggression were coming out of his pores and he wanted to tear some shit up. He sat in his room and drank until the sun came up, just a' counting the minutes until the DNA lab opened. He was gonna go down there and bitch-slap him a nigga named Kelvin Merchant, so that fat-ass fucka just better be ready!

The lab had just opened and Kelvin sat at the front counter trying hard not to squirm. He had to pee real bad but his dick was sore and he didn't wanna touch it, not even to aim it down into the toilet. All morning long he had been reliving his deliciously agonizing memories of his hot night with Bunni. She was a brutal hood bitch. He could still see the vicious look on her face as she inserted his meat in his favorite torture grinder and then ass-mugged him for almost two hours straight.

His dick got hard just thinking about it and Kelvin moaned. After a night like that an erection was the last thing he needed. All that hot blood rushing to his dick, stretching the tender, brutalized skin . . . . He just couldn't help it. He reached under his desk and gripped his wood, wincing as intense pain wrapped around sensual pleasure and shot straight through him. Hell yeah, he was a pain slut. Agony was his eroticism, and he had finally found someone who was willing to hurt him bad enough to make it feel good.

Closing his eyes, Kelvin stroked himself on the sly. He gripped his dick in his fist and squeezed as hard as he could. He damn-near shot off and passed out at the same time from the sheer erotic torture that was radiating through him, and he smiled and sighed as his entire body tingled with joy.

"What the *fuck* is your fat ass grinning about?"

"Oh!" Kelvin's eyes flew open as he wobbled on his stool. "Excuse me, sir! How can I help . . ." His words trailed off as he stared at the tall black man with the killer glare in his red eyes. Dude looked like he'd been out drinking all night, and his whole grill was twisted and scary. "Oh, Mr. Dominion . . . I didn't know you were coming by—"

"Get ya fuckin' ass outside!" Barron Dominion grabbed him up in his collar and yanked him off his feet. The front counter was the only thing standing between them, and Barron kept him yoked up as Kelvin stumbled down the length of the long counter until they were standing face to face.

"We had a *deal*, muh'fucka!" Barron barked and pushed him out the front door. He grabbed Kelvin's fat neck and slammed him up against the side of the building, then dug his thumb deep into the meat of Kelvin's beefy throat.

"What the fuck did I pay your fat ass ten grand for?" Barron thrust a powerful right fist into Kelvin's soft gut, then bitch-slapped him hard upside his head.

"W-w-wait!" Kelvin stuttered as he reached out to protect himself. His fat arms flailed and his enormous belly jiggled. "I c-c-couldn't do anything! It wasn't even me who ran the test! I swear!"

Barron snatched him in his collar again and slammed his head up against the concrete wall. Rage exploded in his eyes and Kelvin thought dude was about to butt him in the forehead, but Barron lowered his aim and drilled him hard in the nose instead.

Hot blood spurted everywhere. "*Ohh!*" Kelvin shrieked and clutched his nose. He liked pain, but not like this!

Barron cursed and slapped the shit out of him again. He gripped Kelvin's throat between his strong fingers like he was going to rip his Adam's apple out, and then he deep drilled him in the gut so hard that vomit splashed out of the fat man's mouth.

"I oughta *kill* your stupid ass!" Barron spit as he let loose with a barrage of hard punches to Kelvin's chest and gut. "You fucked shit up! I should *smash* your stupid ass!"

Kelvin cried as he balled up the best he could and trembled in fear. Mr. Dominion *was* drunk. He was crazy as hell too. Getting his dick ripped by a chick in heels was one thing, but having an ex-football player busting him all in his grill was something else.

"How the fuck did my mother get that fax?" Barron panted when he finally stopped punching the man. "Huh? How did she get it when I paid your dumb ass ten fuckin' grand to send me a negative report?"

Kelvin babbled and whimpered like a submissive little bitch. "I swear, Mr. Dominion. There was nothing I could do!

My supervisor faxed your mother the report! She came in extra early that day, and by the time I got here it was already done!"

He couldn't believe it when Barron Dominion turned him loose and took a few steps back. Barron was a tall, athletic man, and he had the kind of body that Kelvin had always wanted but would never get, no matter how hard he tried. He could tell Barron wanted to fuck him up real good again, and he watched the man struggle to get his rage under control. He watched him lose the battle too.

"*Umph!*" Kelvin shrieked as Barron's fist brutalized his nose again. He heard the crack as his bone broke, but before his mind could register it, Barron's other fist caught him under the chin and snapped his head back on his neck.

"You's a lucky muthafucka," Barron breathed as he watched the fat man slide down to the ground. "You're real fuckin' lucky. 'Cause I feel like killing your ass."

"God!" Kelvin sniffed. "I think you broke my nose!"

"Good. You better not cash my check neither, muthafucka or I'll be back to break your ass next time."

Kelvin cupped his hand under his nose as a steady stream of blood flowed from his nostrils. He peered through terrified eyes as Barron strode over to his fancy white car and climbed inside. He crouched there shaking, knowing his nose was terribly broken but happy as hell that his teeth hadn't been kicked in too.

But Barron was right about one thing. Kelvin *was* real lucky. Because late last night, right before she had locked his dick in a spiked clamp and tied a blindfold over his eyes, Bunni had told him that her friend Mink was gonna tear him off a cool five grand in sweet cash. It was gonna be his reward for hooking her up with a positive DNA analysis that matched the sample they had on file for Sable Dominion.

Kelvin flung the warm blood from his hand as he crawled back inside the building to take care of his busted nose. This was the last time he was gonna do business with those god-damn Dominions. He was gonna tear up the check that crazy Barron had written him for ten thousand dollars, but he was damn sure gonna keep the money he got from Bunni's friend, whether he had earned it or not. The moment she handed it over that money was going right into his vacation account. There was a pain-fest kicking off in Sweden in just a few months, and Kelvin planned on being there!

CHAPTER 45

"Girl yo' ass is a goddamn Domino now!" Bunni raised her shot glass of fuzzy balls in the air tryna come at me for a toast.

"*Dominion*," I corrected her, and clinked my glass of coconut Bacardi against hers. "I'm a Dominion now."

"Yeah! What the fugg I said!" she said and slurped from her glass so hard the brown liquid spilled over and soaked her hand. That cracked her up. "You see what a rich Domino bitch just made me do?"

Ever since Selah had announced the results of the DNA test we had been flying real high, and tonight Dane had invited everybody out to a bar in Dallas so we could celebrate, and of course Barron and Pilar were the two who didn't show up. Not that I gave a damn. I figured they were somewhere together fuckin' like rabbits, which was way cool with me.

Bunni was just a little bit too lifted over the twenty-five grand she had gotten as a reward for finding me, but I was feeling myself too. That little piece of paper from the lab had been the knock-out punch of the decade, and I was walking around poppin' my collar and feeling like I was entitled to a slice of everybody's pie.

Our New York asses had dug in real deep and comfortable

at the mansion during our last few days there, and we had been ordering food and drinks to our rooms and running those servants up and down the stairs like crazy.

We'd gone on a shopping spree earlier, and Dane and Jock had carried mad packages as they followed us around in the bougie white people's mall called NorthPark Center. It seemed like the Dominions had an account at every high-end store up in that bitch!

"Just put this on the Dominion account," I had grinned and told the store clerks left and right. All Dane had to do was show his ID and sign a form, and them clerks got to serving my hood-ass like I was a rich little princess!

"Don't worry," I told Dane a couple of times. "I'll pay it back outta my inheritance money."

Being New Yorkers, me and Bunni were no strangers to dropping big bank on some real lovely gear. We had done it countless times before, so it wasn't like we got all ga-ga over all the expensive shit we were trying on and picking up off the racks. But to actually walk in a store and buy any damned thing we wanted without plopping down a dime was just amazing.

I planned to be real careful though. I knew a hundred grand wasn't gonna last but so long. And with Gutta coming home for his twenty-five large and a warrant that was about to be hanging over my head back in New York, I was gonna have to be watchful about how I dished off my cash. But I wasn't tryna worry about none of that be-good shit tonight because my little rich ass was too busy celebrating!

"So what's your next move?" Dane asked me as we wilded out at the bar and tossed back shots. Fallon was in a booth with her stud chick, Freddie, all deep in a conversation. Jock was on the dance floor dry-fuckin' Bunni, and if watching his little brother humpin' on his squeeze pressed Dane out, he damn sure didn't show it. "You're family now, so are you gonna stay here in Texas with us or what?"

I almost choked on my rum.

"Are you kidding me? No, no, no!" I wheezed. My eyes burned and I coughed up tiny sprinkles of liquor. Hell nah I wasn't staying in no damn Texas! Selah had told Barron to open me up a bank account and deposit my birthday money in it, and as soon as I got my bank card I was out! The first thing I was gonna get was two one-way plane tickets—one for me and one for Bunni. We were going home, and we were flying first class all the way too.

"Remember," I hit Dane with the same lie that I had told Selah, "I was only planning on staying down here for one day! It's been two weeks now, and I really need to get back home. My job, my school, my aunts . . ." I was lying like hell 'cause I didn't have none of that to go home to. "I can't just leave my life floating all up in the air like that. I gotta get back to New York and take care of my bizz."

"I feel ya," Dane said as he packed another blunt with yay and held it under the counter while he rolled it. "But while you're gone you better be thinking hard on that trust fund, ya feel me? If Pop doesn't wake up soon then Barron's gonna take over the company. And if that fool gets the key to the safe where the *real* money is waiting, then you and me both are gonna be ass out."

"Welcome to the family." Uncle Suge walked up behind me and kissed me on the cheek. He left his lips on me for about two seconds too long, and when he pulled away he let them kinda drag across my skin.

I turned around and grinned at his sexy ass.

"Sorry I'm late to your party. But I did bring you something." His hands were empty but his sexy-ass eyes were full of fun.

"What? You got me a present? I love presents! Where is it?"

He nodded toward the door. "In my truck."

I tossed back my drink and licked my lips. "Well what you waitin' for, Big Daddy? Leggo!"

I ran outside and squealed as I jumped up in his big old truck and wiggled my ass around on all that soft leather.

"What you get me?" Being so close to him had me turned the hell on, and as bad as my na-na was leaking I was scared I was gonna leave a puddle on his fly leather upholstery.

He pushed a button and his glove box popped open. I held my breath as he reached inside and took out a silver box that was tied with a tiny pink bow.

"Welcome to the family," he said and passed it to me.

I pried the top off the box and stared at the prettiest pair of diamond earrings I had ever seen! They looked like a pair I had lusted after in Tiffany's but could never get up enough dough to buy. Those babies glinted and sparkled and shined like mad in the darkness of his whip.

I threw my arms around his neck.

"Thank you, Uncle Suge! These suckers are hot as hell!"

"These suckers are too," he said as his big hands slid up my sides and gripped my titties. Our little game was over and I loved that shit. Wasn't nothing timid about the way he jumped on me. He didn't ask for no permission 'cause he knew he didn't need none.

He attacked my lips and ate them shits like they were steaks. His tongue busted up in my mouth like it was a landlord and I was late on the rent. I moaned as he took charge and handled my ass.

Uncle Suge was damn sure sugaring me up right. He had me dripping. I reached in his lap and felt that bulge thumpin' in his pants and my nookie got wet and wild. I turned away from him and backed up halfway in his lap as I banged my plump ass up against his bulge and slid it from side to side.

"Ride 'em, cowgirl," he growled in my ear, and the next thing I knew my little dress was hiked up in the back and Suge had scooped open both of my ass cheeks and lifted me dead on his lap so we could play pony.

"Yeah, ass high, legs wide! That's how we like 'em down here!"

This fool was good. He rested my little frame on his forearms and pushed his meat into an extra-large rubber, then he slid one hand under my thong and the other one slid right up in my pussy.

He started gently glidin' two fingers up and down both sides of my clit with a bangin' rhythm. I arched back against his massive chest and let my juices flow. He took his fingers out and lifted me up slightly, then brought me down on his monster dick, holding me over him while he eased that pulsating hot thang into me inch by inch.

It was all I could do not to flip out in his grip. With both my hands, I reached back and popped buttons off as I ripped his shirt open. He scooted out from behind the steering wheel and helped me spin around.

Once I was facing him, I bent my knees so he could lower me up and down on his lap. I felt like we were on a trampoline the way he bounced that dick around in my coochie. We was fucking rough-neck style all the way, and his windows was getting foggy like a muthafucka!

"Let me hit that oil, baby!" Suge grunted. He slammed up into me and drilled my pussy until I was just about to come, and then he lifted me off him and pushed me down on the bench seat with my legs gapped wide open.

He threw my legs over his shoulders and lifted my hips in the air, then he dove down and put my explosion point directly in his face. His lips covered my clit and he sucked it and rolled it around on his tongue. We were in oil country, and Suge slurped my gushy up like it was some sho nuff bubbling crude.

"*Yummm*, Miss Mink," he pussy-mumbled, "I'd stick my whole head up this fine ass of yours if I could!"

I grabbed the back of his neck and he started mushing his tongue in and out of me like an accordion. I pointed my feet up in the air and hollered as I busted my nut, and after licking my na-na up like his tongue was a wet washcloth, Suge climbed on top of me and pumped me real hard until he busted himself one too.

CHAPTER 46

"So what happens now?" Pilar wanted to know. It was a few days after Selah's big announcement and she was still pissed off. Barron was chilling in a soft leather chair and Pilar was standing behind him massaging the thick knots in his shoulder muscles. "We're just gonna let that bitch get away with this?"

Barron sighed. He put his head back and Pilar leaned over and kissed his lips. She darted her tongue out and slid it across his teeth.

"C'mon, now." Barron turned away, then held her wrists and moved her hands away. "We said we wasn't gonna go there anymore, right?"

Pilar smirked. "That's what *you* said, Barron. Not me. I said we need to go there a whole lot more."

She came around in front of him and sat on his lap. She felt his dick jump as she stroked his neck and let her fingers trail down his chest.

"Seriously," she said. "You're not gonna just let Mink get away with this, are you? I mean, it's bad enough that she's pocketing a hundred grand and her sidekick gets away with twenty-five. But that chick is a fraud, Barron. What's going to happen if she comes after the trust fund? That's a lot of money to throw out the window every year. Are you gonna let her get away with that too?" Pilar saw fire enter Barron's eyes and she felt a spark of heat shoot up from his groin.

"Why can't you just tell her to go away? DNA test or not, get rid of her ass."

"It's not that simple," Barron explained, "and besides, there's a chance that we might actually need her vote . . . but I'm working on some things, and once I have my plans all lined up and in place, Mink is getting dropped."

Pilar moved in on him and gobbled up his bottom lip, sucking it gently and stroking it with her warm tongue. "Hurry up and drop that bitch," she whispered as she arched her back and gyrated her hips on his erection. She shivered as Barron gripped her waist and thrust up to meet the motion of her sweet round ass. "Drop that bitch hard."

CHAPTER 47

Now that I had a bank card in my hand, shit was official and me and Bunni really busted loose. We had the run of the joint. We got the drivers to take us for a spin in all the whips, ran the cooks back and forth bringing shrimp and lobster up to our rooms, and we basically acted like the wild little Harlem guttersnipes that we were.

I couldn't wait to get my ass back to New York! Yeah, Texas was real cool and all that, but I was feenin' for the City That Never Sleeps. And even with the DNA proof staring at them in black and white from the lab, not everybody wanted to accept the fact that I was part of the family.

Me and cousin Pilar had had us a little showdown, and I was all for that shit because it was definitely overdue. She got up in my face and called me a gold-diggin' piece of street meat, and I called her a string of foul bitches too.

"Oh shut the fuck up, you broke-ass trick!" I let loose on her like I had a gat under my tongue. "You just salty because you're not *me*! But I tell you what, ain't nobody stupid around here. That little kissin'-cousin thang you and Bump-Boy got going on is about to blow straight up, ya heard? You better keep diggin' deep in his pocket stash while you can, stupaholic,

because that dude is *never* gonna marry you." I looked her up
and down and then patted the round hump of my ass. "He
might dig you out, but you really ain't his type."

Selah wanted me to stay in Texas and she just couldn't stop
telling me.

"I can't believe you're leaving me when I just got you
back," she cried as her mascara ran down her face.

I put my hand on hers. I had been so hyped over getting
that hundred grand that I hadn't really thought about how
pulling up outta Dallas was gonna make her feel. It seemed like
everybody had their own crazy reasons for wanting me to stay
in Texas. Suge and Dane wanted me to stay so I could get
down on their squad when it came time to cast some kinda
upcoming stockholder vote. Jock wanted me to stay 'cause his
horny ass was still tryna get up in Bunni's funky stuff. But
Selah wanted me to stay because she was convinced that I was
her long-lost daughter, and based on that, she loved me.

"I'ma come back real soon," I lied. "I promise I won't be
gone too long, and I'll call you a lot too, okay?"

Selah looked a wreck. She'd gotten real clingy and mushy
on me over the past few days. She wanted to know every damn
thing that had jumped off in my life ever since kindergarten,
and I wasn't tryna drag up no old crazy memories of how I
had lived with Jude, so I created some new scenarios and fed
her a whole lotta bullshit that just made her cry even harder.

I tried to let Selah hug me as much as she wanted to. It
wasn't that I didn't like being touched like that, I just wasn't
used to it. I hated to admit it, even to myself, but she was a
damn good mark. While she had been busy all this time hoping I was her daughter, I had been busy puttin' in work. Coming to Texas had been a bomb opportunity to turn some fast
money, but now I was ready to break out so I could go on with
the rest of my fun little life.

But for Selah, this *was* her life. She had spent so much energy feeling guilty about losing Sable and grieving over her daughter that it had become all she lived for. And now that she had found me, and especially since I was making moves to jet back to New York so soon, she looked real sad and lost.

I hated it for her, I really did. But I knew leaving was the best thing for all of us, and when she asked me if I wanted to go back to the hospital and see Viceroy one last time, I almost screamed out, *Hell the fuck no!*

Because even though that man couldn't talk or point his finger, the look in his good eye and the way those machines started beeping and lighting up as he stared up in my face told me that somewhere in that damaged head of his, Viceroy knew the truth about me. And I knew without a doubt that if he ever got better and had a chance to bust me out to Selah and the rest of the family, he damn sure would.

CHAPTER 48

Finally! We was up in the air celebrating like a mutha! I was so hyped that I coulda flown that plane back to New York my damn self. I had a Coach wallet full of dough, a bank account that was loaded, and nothing but fun new opportunities stretched out in front of me for as far as I could see.

Bunni was lifted too. We had smoked some chronic with Dane before we got in the limo to come to the airport, and right now we were sitting in the first-class cabin in extra-wide seats as Bunni ran them lil flight attendants back and forth with all her fifty thousand requests.

"So check it out. This is how you should do it, Mink." She batted her false eyelashes and counted off on her fingers. "You got a hundred grand, right? Okay, the first thing you need to do is throw that nine grand on your warrants so they don't toss your ass under the jail. After that, we should go in half and half and get us a little weight—maybe fifteen to twenty g's worth—and flip it a couple of times. Not in my building, 'cause that fool Punchie is probably still gunning for you, but maybe somewhere uptown. I got a few places in mind."

She snapped her fingers and the waitress brought her another shot of Hen-Hen on the rocks.

"After that, you gotta put Gutta's twenty-five racks to the side for when he gets outta jail, and you better find him a new apartment and get his shit outta storage too! That nigga don't play when it comes to his cream, so we definitely gotta sit on that money and don't touch it this time or we could end up dead. But that still leaves us a whole lot more cash to play with!"

"Damn right! Maybe we should take a vacation," I said with my eyes lighting up. "We should take Peaches with us too."

"Yeah! Yeah! Let's take our asses to Jamaica! We gon' eat summa dat good roti and smoke some trees and get one a dem long-dick island boyz. Wha' you know about dat shit mon?"

"You so stupid!" I howled. "Jamaicans don't sound nuthin' like that!"

"Whateva." Bunni waved her hand. "However they sound, I want me one that ain't never left the island. Not one of those dreads that be running around in New York!"

"Well, wherever we go, our asses still gotta shop!" I giggled and took another sip of my drink. "I mean, how we gonna look busting up in Club Wood flossin' some ancient shit? I need new gear from my wig to my shoes, baby. I feel like hitting a few hot parties when we get home too. You know I wanna make the rounds styling all my new shit so them hater-bitches sitting on your front stoop can faint!"

"Hell yeah!" Bunni screamed all loud and made the flight attendants look at us like we was crazy. "Let's do that shit, girl! 'Cause ain't no party like a New York party, and a New York party don't stop!"

CHAPTER 49

Barron rode in the backseat of the limousine holding his crying mother in his arms. They had just dropped Mink and Bunni off at Dallas/Fort Worth International Airport, and Selah was so broken down by the departure of this lost-and-found daughter of hers that it made Barron hate Mink even more. He glanced back at his brother Dane, who was sitting in the row behind them.

"Is she all right?" Dane whispered, and reached over the seat to pat his mother's shoulder.

Barron shook his head real quick. Hell no, she wasn't all right. How the hell could she be okay when that little Harlem bandit had run up in her world and pulled a stickup on her heart?

Barron was fuming, and he swore that no matter what happened with the board's vote at Dominion Oil, Mink wasn't getting another dime of his family's fortune. He was busy pulling together the threads of a scheme in his head when his cell phone buzzed and he reached to answer it.

He frowned when he glanced at the caller ID, then he turned slightly away from his mother and barked into the phone, "Hello?"

The wimpy-ass voice on the other end brought out the beast in him, and Barron had a satisfying flashback of drilling his fist into this idiot's grill and breaking his fuckin' nose.

"Um, yes, Mr. Dominion?"

"What do you want?"

"Um, hi. This is Kelvin Merchant at Exclusively DNA. . . . I'm sorry to bother you, but I just got a report back that I thought you might be interested in. And you know, after what happened the last time we met, I just don't want to take any chances or mess anything up again."

"Man, what the hell are you talking about?"

"I'm talking about a lab report. We had another specimen come in this week from a young lady in Philadelphia. I was asked to run tests on her sample and compare the results to your sister Sable's DNA."

"Yeah, okay? And?"

"Well the results just came back, and I know you probably don't wanna hear this but . . . umm . . . we've got another match."

To Be Continued . . .

Discussion Questions

1. Mink LaRue is a beautiful and cunning con artist who is all about getting her hands on some quick money. Can she handle the shrewdness and power of the Dominion family? Or is she in over her head?

2. What kind of doubts and suspicions would you have had if someone like Mink showed up at your door on a crazy misadventure?

3. What kind of friend is "Bowlegged" Bunni? Was taking her to Texas a good idea?

4. Barron was cool on Mink immediately. Do you think he would have responded to her in this manner if she wasn't so sexy and he wasn't battling such an intense erotic attraction to her?

5. Pilar is digging for gold. In your opinion, are her and Barron "kissing cousins" or are the traditional family barriers irrelevant because Barron is adopted?

6. What did you think about the shower scene between Barron and Pilar? Was Barron wrong for getting it on with Carla while Pilar was hiding in the bathroom? Should Pilar have come out and let Carla know she was there?

7. Uncle Suge is a skirt-chaser. What do you think are his true intentions toward Mink? Does their relationship violate any taboo family boundaries?

8. Selah is obviously guilty because of her role in losing Sable. Do you think her guilt is clouding her judgment when it comes to Mink being her daughter?

9. Jock witnessed a tragic event in the pool house. Will Mink finding out about it come back to bite him?

10. Viceroy Dominion is still in and out of consciousness while his family and the financial empire he built is facing a state of chaos. What do you think he was saying with his eyes when Mink looked down on him in that hospital room?

Up Next

Sexy Little Liar

In stores November 2012

CHAPTER 1

New York was my shit! Our plane had just landed at JFK, and after ballin' hard on a crazy misadventure down in fabulous D-Town, me and Bunni were hyped as hell to be back in the Big Apple.

We had dipped outta Manhattan with nothing going for us except mad dreams and devious schemes, and after working our grind and flipping the state of Texas upside down, we were rolling back in town with more dough than we had ever baked before.

"We need a taxi!" My best friend and partner-in-grime hollered as a bellman wheeled our luggage outta the crowded terminal. Bunni was posted up in a bright pink cat-suit and a matching pair of silver-buckle gladiator sandals, and I was rocking a platinum-white Glama-Glo wig that had big orange streaks down the bangs, and an orange and white tank top tucked into a skimpy white tennis skirt that barely covered my apple ass.

For two hood-bound Harlem girls, me and Bunni had crazy suitcases everywhere, and every last one of them was stuffed with mad jewelry and the hottest designer gear that money could buy.

I had recently become an official member of the Dominion oil family of Texas, and using my new status as the once-missing and now-found oil heiress Sable Dominion, me and Bunni had hit the rich folks' mall in Dallas and killed every store in sight. I mean we ransacked that mall like a pair of greedy cat burglars, *oohing* and *aahing* as we touched, and admired, and tried on every damn thing we saw. We shopped like fiends for hours, and we didn't come up for air until we were broke-down tired and all twenty of our toes had corns.

"Now, see there, Mink," Bunni rolled her eyes and sucked her teeth as she struck a funky pose on the sidewalk outside the terminal. Bunni had a real stank shape and she always dressed to show that shit. Almost every dude who zipped into the terminal stole a quick peek at her round titties and bouncy ass as he passed by. "I knew we shoulda called us a limo before we left Texas. We got mad ends now, baby. How we gonna look pulling up around the way in some beat-up yellow cab?"

Bunni had it right. Image was everything in our hood, and I was damn sure tryna elevate mine. I was *not* the same con-mami Mink LaRue from the 'jects who had skied up outta New York just a few weeks ago. After chilling in a phat mansion and ballin' around town in half-a-million dollar whips, I had the head and it was sure nuff big too.

"That's okay," I told Bunni. "We gonna roll with it for right now," I said and grabbed her arm as I pulled her toward a waiting cab. "But this is gonna be our *last* damn time slumming around in a hooptie, okay? We's paid now, mami! Our pockets are *swole!* As soon as we hit Harlem I'ma lease us a limo and a driver too, cool?"

We climbed our booties in the back of the cab and left the driver and the porter standing outside tryna figure out how to cram all our stuff in the trunk. It seemed like just yesterday that we had climbed in a cab at the Dallas International Airport and headed toward the Dominion Estate where we were on a mission to pull the biggest scheme of our lives.

It had all started when Bunni walked into the Food Land up the block from her crib and saw my picture on the back of a carton of milk. The National Center for Missing Children had just kicked off a new campaign aimed at some of their biggest cold cases, and a three-year-old girl named Sable Dominion—a rich little oil heiress who had been kidnapped from a midtown drugstore—was one of their featured kids.

Bunni had taken one look at Sable's age-progressed photo and swore all out that the rich chick was *me*. She said me and Sable looked so much alike that my own mama wouldn't be able to tell us apart. And she was right. I was a dead-ringer for the missing little girl, and we even had the same birthday too.

We did a few Google searches and damn near flipped out when we found out that not only was Miss Sable about to come into a hundred grand inheritance on her twenty-first birthday, but if Bunni pretended to turn me in, she could get a crack at the twenty-five thousand dollar reward money that the Dominions were offering to anybody who coughed up information that led to Sable's return.

Well desperate times damn sure called for a desperate hustle, and me and Bunni almost burnt our brain cells out tryna cook up a scheme to get our hands on that Dominion dough. We were broke as hell and we needed that shit. Not only was Bunni and her brother Peaches about to get booted outta their tenement apartment, but a psycho drug dealer named Punchie Collins was tryna kill me for ganking him outta some ends *and* I had a shitload of court-ordered fines to pay up real quick, or else a warrant was gonna be issued for my arrest.

And if that wasn't enough to light a fire under my big ass, my gangsta boo Gutta was finishing up a little bid upstate and he was about to be back on the streets in a minute, and I do mean on the *streets* too! See, Gutta had left me sitting on a stash of twenty-five g's, and he needed that money to rebuild his drug empire as soon as he hit the bricks. But a rat like me just couldn't help nibbling. A grand here, five grand there, shoes, wigs, chronic, jewels and parties . . . *shiiit* . . . me and Bunni had burned through Gutta's cash so fast that before his bid was even halfway over his crib was a wrap and so was all his loot.

Pulling off a hustle for Sable's hundred grand was my last crapshoot, my final shot at street redemption, and me and Bunni had used every flim-flam in the book to convince those super-rich black folks in Dallas that I was really the kidnapped daughter that they had lost so long ago. We'd busted up at their estate in the middle of their Fourth of July barbeque, and you can trust and believe that we set that joint on fire!

Those Texas folks didn't know what to do with me as I laid my slick Harlem flow on their asses. In no time at all I had Sable's mother, Selah, eating outta the palm of my hand, and my fine-ass play "uncle" Suge Dominion had done a damn good job of eating out the rest of me!

Bunni had played her role like a champ too. She'd scammed her way up on a freaky pain slut named Kelvin Merchant who worked at the DNA lab, and in return for whipping his ass and pinching his balls, Kelvin had hooked us up with a fake DNA report that guaranteed me a slice of the Dominion family pie.

With the DNA results on the table, I had rolled outta Dallas with a hundred-grand in my bank account, and Bunni made out like a street bandit with twenty-five large in reward money for all her hard work. All in all, it was the biggest hustle of our guttersnipe lives, and we were amped up and feelin' ourselves for pulling off a gank so lovely. All I had to do now was pay my fines to the city of New York, tear off some ends to crazy Punchie Collins, and stash twenty-five grand in Gutta's safe to keep that fool from slumping me when he came home.

After that, life was gonna be one big freaky-ass party, and as long as I handled my bizz I could get as wild and loose as I wanted to! *Hell yeah*, my blood surged with hood excitement as our taxi pulled up outside of Bunni's building and the hater-bitches on the front stoop got to peeping all in the windows. *Handle ya bizz, Miss Mink LaRue!* That's all a slick hood chick like me had to do.